THE DEVIL'S MONK

*The Thomas Potts Mysteries by Sara Fraser
from Severn House*

THE RELUCTANT CONSTABLE
THE RESURRECTION MEN
THE DROWNED ONES
SUFFER THE CHILDREN
TIL DEATH DO US PART
THE DEVIL'S MONK

THE DEVIL'S MONK

Sara Fraser

severn House

This first world edition published 2015
in Great Britain and the USA by
SEVERN HOUSE PUBLISHERS LTD of
19 Cedar Road, Sutton, Surrey, England, SM2 5DA.
Trade paperback edition first published 2015
in Great Britain and the USA by
SEVERN HOUSE PUBLISHERS LTD.

British Library Cataloguing in Publication Data

Fraser, Sara author.
  The Devil's Monk. – (The Thomas Potts mysteries)
  1. Potts, Thomas (Fictitious character)–Fiction.
  2. Murder–Investigation–Fiction. 3. Police–England–
  Redditch–Fiction. 4. Detective and mystery stories.
  I. Title II. Series
  823.9'14-dc23

ISBN-13: 978-0-7278-8502-9 (cased)
ISBN-13: 978-1-84751-604-6 (trade paper)
ISBN-13: 978-1-78010-655-7 (e-book)

All Severn House titles are printed on acid-free paper.

Severn House Publishers support the Forest Stewardship Council™ [FSC™],
the leading international forest certification organisation. All our titles that
are printed on FSC certified paper carry the FSC logo.

Typeset by Palimpsest Book Production Ltd.,
Falkirk, Stirlingshire, Scotland.
Printed and bound in Great Britain by
TJ International, Padstow, Cornwall.

ONE

Parish of Tardebigge, Worcestershire.
Monday, 13 July, 1829

The overnight breezes had died away, and in the clear sky the crescent moon was fading as dawn spread. Concealed in a copse of thick woodland, the tramp lying upon a makeshift bed of fern and bracken grunted and stirred into bleary-eyed consciousness. Casting aside the soiled greasy blanket, he clambered stiffly to his feet, limped to the edge of the trees and stared across the river-bisected valley towards the broad outcrop of steeply rising ground where several tall chimney stacks marked the northern edges of the Needle District of Redditch Town and its satellite villages straddling the Worcestershire–Warwickshire border.

He fingered the long, thick stubble on his grimy face and throat, and thought, Well, before you goes any further, my bucko, you'd best get down to that water and get rid o' this lot.

He collected his blanket and large canvas bag and made his way to the river where he stripped to the waist, laved away the grime on his face and neck and carefully trimmed the stubble with a cut-throat razor. Afterwards, he took a battered military shako and shabby red uniform tunic from the bag and put them on. Stood to 'Attention', saluted smartly and announced out loud: 'Corporal George Maffey, Sir. Fourteen years' service in the Thirty-second Foot, Sir. Invalided out after Waterloo, Sir.'

He repacked and shouldered the bag, then limped along the bank. The pasture he was in had very recently been harvested and as he was passing a large, newly thatched haystack he halted abruptly, staring hard at the motionless figure sprawled on the haystack's wide, flat stone platform. He took a few steps towards the figure, and again halted abruptly.

'Fuckin' hell's bells! Who smashed your head in!' he grunted, and limped as fast as he could towards the nearby turnpike road.

Gripped in the terrible nightmare of a woman's anguished screams dinning in his ears, Tom Potts was thrashing about in his narrow cot, shouting in desperate frustration, fighting with all his strength to break through the impenetrable black cloud that enveloped him.

Amy Potts rushed up into the dark garret, a lighted lamp in one hand, a bucket full of cold water in the other. She bent to place the lamp on the floor, then hurled the cold water into her writhing husband's face.

He jerked upright, gasping and choking for breath as she berated furiously, 'You're doing it again, you great fool! Waking me up and destroying my rest! You're driving me out of me bloody mind!'

Full awareness came to Tom and, wiping his face upon the bed sheet, he ruefully apologised. 'I'm truly sorry, my love, but it was the same nightmare again. I could hear your screams and couldn't come to your aid.'

'Ohhh, "I'm truly sorry, my love, but it was the same nightmare!"' She spat the words back at him, then turned and went down the narrow stairs, shouting, 'You can cook your own bloody breakfast! I'm going to the Fox for mine!'

He sighed despondently, levered his exceptionally lanky body from the bed, pulled on a shirt and breeches, slipped his feet into boots, lifted the lamp and made his own way downstairs.

The slamming of the outer door signalled his wife's departure and he could only sigh sadly, thinking: How much longer is this terrible moodiness of yours going to continue, Amy?

As George Maffey limped up the steep Fish Hill, which led up on to the wide central plateau of Redditch Town, the early 'Waking Bells' were ringing out from Needle Mills and workshops, rousing from sleep the mass of the town's population who earned their living from that industry.

When he reached the broad, flat triangular Green he stood for a few moments, staring at the rows of buildings which enclosed it.

A man emerged from a nearby house and Maffey accosted him. 'I needs to speak wi' a constable straight away, Master. Can you please name one and direct me to him?'

'Ahhrrr, I can, Soldier Boy. He's called Tom Potts and he lives in the Lock-Up down the bottom there. That place that looks like a little castle.'

'Thank you kindly, Master.' Maffey limped on towards the grey-stone castellated building standing on the eastern corner of the Green's triangle; separated from its neighbours by the bordering roadways which merged then forked again to continue eastwards.

He mounted the three steps on to the narrow stone platform which fronted the building and tugged on the long, thin iron bell pull which hung at the side of the large Gothic-arched, metal-studded door.

Bells jangled inside the building and after a brief interval the door creaked open. Maffey blinked in surprise as a half-dressed elongated figure appeared in the doorway and enquired in the accents of an educated Gentleman, 'Good Morning to you, Soldier. Can I be of assistance to you?'

'Might you be Tom Potts, the constable?' Maffey queried, frowning doubtfully.

'Yes, indeed I am.' Tom could not help but smile wryly at his caller's expression.

Maffey immediately stiffened and saluted smartly. 'Corporal George Maffey, Sir. Fourteen years' service in the Thirty-second Foot, Sir. Invalided out after Waterloo, Sir.' He held out a folded piece of parchment. 'Here's my license to beg, Sir, which I'm hoping to get your kind permission to make use of in this parish, Sir.'

Tom took the proffered parchment and briefly scanned its contents, then handed it back. 'Very well, Corporal Maffey, your license looks to be in order, so you may beg throughout this parish. But I must warn you not to beg aggressively, or to pester those who are reluctant to give.'

'Ohhh, I'd never do that, Sir. I'm a man of honour, I am,' Maffey assured him.

'I'm sure you are, Corporal Maffey. Now if you'll excuse me, I have urgent tasks to fulfil.'

Tom stepped back and began to close the door, but Maffey stopped him. 'Hold hard, Sir, if you please. I've stumbled on to summat this morning down in the valley that you really must needs see for yourself. It's a dead 'un, Sir. And although I've seen more dead 'uns that I can wish to recall, this one is summat real extraordinary, Sir. You needs to come see it for yourself; it's real extraordinary, so it is.'

TWO

'There now, Sir, what did I tell you? It's real extraordinary, aren't it! You'd have to travel a lot o' miles afore you'd see the likes of this dead 'un again, Sir!' Maffey's manner was that of a showman presenting his latest attraction.

Tom's dark eyes were intently studying the corpse lying sprawled with out-flung arms and legs, its blood-caked, bulging-eyed features and head grotesquely distorted and surrounded by a pool of coagulated blood and brain matter. Although dressed in a man's long-sleeved waistcoat, loose-fitting shirt, breeches and ankle boots, it had the long hair of a woman and Tom bent to loosen the shirt laces and confirm the swell of feminine breasts.

The sun was now well risen and the burgeoning warmth had roused the flies which were swarming on to this feast of blood and body wastes.

Tom's mind was racing as he gently fingered the woman's neck, shoulders and upper arms before straightening upright and asking his companion: 'Corporal Maffey, might you have a blanket in your bag that you could sell me? I promise to pay you well for it.'

Maffey hastened to present Tom with the blanket, and Tom used it to carefully cover the dead woman. 'Corporal Maffey, will you place yourself under my direction for this day? I'll pay you for your services,' Tom requested.

The other man flashed up a rigid salute. 'Corporal Maffey is now enlisted in your service, Sir. Please to give me your orders, Sir.'

He listened silently while Tom gave long and detailed instructions.

In the kitchen parlour of the Fox and Goose Inn, three of the women seated around the table had devoured breakfasts of freshly baked bread plastered thickly with beef dripping and washed down with foaming tankards of ale. The fourth woman had eaten nothing, and taken only a few sips from her tankard.

Appetite satisfied, Gertie Fowkes, the fat, florid-featured wife of the innkeeper, Tommy Fowkes, gusted a belch of satisfaction and narrowed her puff-balled eyes at the fourth woman.

'Now then, Amy Potts, let's hear what the problem is. You sitting there again wi' a face like a wet week and not ateing a morsel? What's up wi' you?'

'Nothing's really up wi' her, Mam. She just wants us all to keep on feeling sorry for her. You'd think she was the first woman in the world to miscarry a babby, wouldn't you?' Gertie's daughter, Lily, a physically younger version of her mother, sneered spitefully. 'She should do what the rest of us women do. Just get over it and get pregnant again. That's always supposing that Tom Potts is able for it, o' course. Because these days he looks like he arn't got the strength to kill a bloody gnat, let alone give his Missus a good seeing to.'

Buxom barmaid, Maisie Lock, long-term friend and confidant of Amy Potts, immediately offered battle. 'It's easy for you to say that Amy should just have another try at birthing, aren't it, Lily. Seeing as how youm too fat and nasty to have ever managed to get any bloke to babby you.'

'That's enough o' that, you pair!' Gertie Fowkes snapped sharply and ordered. 'Now set about finishing your chores this instant, or I'll be taking a stick to both your arses. Go on! Bugger off!'

Huffing and puffing indignantly, the pair obeyed and, as the door closed behind them, Gertie Fowkes smiled kindly at Amy and said gently, 'Listen, my duck, it's nigh on five months since you lost that babby. You should surely be getting over it by now. It's just one o' them natural things us women have to bear. God only knows I've lost enough of them in my time. But as soon as you gets another little mite stirring in your belly, I guarantee you'll feel as right as rain again!'

Amy made no reply, only sat silent with her head bowed and hands clasped upon her lap.

The older woman, who loved Amy almost as if she were her own daughter, sighed sadly as she mentally contrasted this pale-cheeked, drawn-featured, depressed young woman with the vibrant, rosy-cheeked girl of five months past.

Amy suddenly drew a hissing intake of breath and lifted her head. 'Listen, Mrs Fowkes, I need to tell you something, but it must be kept secret between you and me, and you mustn't breathe a word about what I say to anybody.'

The older woman didn't hesitate. 'If you tells me you wants it kept secret, my duck, then I'll carry it untold to me grave. Now am you going to tell me that your man is serving you ill? Because if he is the bugger will have to answer to me for it!'

'Oh, no!' Amy denied vehemently. 'Tom has never ever treated or spoke to me harshly, although I aren't let him share my bed or lay a finger on me since I fell pregnant. Nor even this morning did he turn on me when I chucked a bucket o' water over him in his bed. He's a truly good, kind man, which makes me feel even worse about what I wants to say now.'

'Which is?' Gertie Fowkes frowned doubtfully.

'That I wants to leave him, and come back here to live and work,' Amy stated firmly.

'You can't mean that?' the older woman screeched in disbelief.

'I do mean it,' Amy declared.

'But respectable, good living women like us never ever leave their husbands!' Gertie Fowkes was shouting agitatedly now. 'No! Not even when they've got a rotten bugger who knocks 'um about and keeps 'um in rags! Women who leave their husbands always goes to the bad, and become dirty prostitutes that every decent woman spits on!'

The door slammed open and the rotund figure of Tommy Fowkes filled the wide doorway. 'What's all this bloody racket, Missus Fowkes? What'll my customers say when they comes in and hears you blarting and screeching like a bloody slum bitch?' he demanded angrily.

'They can say whatever they got a mind to say, Master Fowkes, because I don't give a bugger for any of 'um! Nor for you neither, come to that!' she shouted defiantly.

Dismayed that she had inadvertently caused this heated confrontation between the couple, Amy immediately rose and went to stand facing the man.

'It's my fault that Mrs Fowkes is so upset, Master Fowkes.'

Tommy Fowkes, who had always favoured Amy, smiled down at her. 'Why so, Amy? What have you said to upset her?'

Amy swallowed hard and summoned all her resolve. 'I told her that I wanted to leave my husband and to come back here to live and work.'

'What!' Tommy Fowkes could not believe he had heard her correctly.

During the years that Amy had lived and worked at the Fox and Goose she had come to know Tommy Fowkes's character very well, and now she used that knowledge.

'I was a good, honest barmaid, wasn't I, Master Fowkes? I know that there'll be people in this town who'll think that I've loose morals because I've left my husband and, like they always do, men will be throwing their money over the counter and buying drinks for all the house to try and impress me. But you know very well that I'd die before I'd ever bring any stain upon the good name of the Fox.'

While Amy was speaking, Gertie Fowkes's own sense of guilt began to torment her. She felt that it was her fault that Amy had been forced to tell Tommy Fowkes the shared secret that she, Gertie, had just sworn to take to her grave. Now she intervened.

'Me and Master Fowkes both knows that youm a good living wench, my duck, and you always has been. You can come back whenever you chooses, can't she, Master Fowkes?'

Tommy Fowkes was savouring this moment. He relished the fact that by taking her in he would cause Tom Potts a great deal of chagrin.

Tommy Fowkes had always disliked Amy's husband for the simple reason that the man had been born, educated, and invariably behaved as a Gentleman was expected to behave. That fact alone made Tommy Fowkes, who had most definitely never been any sort of Gentleman, feel resentfully inferior to Thomas Potts.

His sweaty, florid features now beamed benevolently at both

of the women. 'O' course our Amy can come back here to live, Missus Fowkes. It'll be like having our own daughter come back to us, won't it?'

THREE

I t was early afternoon when the horseman, Doctor Hugh Laylor, reined to a halt at the haystack and nodded towards the blanketed corpse.

'Well now, Tom, I take it that's the female that your messenger spoke of? I must apologise for not coming sooner, but there were patients needing my urgent attention.'

Tom smiled at this exceptionally handsome, elegantly dressed friend. 'I'll wager that those particular patients were ladies, Hugh.'

'Of course.' Laylor chuckled and dismounted. 'Now, let's take a look at the specimen.'

Clouds of flies buzzed up from the blanket and the mingled stench of blood and body wastes were palpable as Tom uncovered the dead woman.

'By God! She's been sorely ill-used!' Hugh Laylor exclaimed as he knelt to stare closely at her. 'She looks as if she's been trampled by a herd of beasts.'

'Well, there are spatters across the platform to indicate that she was hit with weight and impact enough to spray the blood widely,' Tom rejoined. Then asked, 'Will you do the post-mortem? Blackwell will be back in the parish this afternoon, and I'm sure he'll agree to you doing it.'

'Certainly I will! The longer I look at this wench the more eager I'm becoming to get her on to my slab.' Laylor paused, then grinned. 'I assume that you'll be happy to assist me at the work?'

Tom nodded. 'You assume correctly, my friend.'

His companion's mood abruptly sobered, and he burst out: 'By God, Tom! If there were any true justice in this life, it should be you leading this post-mortem and I assisting. If your father's death had not left you and your mother penniless, you would now be a Licentiate of the Colleges of Physicians and Surgeons both, instead of being a dogsbody Parish Constable under that useless bastard, Aston!'

'I won't be under his rule for ever, Hugh. And strangely enough, I like being a Parish Constable.' Tom chuckled wryly. 'There are moments when I believe that in a previous life I was a bloodhound, because I do so relish tracking down lawbreakers.

'Now, I've sent for Ritchie Bint to come with a handcart, so when he arrives we'll take her directly to your house.'

'We?' Laylor queried doubtfully. 'I don't think my patients will appreciate my working as an undertaker's handcart pusher, Tom. Why don't you just send for Jolly's horse and cart?'

'Because I don't want word of this spreading until we know more about what's befallen this poor creature. Don't worry, I'll not trouble you to push the handcart. Ritchie and myself are perfectly able to manage that without your aid.'

'A capability which at this moment truly makes me appreciate you even more than I do normally.' Laylor chuckled, remounted his horse and cantered away, calling back over his shoulder, 'I'll have everything prepared for your arrival, my friend. I'm sure you'll find something to occupy yourself with while you're waiting for Bint.'

Tom could only nod grimly. He had already closely scrutinized the stack, its platform and near surroundings. Now he began moving in ever-widening circles around the platform, painstakingly searching the mowed ground for bloodstains, tracks and possible weapons.

Hours passed and Tom had found nothing when he was hailed from the river bank pathway and looked up to see his scar-faced, sandy-haired, muscular Deputy Constable Ritchie Bint pushing a handcart with George Maffey.

Bint left the handcart and ran to Tom. 'I hear we've got a dead wench on our hands, Tom.'

'Indeed we have, Ritchie, and it looks to be a nasty business,' Tom confirmed gravely.

'Where is her?'

'On the stack platform.'

At the stack Tom removed the blanket from the dead woman. 'Do you see any likeness to anyone you know, Ritchie?'

The other man shook his head. 'Her head's so fucked up, I couldn't name her even if her was me own kin.'

Maffey brought the cart to the edge of the platform. The three men carefully transferred the woman on to it and re-covered her with the blanket.

Maffey saluted Tom. 'I'm dreadful sorry I took so long to do these errands, Sir, but I had troubles finding both Gentlemen.'

'I'm sure you did, Corporal Maffey. I always have great difficulty in finding them myself, particularly when I'm in sore need of their services.' Tom grinned. 'You've done good service for me and I am very grateful to you. As soon as we complete our business I'll take you to the Lock-Up and pay you.'

It was early evening and the sun was setting when Tom and Maffey finally returned to the Lock-Up. Maffey sat down on the stone steps while Tom unlocked the main door and went inside, calling, 'Amy, I'm back, and there's a Gentleman with me who needs some refreshment.'

There was no reply and Tom called again, but was still met with silence. He went along the broad passage between the locked and barred cell doors and up the stone staircase to check the living quarters on the upper floor, then continued on up the wooden steps to the garret. All the rooms were neat and tidy, and his cot had been remade with fresh bedding.

'She'll be out visiting her family or her friends,' he accepted and, unlocking the iron-bound chest in the corner of the garret, he took coins from the money pouch stowed inside it and returned to the ground floor.

In the kitchen alcove, next to the rear door which led into the enclosed spiked-walled yard, he portioned out bread and cheese on a platter, filled a pewter tankard with ale drawn from the trestle-mounted keg and carried them out to the front platform.

'Here's some supper, Corporal Maffey, and here's the cost of your blanket and the wage for the work you've done for me.' He pressed two silver crown coins into the man's hand.

'Fuckin' hell's bells, Sir! I warn't expecting to get ten shillings!' Maffey exclaimed in shock. 'I thought I'd not get more than a shilling at best. You're a true Gentleman, Sir! And if there's ought else that you wants me to do for you, then you've only to ask it of me. It won't cost you a penny piece neither, Sir.'

Tom shook his head. 'Not at present, Corporal Maffey, but many thanks for your offer. When you've finished your victuals, just tug the bell pull and leave the tankard and platter outside the door. If you want lodgings for the night, go to Mother Readman's house in the Silver Square. Tell her I sent you and she'll find you a bed, a fire to cook at, and drink and victuals as well if you want them. All at a very fair price. I bid you Good Night, Corporal Maffey.'

'And a Good Night to you, Sir.' Maffey stiffened to attention and saluted as Tom stepped back inside and closed the door.

His own sharp pangs of hunger impelled Tom to return to the kitchen alcove, cut himself some slices of bread and cheese, draw a tankard of ale and sit down to eat. As his stomach pangs eased his thoughts turned towards the gruesome condition of the female corpse, and pity for her flooded through him as he thought: I could feel so many broken bones. The poor girl must have suffered unspeakable agonies while she was being killed. Whoever served her so is truly an evil savage. I'll relish bringing him, or them, to the gallows.

Even as this last thought crossed his mind, he chided himself: Come now, why am I already assuming that she's been battered to death by some man, or men? It might have been females who did this to her.

He sat pondering the questions reverberating through his mind. Was she alive or already dead when she came to the stack? Was she brought there by force, or did she come willingly? Why was she wearing a man's clothing?

The bells jangled loudly.

That'll be Maffey leaving, Tom thought. I'd best take the things in before somebody pilfers them. He put his platter to one side and walked to the front door. As it creaked open he exclaimed with pleasure, 'Oh, you're back, my love!'

He pulled the door fully open to allow Amy to enter. Bonnetless, wearing no shawl over her gown, she stayed motionless, staring nervously at him.

He frowned with concern at her troubled expression and

questioned anxiously, 'What's the matter? Is there something amiss with your family?'

She gave a slight shake of her head.

'Amy, what is it? What's troubling you?' He stepped towards her, reaching out his arms.

She recoiled from him, shaking her head and telling him, 'No, Tom! No! Don't touch me!'

He let his arms fall to his sides and questioned anxiously again, 'Amy, what ails you? Are you ill or in pain?'

She drew a long, shuddering breath and blurted, 'I've come to tell you that I've moved back into the Fox to live.'

He could only stare at her in shocked bemusement, and she went on hurriedly: 'It's no fault of yours, Tom – it's me who's to blame for this. I just can't live here with you at this time. Don't follow me now because I'll not speak with you, and I've told Tommy and Gertie Fowkes to bar you from the Fox till I tell them different.'

She turned and, lifting her skirts to her knees, ran back across the Green, her long blonde hair tossing about her shoulders.

Tom stood as if transfixed, desperately wanting to go after her but unable to force his limbs into motion. He watched her reach the inn door, where the waiting Gertie Fowkes and Maisie Lock enfolded her protectively as they all disappeared into the building.

He heard a cough and turned to face George Maffey, standing on the platform a couple of paces from the door.

Maffey coughed again, then said tentatively, 'If I might make so bold, Sir, I reckon it would be for the best if you went back inside. There's them who're taking a deal of notice of you.'

Feeling dazed by what had happened, Tom turned his head and saw that curious onlookers were gathering. 'Yes, Corporal Maffey, you're right,' he agreed wearily. 'It would be for the best.'

'Here's your things, Sir.' Maffey stepped forwards and handed him the tankard and platter, then saluted and urged, 'Don't stay here any longer, Sir. You go back inside now and spoil these nosey buggers' entertainment.'

Tom silently stepped through and closed the door, then slumped back against its thick boards as despair overwhelmed him. 'Oh, God, what shall I do?' he groaned aloud. 'What *can* I do?'

Knowing Amy's character, he accepted that it would be fruitless for him to go to the inn and try to speak with her while she was in her present mood.

His thoughts ranged back over the previous year, and how Amy's attitude towards him had soured when she had become pregnant.

Truth to tell, he thought, I feared this might happen. But after she lost the baby I just didn't dare to talk with her about her moods and tempers. Bloody coward that I am, he accepted miserably.

The memory of that terrible night when Amy had miscarried, only weeks from the estimated time of birth, flooded back. Her screams of agony had reverberated through the Lock-Up as in the garret bedroom the man-midwife and his female helpers battled to deliver the dead baby boy from her womb.

He, Tom, banned from the birth chamber by the deeply engrained strictures of age-old custom and usage, could only stand helplessly at the foot of the wooden staircase, cursing himself for his own impotence to free her from such agonies of pain and anguish.

The bells suddenly jangled and hope sprang up. *She's come back!*

He pulled the door open and found himself staring into the fat, florid features of Gertie Fowkes.

'Now then, Tom Potts, step aside and let me come in. I needs to have a talk wi' you.'

Crestfallen with disappointment, he obeyed and she entered, telling him, 'Now don't you fret too much about Amy. We'll take good care of her. You must just bide your time until her gets over losing that babby. You've got to remember that losing a babby that close to birthing can fill a woman's mind wi' strange fancies and turn her against him that put the babby into her belly in the fust place. I've seen it happen time and time again.'

She lifted her hand and pointed her forefinger at Tom's face, repeatedly jabbing it towards him to emphasize her next words. 'But them strange fancies don't always last, Tom Potts! As time passes they can leave that woman's mind bit by bit until theym all gone and she's her old self once more. I've seen it happen time and time again. So my advice to you is to let her alone and not go pestering her to come back to you. I knows that you've been a good, kind husband to her, and I'm certain sure that sooner or later she'll come to her right mind and want to be wi' you again. But mind what I say, Tom Potts, and do as I'm telling you if you wants her back. Just leave her be for the present!' With a final emphatic jab of her finger, she turned and left him.

The hope that had so suddenly flared and been extinguished now flared again in Tom, and he called after Gertie Fowkes's receding figure, 'I'll do what you advise, Mistress Fowkes, and I sincerely thank you for that advice.'

FOUR

Tuesday, 14 July, 1829

I t was late afternoon and the two men had been working on the woman's corpse since early morning.

'I think that we've done enough, Tom, do you not agree?' Hugh Laylor straightened his back and stared questioningly across the dissecting table at his friend.

Tom Potts also straightened to his full height and nodded. 'More than enough, Hugh. I've never before seen so many multiple blunt-force injuries.'

'Nor I.' Laylor drew a long, hissing breath, then intoned grimly, 'Fissure fractures of skull and spine, ribs and clavicle, hips, pelvis and upper and lower limbs.' He pointed to the row of buckets on the floor which were half filled with bloodied liquid and bodily organs. 'Lacerated foetus and womb, liver lacerations, lung lacerations, spleen and kidneys damaged. Multiple lacerations of the outer epidermis. Every body region has suffered injury! It's as though she's been smashed with heavy hammers. Whoever did this to her should be burned alive, and I'd gladly light the flames.'

Tom could only nod in rueful agreement. 'Me also, and I'm going to do my damnedest to find who did this to her. But for now I think that we should put her back together as tidily as we

can and lay the foetus with her in the coffin. I'll get her back to
the Lock-Up and then report to Blackwell.'

Dusk had fallen when Tom walked to the imposing Red House
at the top of the Fish Hill, which was the dwelling place of
Joseph Blackwell Esq., Lawyer, Coroner and Clerk to the Select
Vestry, Clerk to the Magistrates and Senior Overseer to the Poor.
He was also the Director of the Parish Constabulary and Tom's
de facto immediate employer.

When Tom tugged the bell pull the door was opened almost
immediately and he was met by the pallid, deeply-lined, ageing
features of small, frail-bodied Joseph Blackwell.

'I'm going for a stroll, Constable Potts. You may walk with
me and make your report on the post-mortem.'

'Very well, Sir.'

They left the house side by side, and as they walked Tom took
shorter steps so that his companion might keep up with him more
easily.

Blackwell snapped curtly, 'Do not trouble yourself to so
awkwardly shorten your step, Constable. I was a champion pedes-
trian in my youth, and am perfectly at ease in matching your
normal walking pace.'

'Very well, Sir.' Tom obediently lengthened his steps.

'What have you to report to me?' Blackwell asked, and listened
intently while Tom gave a full account of the post-mortem
findings.

When Tom finished speaking, Blackwell mused aloud, 'From
your description, it appears that this female has been rendered
virtually unidentifiable. How can you possibly achieve any
successful investigation into her identity?'

'Well, Sir, both Doctor Laylor and myself are of the opinion
that she was a young woman carrying a foetus approximately
two or three months in development. Her hair was black with
no trace of grey. Her teeth, although damaged and broken now,
were free of decay, and there was no shrinkage of the gums from
them. Her flesh appears well nourished and her bones to be free
of rickets. We also discovered that the third and fourth fingers on
both of her hands were peculiarly deformed by malformation of
the proximal, middle and distal phalanx joints, which we judged

to be birth defects. So I already have knowledge of her as a starting point for my investigation.'

Blackwell's thin lips twitched momentarily, and he exclaimed pettishly, 'Goddamn it, Constable Potts! You appear to be taking it for granted that I'm going to make free of the parish coffers by paying Ritchie Bint to carry out your parish duties, so as to enable you to go gallivanting around like a hound following the scent of prey! I don't think that My Lord Aston will take very kindly to that idea.'

It was Tom's lips which now twitched in grim amusement as he replied gravely, 'With great respect, Sir, it's well known throughout the whole of the Midlands that My Lord Aston doesn't take kindly to any ideas but his own, but that he listens very carefully indeed to any suggestions that you may venture to offer him.'

Blackwell halted and turned to stare searchingly into Tom's eyes. 'Tell me, Constable Potts, will your separation from your wife not adversely affect any investigation you might be engaged upon?'

Tom was not shocked by his companion's knowledge of Amy's leaving. He had long since known that Blackwell was like a spider sitting at the centre of a widespread web of informants.

Now he shook his head and replied quietly, 'Indeed it will not, Sir. Truth to tell, I welcome this investigation. It will prevent me from constantly dwelling upon my current matrimonial difficulties.'

Without any hesitation, Blackwell nodded acceptance. 'I fully accept that assurance. You may notify Bint that he is to cover your duties when necessary, and you may make use of my stable when you're in need of a mount. Now tell me how you intend to open your investigation.'

'My first call will be upon Farmer Parkman. It's his land and haystack, and he may well have tried to find me at the Lock-Up as soon as the word of her discovery reached his ears. I've no doubt that it's already common gossip throughout the entire district.'

His companion emitted a reedy chuckle. 'Well, you know the old saying hereabouts, that if somebody in Redditch drops a fart at the sunrise then, come the sunset, the stink of it will have

filled the nostrils of everyone in the Needle District. So I'll bid
you Good Night and Good Hunting, Thomas Potts.'

FIVE

Wednesday, 15 July, 1829

T om rose in the darkness of early morning and walked to
the isolated farm, arriving as dawn was breaking. Farmer
Andrew Parkman was already in the farmyard giving
instructions to the sizeable group of men and women haymakers
carrying scythes, rakes and pitchforks.

When he saw Tom, Parkman ordered the group harshly, 'Right
then, get to your work, and remember, if come nightfall I'm not
satisfied with what you've done I'll kick your bloody arses all
the way back to Paddy Land!'

The straw-hatted, shaggy haired, bearded men led the way and
their bonneted, shawl-swathed women followed. As they went
past Tom they eyed his unusual height, exchanging voluble
comments in their native Irish tongue and emitting roaring bursts
of laughter.

Andrew Parkman also came towards Tom, who as always could
not help but marvel at how closely the farmer resembled the
apocryphal 'John Bull' with his broad red features, bulky build
and style of dress.

'Where the bloody hell was you yesterday arternoon, Master
Potts?' Parkman challenged angrily. 'Was you a-skulking behind
the bloody door when I was a-ringing your bloody bells?'

'No, Master Parkman. I was going about my duties,' Tom
replied quietly.

'Well, why didn't you come and tell me what you found on
my land afore you went blabbin' about it all over the bloody
parish? There was dozens o' cheeky bastards come poking around
in my fields last night. The buggers was tearing chunks out o'
my new stack and shouting that they was looking to find how
many more dead 'uns I'd got hidden in there! They'd have torn

it to bits if I hadn't stung their arses wi' buckshot and chased them off!'

'I truly regret that I haven't been able to call on you until now, Master Parkman,' Tom apologised. 'However, I can tell you that the body was that of a young woman who was dressed in a man's waistcoat, shirt, breeches and boots.'

'Dressed like a bloke?' Parkman's broad features displayed instant interest.

'Yes indeed,' Tom assured. 'Do you know of any young women hereabouts who favour such a mode?'

Parkman shook his head. 'No.' He then grinned and added, 'But I knows a few blokes who by rights ought to be wearing petticoats.'

'Tell me, Master Parkman, did you see anyone on that field before the mowing? Any couples, local people or strangers, perhaps?'

'No, and if I had of done, I'd have run 'um off in double quick time. I don't allow anybody to wander over my property, and all my regular hands knows that very well.'

He paused before offering eagerly, 'I'll come and take a look at that dead wench. I might know her, or seen her about sometime.'

'Sadly, Master Parkman, you seeing her would serve no purpose. Her features and head have been so disfigured as to render her virtually unidentifiable,' Tom told him quietly. 'But, if you should by chance learn about any women who have disappeared from their homes or the places they frequent, I'd be very grateful to you for informing me of it.'

Parkman's expression showed disappointment, but he nodded. 'It's a pity I aren't going to see her, but if I does hear anything then I'll let you know.

'There's none o' my hands missing, and the Paddies am all present and accounted for. And, speaking of them, I've got to go and keep an eye on the buggers, or they'll be skylarking about and costing me time and money.'

'Please spare me some moments more, Master Parkman,' Tom entreated and, when the farmer concurred, asked several questions before they parted.

As Tom walked slowly back towards the turnpike road all his

thoughts centred on the dead woman. The work on the stack and field was completed on Saturday evening. Around noon on Sunday morning, Parkman had given it a final inspection. So the woman was left at the stack at some time between Sunday afternoon and dawn on Monday. Judging by the amount of blood and brain matter pooled around her head and the spatters on the platform and side of the stack, he was pretty sure she'd been killed there. When he first touched her it was near seven in the morning, and there were degrees of rigor mortis in her neck muscles, upper arms and shoulders. When they'd got her to Hugh's house it would have been about eight o'clock that evening, and there was almost total body rigor. And when they began the post-mortem at fifteen minutes past six o'clock the following morning, the rigor was easing from the neck muscles, upper arms and trunk.

He did some mental arithmetic and decided that she was killed somewhere around midnight on Sunday. Tom's thoughts then turned to another facet of the case: why did the killer make no attempt to hide the body? He answered his own question: God only knows!

When Tom reached the road which led up on to the central plateau of Redditch he was shouted at by an old man who was leaning on a crutch in the entrance of a winding lane. Tom recognized the long white beard, ankle-length brown smock and schoolboy's floppy-topped tasselled cap and sighed ruefully.

The man was Methuselah Leeson, who was regularly committed for brief stays in the Parish Poorhouse when his mental eccentricities became too extravagant for his aged wife to cope with.

With the dead woman uppermost in his mind, Tom's first impulse was to wave in reply and walk on. But then he reprimanded himself for his lack of good manners, and went to the other man to enquire politely: 'Good Morning, Master Leeson. Can I be of service to you?'

'Service to me, Constable Potts?' Leeson's rheumy, watery eyes and toothless mouth gaped wide and his quavering tone was one of utter disbelief. 'You? Be of service to me?'

'Well, I assumed that was why you called to me, Master Leeson.'

Cackling with laughter, the old man slowly shook his head from side to side.

Tom struggled to keep his burgeoning impatience from his tone. 'Master Leeson, I've many pressing affairs to attend to. So if you have no need for my services, I must beg you to excuse me.'

Leeson winked knowingly. 'Oh, yes, Constable Potts, and I knows very well what them pressing affairs be. Don't I just! You wants to know who it is that's butchered that dead wench on Andrew Parkman's stack platform. Don't you just!'

'Indeed I do, Master Leeson,' Tom confirmed. 'And that's why I must now leave you and go about that business.'

Leeson winked and cackled again with laughter.

'I bid you Good Day, Master Leeson.' Tom turned to leave, but the other man's bony hand suddenly clamped down upon his arm and halted him.

'There's nothing you needs to do about finding out who butchered the wench, Constable Potts, because I can tell you this very instant who it was who done it.'

'What?' Tom gasped in shock. 'What are you saying?'

'I'm saying that I knows who the murderer is.' Everything in Leeson's voice, expression and posture radiated his surety. 'Last Sunday night I was having a wander about and the wind rose and blew real hard. I could hear the wench a-blarting while her was being butchered, and a bit later on I met the evil bugger running away. And I knew who it was that very same instant as I clapped me eyes on him.'

Tom's heart was pounding with shock and excitement as he urged, 'Tell me, Master Leeson! Tell me his name!'

Leeson's eyes bulged, flecks of spittle sprayed from his toothless mouth as he shouted hoarsely, 'It's the Devil's Monk what done it!'

'Who?' Tom demanded, bewildered.

'I was standing in the middle o' the meadow when he come rushing past me, as fast as the wind was a-blowing. He was all dressed up in them white robes he wears, and he come so close to me that when he went past his robes swept all over me, and nigh on took me along wi' 'um. I shouted at the bugger, so I did, but he just kept scarpering as fast as the bloody wind was a-blowing.'

'Where does this man live?' Tom asked.

'Well, he used to live down the bottom there, o' course.'

Leeson jerked his thumb eastwards to indicate the winding lane behind him which was dotted along its length with ancient thatched cottages. 'But when he went to the bad, he buggered off and ended up a-living in the woods.'

This time Leeson's thumb jerked westwards towards the distant woodlands.

Before Tom could ask another question, he was interrupted by the furious screeching of the diminutive old crone hobbling along the lane towards them, brandishing a rusty hatchet above her mob-capped head.

'Get back here, you barmy bugger! I told you to stop in the house, didn't I! Get back here afore I has your bloody guts for garters!'

She glared at Tom. 'Who be you? And what's you been a-doing wi' my husband?'

'I'm Thomas Potts, and I . . .'

She cut him short. 'Hold your bloody tongue and bugger off from here afore I cuts your bloody yed off!' She waved the hatchet threateningly before his face.

Tom involuntarily took a backwards step, protesting, 'I mean your husband no harm – I was only talking with him.'

Methuselah Leeson howled in pain as his wife grabbed his long beard with her free hand and hobbled back along the lane, dragging him with her.

It took Tom a couple of seconds to realize that Methuselah Leeson's crutch was left abandoned on the ground and the old man appeared to be managing to move very well without it. He smiled wryly. 'It just goes to prove needs must when the Devil drives.' He continued on his way towards the town, mulling over what the old man had told him.

Reaching the central crossroads, Tom noted that the main door of the chapel was wide open and entered the building, calling, 'It's Tom Potts. Are you here, John?'

'I am indeed, Tom.' Footsteps echoed on the paving and a man came from the shadows.

John Clayton, curate of the Chapel of St Stephen on the Green, was an unusual type of clergyman. He stood six feet in height, with an exceptionally powerful physique, his rugged ugly features bearing the mementoes of bare-knuckle boxing bouts.

'Do you bring me news of the burial?' Clayton questioned.

Tom shook his head in negation. 'Blackwell's given me no date for it yet. The poor woman will have to remain as my guest for the time being.'

'Have you made any progress with your investigation?'

'I think that I may have. I've just met up with Methuselah Leeson, and he spoke of a man with the strange nickname of the Devil's Monk.' Tom went on to relate what Leeson had told him.

'So, you surmise that the poor woman was murdered by this Devil's Monk, who wears white robes?' Clayton's lips quirked.

'Why are you looking at me like that?' Tom queried curiously.

Clayton returned question with question. 'Where did you say that Leeson said this fellow used to live?'

'Well, he jerked his thumb towards the end of the lane he lives in himself.'

'That's the lane that leads to the Bordesley Abbey Meadows, is it not?'

'Yes. Do you know this fellow then?' Tom pressed.

'Not personally.' Clayton grinned broadly as he shook his head. 'The Bordesley Abbey monks were Cistercians and wore white habits. One of them raped and killed a woman, and the legend is that the Devil took him in. Local superstition has it that the Devil's Monk returns here at times to rape and kill again.'

Clayton shook his head and smiled pityingly. 'Poor old Methuselah. His childhood memories of the story are afflicting him.'

Tom shook his head and groaned in self-disgust. 'I fear that I'm starting to lose my own commonsense. What possessed me to give the old sod any credence in the first place, knowing his history of lunacy as I do?'

The clergyman reached out and patted Tom's shoulder, reproving him jovially, 'Don't you dare begin displaying any self-pity, Constable Potts. You must continue to be the only man in this parish whom I can look up to both in height and strength of intellect.'

Tom drew a deep breath, smiled and nodded. 'I'll do my utmost not to fail you, Reverend Clayton.'

'I'm going to the Crown in a little while to refresh myself. Will you join me?' Clayton invited.

'Regretfully I can't, John. I've many enquiries to make, so I must bid you Good Day.'

'Good Day, Tom.'

Tom spent the entire day trudging from door to door in the outlying environs of the town, fruitlessly enquiring about missing girls or women, and it was evening when he returned to the Green. The sounds of voices and merriment came from the lighted windows of the Fox and Goose, and as he passed he thought he heard Amy's melodious laughter. Sadness overwhelmed him, and he had to exert all his willpower not to run through the door of the inn.

'Remember what Gertie Fowkes said to you!' he reiterated over and over again as he forced himself to continue trudging doggedly on towards the bleak sanctuary of the Lock-Up.

But all through the sleepless hours which followed, the raw grief of his parting from Amy continued to rend him.

SIX

Thursday, 16 July, 1829

In the dark corner of the rear yard, naked to the waist and bent double, Tom drew shocked breath as the pump water jetted over his head and shoulders. He continued working the long handle until the dulled senses engendered by lack of sleep were enlivened by the icy impacts and his thoughts were clear: I must go and see Amy's parents before I do anything else today.

By sense of touch he shaved his cheeks and throat with a cut-throat razor, then dried himself with rough towelling, rubbing hard to warm his chilled flesh. He brushed his teeth with powdered wood ash and, chewing a sprig of parsley to freshen his breath, went back inside and up the flights of stairs to his garret bedroom.

As he dressed the wall clock in the living room below struck four times.

'It'll be sunrise in an hour. If I move fast I can maybe catch Josiah before he leaves for the Grange.'

No moonlight showed through the heavy cloud, and all was still and quiet as Tom crossed the Green, turned southwards along the High Street, mounted the Front Hill and followed the long, straight, gently rising ridge of the Mount Pleasant roadway which led to the village of Headless Cross a mile distant.

As he neared the Headless Cross tollgate, he left the road and went down a steep decline of trees and brushwood towards the isolated cottage where Amy's family lived. A glimmer of candle-light showed from one of its small windows, and he halted some distance away. How best to tell them? Tom wondered and swallowed hard, felt his mouth drying with apprehension and, fighting the urge to turn and head back up to the roadway, forced himself to approach the cottage.

'Halt! Who goes there?'

The harsh shout shocked Tom to an abrupt standstill. He turned his head and saw the face of his father-in-law grinning at him from between the parted branches of a nearby bush.

Laughing heartily, Josiah Danks, veteran Royal Marine and current Head Gamekeeper on the Earl of Plymouth's Hewell Grange Estate, walked up to Tom and clapped him on the shoulder. 'Fuckin' hell, Tom, you'd make a useless poacher! I've been right at your heels since you left the road and you never heard me.'

Tom drew a long, deep breath and shook his head. 'I fear that I'm also a useless son-in-law, Josiah, and when I tell you about Amy and myself—'

The other man instantly interrupted him. 'There's no need for you to tell me what our Amy's done. She come yesterday to see me and the Missus. And she told us what we already knew: that what she's done is none o' your fault because you've always been a good husband to her.'

'Oh, no!' Tom protested forcefully. 'I should have known how very unhappy she is, and . . .'

'Shush!' The other man clapped his hand across Tom's mouth. 'You've nothing to blame yourself for. Youm a very clever man, with more book learning than a dozen parsons. But when it comes to women you knows next to nothing! Theym all born flighty-yedded! All you needs to do is just leave Amy be at present, and in God's good time she'll come running back to you.'

Tom's relief at Josiah Danks reaction to what had happened was so intense that he felt tears stinging his eyes and was momentarily unable to speak.

'Now come in and have a bite o' breakfast wi' me,' Josiah Danks invited.

Grateful for the offer though he was, Tom above all else needed to be alone with his own thoughts. 'Thank you for your kindness, Josiah, but I really do have very urgent business to attend to. Have you heard about the dead woman who's been found?'

'I reckon the whole o' the bloody parish has heard about her by now.'

'Have any of the women from the Grange or estate gone missing?'

'I've not been told of any, but one of our dairy maids was frightened by bloody poachers one night last week. That's why I've been out at night since then looking for the buggers. It might be that the wench down on Parkman's farm ran across some poachers and they've done her in to keep her silent.'

'That's something I'll bear in mind, Josiah. It's certainly a possibility.'

They shook hands and parted, and as Tom returned up the steep slope to the roadway he felt his spirits lifting, and the strengthening confidence that both Josiah Danks and Gertie Fowkes had given wise advice which would bring Amy back to him. And when I run this killer to earth that will surely help to make Amy proud of me and readier to return to me, so I've no time to lose, Tom thought as he quickened his pace.

When he reached the town he went to the terraced tenement where the Town Crier lived and knocked on the door.

The neighbouring window casement opened and a woman's frowsty mop of hair poked out from it. 'There's nobody there. He went out first thing this morning to go and do some Crying down Studley way.'

'Thank you, Ma'am. I'm sorry to have disturbed you.'

'Has you caught that bad bugger that killed that wench?'

'I'm afraid not, Ma'am,' Tom admitted.

'Then you'd best get a bloody move on and catch him afore he kills another poor wench, hadn't you!' she shouted angrily. 'It's about time you did the bloody job youm supposed to do! Instead o' coming round here hammering on bloody doors and frightening them like me, who has to work all bloody hours to pay your bloody wages. Youm naught but a useless long streak o' piss, with your nose stuck up the Gentry's arseholes!' The frowsty head withdrew and the casement window slammed shut.

Tom could only shrug, having long since accepted that the vast majority of the Needle District's poorer inhabitants regarded him as being a willing tool of the ruling class of Aristocrats, Landed Gentry and Needle Masters. Those possessors of wealth and power who, by popular belief, all spent lives of idle opulence while forcing those born beneath them to spend their lives toiling in abject poverty.

He set off to walk the three and a half miles south-east to the village of Studley.

'OYEZ! OYEZ! OYEZ! To be sold by auction on Tuesday the twenty-fifth of July at the Unicorn Inn, Redditch. A Freehold Estate, tithe-free. Consisting of a substantial dwelling house with barns, stabling for eight horses . . .'

Tom had clearly heard the ringing of the brass bell and the stentorian shouting while he was distant from the sharp bend which would bring him to the front of the Barley Mow Inn, Studley Village.

'. . . and other outbuildings, and forty-eight acres of excellent arable meadow and pasture district in a high state of cultivation . . .'

Tom rounded the bend and saw his quarry standing outside the main entrance of the inn without any visible listeners other than a solitary small boy.

'. . . situated and being at Abbots Morton in the County of Worcester. GOD SAVE THE KING!'

Old, bent-bodied Jimmy Grier, garishly resplendent in his plumed tri-corn hat, scarlet waistcoat, green tailcoat, purple knee breeches, scarlet stockings and silver buckled half-boots, gave another loud ring of his bell, then turned and greeted Tom with a scowl.

'Now then Tom Potts, if youm come to ask me to Cry the finding o' that murdered wench, then I'll tell you straight to save your breath and the parish coffer money, because I doubt there's a living, breathing soul in these parts who don't already know about it.'

'I don't doubt it either, Jimmy, but I want you to Cry another message.'

'Which is?'

'The Constable of Tardebigge Parish seeks information about any young woman who on occasion wears men's clothes. A reward will be paid to anyone giving her name and present whereabouts to Constable Thomas Potts at the Lock-Up, Redditch Town. The informant's name will remain a secret known only to Constable Potts.'

'And where do you want it Cried?'

'All over the Needle District, including Alcester, Alvechurch and Feckenham.'

'I shall want double fee for Alcester, because o' the time it'll take walking.'

'You'll get it,' Tom accepted.

'Right then, I'd best make a start.' Grier rang his bell and roared, 'OYEZ! OYEZ! OYEZ! . . . The Constable of Tardebigge Parish seeks . . .' He continued on, repeating word perfectly the exact message that Tom had just imparted, and ending with the obligatory, 'GOD SAVE THE KING!' and a final ringing of the bell. Then he told Tom, 'I'll go and Cry Alcester now, and do Sambourne and Coughton on me way back. You can pay me when I've done all the district, Tom Potts.'

'I'll do that, Jimmy,' Tom assured him, and Grier left.

A burly figure, clothed like Tom in a fashionable top hat, tail coat and pantaloon trousers, exited the inn and greeted him. 'This is well met, Tom Potts.'

'And for me likewise, Will Shayler.' Tom smiled.

He and William Shayler, Constable of Studley Parish, had cooperated on previous occasions and held a warm regard for each other.

'I was expecting to see you, Tom, after what's happened. Needless to say, I'm more than willing to help you all I can. But I arn't yet heard of any wench from around here going missing.'

'It's early days yet, Will. I'm having a reward for information

Cried throughout the all the district, so hopefully something might come of it.'

'Well, you know where to find me if you needs any help.'

They shook hands and parted.

SEVEN

Sunday, 19 July, 1829

The morning service had ended and the Reverend John Clayton took post outside the main door of the chapel to say farewell to his flock. As always the Private Pew Holders led the exodus. The wealthy, powerful Needle Masters who had propelled the Needle District to its world pre-eminence in the production and trade of that commodity. The Ladies and Gentlemen of independent means. The affluent people of multiple property ownerships.

The next to leave were the Rented Pew Holders. These were the more prosperous farmers, traders, innkeepers and shopkeepers who aspired to rise in society.

Last to exit were the most numerous groupings of the congregation, who sat packed together on hard wooden benches at the rear of the nave and up in the overhanging steeply-banked galleries: the clerks, overlookers, artisans and those sundry elements of the 'respectable' population of 'lowly birth' who were eager to 'better themselves'.

John Clayton tried to treat all of the congregation with an equal courtesy, and so always remained standing by the door saying his farewells until the last worshipper had left.

Tommy and Gertie Fowkes were Rented Pew Holders, but their narrow pew could only accommodate the couple themselves, which meant that their daughter, Lily, was forced to sit in an upper gallery in lowly ranked company with the two barmaids, Amy and Maisie. By the time the three girls made their exit, the senior Fowkes were already halfway back to the Fox and Goose.

'You two go on,' Amy told her companions as they reached the chapel gate. 'I need to pop back for a quick word with John.'

'I don't think he'll take kindly to a skivvy calling him so familiar. You'd best remember that now youm just a common barmaid again and address him as Reverend Clayton,' Lily Fowkes advised sneeringly.

'And you'd best remember that I'm wedded to a man born a Gentleman, and that John Clayton looks upon me as the Lady Wife of that Gentleman and considers me his personal friend,' Amy riposted.

'Which is a bloody sight more than he'll ever consider you to be, Lily Fowkes,' Maisie Lock giggled. 'All he sees when he looks at you is a bloody "on the shelf"!'

'Youm calling me an "on the shelf"!' Lily Fowkes exclaimed indignantly. 'That's rich coming from somebody who's been shagged and left on the shelf by a dozen or more blokes at the very least!'

Amy lost patience. 'Give over now, both of you! I'll see you later.' She turned and went back.

John Clayton exchanged a few pleasantries with the final leavers, then looked gravely at Amy. 'I'll wager I know what you want to ask me, my dear. So I'll tell you that Tom is trying to show a brave face to the world, but I know that in his heart he is grievously unhappy.'

'I don't deliberately choose to hurt poor Tom.' Amy's eyes were troubled. 'And truth to tell, I hate myself for doing so. But if I'd stayed with him we would have ended up hating each other.'

'Why so?' Clayton's ugly features showed puzzlement. 'Tom would never have been unfaithful or ill-used you, and I'm sure that you would never have been untrue to him.'

'That's as maybe.' Her eyes suddenly filled with tears, and a rising note of hysteria entered her voice. 'But sooner or later he would have pestered me to do my duty as a wife with him, and that's what I could never do with him again. He planted a dead babby in my womb! That I carried for five months knowing in my heart it was dead. Well, everybody knows that if the first babby a man plants in you is dead, then more than likely so will all the others that he plants in you be. I can't risk going through that again! I'd sooner be laying in my own grave!'

Her voice choked and she turned and ran, leaving John Clayton staring after her, concerned.

Outside the Lock-Up there had been a noisy, smelly, constantly fluctuating crowd since daybreak.

Ritchie Bint was on the platform, guarding the door which at varying intervals opened to discharge a man, woman or child. Each time this happened the waiting crowd surged towards the platform, shouting and gesticulating to catch Ritchie Bint's attention. He would select one of these applicants and allow them to enter the building, then bellow threateningly at the loudly protesting unsuccessful applicants.

'If you don't shut your cakeholes I'll be shutting 'um for you, and then you'll never get to spake wi' Constable Potts!'

Well aware of Bint's prowess as a bare-knuckle prize-fighter and tavern-brawler, the crowd would quieten, but only until the exit of the previous entrant.

Inside the Lock-Up, Tom had pulled a table and stool into the central corridor and set out an ink pot, quill pens and a sheaf of paper on this makeshift desk. As each entrant came to the desk, Tom initially asked the same set of questions.

'What is your name? Age? Address? Place of work? Do you know of any female who is missing from the places she normally frequents? Do you know personally, or have heard of, any female who at times wears male clothing? Has this female any deformity of body that you can describe to me?'

Almost inevitably the last three questions were answered with fervent assurances of such personal knowledge, and Tom was treated to many bizarre descriptions of female deformations and outlandish fashions of dress.

Another constant uniting all these interviewees were their demands to see the corpse and to be given the payment of the promised reward there and then.

Tom's firm refusals led at times to heated arguments and verbal abuse but, to his relief, no physical assaults.

It was a welcome respite when instead of yet another reward-seeker, Ritchie Bint ushered in Joseph Blackwell.

'Good Afternoon, Constable Potts,' Blackwell greeted. 'How is your investigation progressing?'

Tom bowed. 'Good Afternoon, Sir. As yet with no result.' He hesitated, then tentatively suggested, 'Perhaps if I placed notices in the Worcester and Birmingham newspapers it might help to quicken the identification?'

The other man shook his head dismissively. 'The Vestry will not sanction the expense of placing the notices. They are already complaining about the parish having to meet the expense of paying Bint to perform your duties while you investigate the death of a tramper woman who apparently has no connection whatsoever with this district.' Blackwell's thin lips momentarily quirked in a grim smile. 'But you may continue your investigation into her death. At the very least it will certainly help to distract you from your current matrimonial difficulties.'

Tom could not help but nod in rueful appreciation of this ironic sally. 'Indeed so, Sir. However, I believe I may still be able to find a little time to feel sorry for myself.'

Blackwell chuckled dryly. 'I don't doubt your capacity to do so. Now, is there anything else you require of me at this time?'

'Well, to begin with, Sir, I do think it best if the woman is buried as soon as possible.'

'Yes, I'm aware of the very unpleasant odour emanating from that cell over there. You may arrange to have her buried as quickly as possible. I'll leave you to continue interviewing your visitors, Thomas Potts. I wish you good luck in that task.'

'I fear I'll need a good deal of that, Sir,' Tom wryly acknowledged.

EIGHT

Monday, 20 July, 1829

Fortunately for Tom's capacity for tolerance, the numbers of reward-seekers coming to the Lock-Up was greatly diminished, and by mid-morning he had finished interviewing the final unsuccessful applicant. With relief he left the building and walked down the Fish Hill into the valley of the Arrow River.

The more prosperous of the local population buried their dead in the various church and chapel graveyards of the Tardebigge Parish, as Tom had buried his own mother in the graveyard of the Tardebigge Parish Church during October of the previous year.

The poorer people utilized the Old Monks Graveyard adjoining the multi-mounded site of the ancient Bordesley Abbey. One section of that graveyard was the Paupers' Plot, where the destitute dead were buried at the parish's expense.

'Has you come to pick out a nice plot for yourself, Master Potts?' Hector Smout, the aged, gnarled-featured gravedigger cheerily greeted Tom on his arrival at the graveyard. 'That's a very wise thing to do because there aren't a deal o' room left to choose from. There's too many bloody furriners come to live in the parish lately, and theym a dying off like bloody flies, so they be, and taking the grave plots that by rights belongs to us local folk.'

Tom grinned amusedly and countered, 'Come now, Master Smout. Like the people you refer to, I'm not originally from this parish. But I was born in England of English stock, and that makes me a true Briton. As are the vast majority of these other newcomers that are settling hereabouts.'

The old man brayed with laughter. 'As far as I'm concerned, anybody who aren't bred and birthed in Tardebigge Parish is naught but a bloody furriner. Now does you want to choose a plot for yourself, or not? Because I'se got work to do.'

'I need a pauper plot as soon as possible, for the dead woman who was found on Andrew Parkman's land.'

'You can have it this very hour.' Smout pointed his long-handled spade at a large excavation. 'I'm just opening that 'un up for a bloke that's coming down from the Poor'us anytime now. There's only three long-timers in it at present and theym well rotted down. So after I've flattened them, your wench and the new bloke 'ull be plenty deep enough.' He hawked and spat, then growled contemptuously, 'That'll please the fuckin' Vestry, won't it? Does you know that them rotten, skinflint bastards never gives me a penny more on me wages, no matter how much land I saves for the parish by cramming the paupers in tighter every year that passes!'

'Well, thank you very much, Master Smout,' Tom told him

sincerely. 'You've done me great service by offering me this space. I'll go straight and make arrangements for the coffin to be brought here.'

'You'll have to be a bit sharpish about it then, because I knows that Parson Clayton has got another funeral to do at the Tardebigge Church later this afternoon.'

'I'll make haste,' Tom assured, and was turning away when Smout asked, 'Am you any nearer to finding who killed the wench?'

'Sadly, no.' Tom shook his head.

'But me neighbour, Methuselah Leeson, reckons he told you days ago that he saw who did it.'

'Come now, Master Smout, you surely can't believe that a long-dead monk is able to kill anybody?' Tom chided gently.

'No, o' course not!' the other man irritably denied. 'But what I'm saying is that Methuselah might have gone doolally, but if he says that somebody wearing white stuff run past him that night, then I for one believes him. He's always been a man who speaks the truth.'

Smout pointed his spade eastwards. 'There's a deal o' bloody furriners whom lately settled on that side down towards Ipsley and Studley way. I reckon you needs to be looking among them for the bugger who killed that wench.'

'I shall certainly do as you advise, Master Smout.' Tom proffered a verbal olive branch. 'Just as soon as I've made the necessary arrangements to have the woman brought here and notified Reverend Clayton that he now has two burials instead of one.'

As Tom walked back towards the town centre he found himself thinking hard about Hector Smout's support of Methuselah Leeson. Could it be that Leeson really did see the murderer making his escape? And the man he saw was perhaps dressed in a white smock? He turned his thoughts toward the task of conveying the dead woman's coffin down to the graveyard. At this hour the carters would all be out working and the dead man from the Poorhouse would be brought by way of the Red Lane. He'd have to borrow the four-wheeled handcart from the Red House stable and see if someone there could help him load her coffin on to it.

But when Tom took the handcart from the stable there was no one there to ask for help.

The local celebrants of Saint Monday always ensured that there would be more than a few individuals neglecting their work to continue the weekend's carousing; however, the Saint Monday celebrants were invariably hostile to the Parish Constabulary.

'There's nothing else for it; I'll just have to try among them, and risk getting bombarded,' Tom reluctantly decided.

Parking the handcart outside the Lock-Up, he went to the Red Lion inn which stood at the arched entrance to the long slum alleyway known as the Silver Street. As he nervously entered the smoky, odorous Tap Room, the sounds of loud talk and laughter stilled and the hostile stares of men and women greeted him.

Tom drew a deep breath to steady his racing heartbeat, and forced a smile. 'Ladies and Gentlemen, I've not come to spoil your enjoyment. I'm in need of a strong man to help me lift a single load. It'll take only a minute, and I'll pay him a full shilling for his help.'

'Fuck off, Jack Sprat!' a woman shouted, and almost instantly a dozen other voices roared in concert.

'Fuck off, Jack Sprat! Fuck off, Jack Sprat! Fuck off, Jack Sprat!'

Others shouted threats of physical assaults.

Tom hid his apprehension of this threatened violence, made a dignified withdrawal from the room and walked away to try elsewhere.

Four alehouses, two inns and four taverns later, he was losing hope, and then in the distance saw a red-coated figure.

'Thank you, God!' he breathed in gratitude and broke into a run, shouting, 'Corporal Maffey! Stand fast, Corporal Maffey!'

The man's eyes were wary until Tom explained his need of help, and offer of payment.

Maffey saluted smartly. 'Give me your orders, Sir.'

Back at the Lock-Up, it took all of their combined strength to drag the coffin from the cell and lift it on to the handcart.

As on so many previous occasions during his life, Tom was sadly conscious of his lack of physical prowess. Now he was doubting his capability to push this load the considerable distance to the Old Monks Graveyard, or to control it on the steep descent of the Fish Hill.

Maffey was also conscious of Tom's lack of physical prowess, and he offered, 'I'll help you bury this poor wench, and I want no payment for it, Sir. I'm doing for the memory o' some old comrades in the wars, who never had anybody find where they fell and give them a Christian burial. God pity 'um!'

Tom was deeply moved by his companion's words. 'This is a truly kind gesture you're making, Corporal Maffey, and I'll consider it an honour to have you beside me.'

With Tom in the front shafts of the handcart and George Maffey pushing on its rear, they set out from the Lock-Up and almost immediately attracted attention. Heads poked from windows and onlookers came out from doorways of the neighbouring buildings, some shouting.

'Who's that you got in there?'

'Where you going with it?'

George Maffey called back to one persistent questioner, 'It's the murdered wench.'

This information spread like wildfire, and an excited crowd materialized with astonishing rapidity, clustering around the handcart, bringing it to a halt.

Tom, aware that the funeral cart from the Poorhouse must already be at the Old Monks Graveyard, told the blockers, 'Parson Clayton is waiting at the graveyard for us. We need to be there as quickly as possible. Show some respect for this poor woman by clearing the way and letting us pass.'

On the roadway a large, high-roofed wagon had been forced to halt by the crowd and the young man sitting beside its driver jumped down and came forwards, asking, 'What's happening here?'

Eager voices quickly told him and he frowned. 'Burying a murdered woman, you say?'

'Ahr, so I does,' his informant asserted. 'Beat to death wi' hammers so her was, nigh on a couple o' weeks past, and left on a fuckin' haystack down on Parkman's farm.'

'Beat to death with hammers?' the young man exclaimed disbelievingly.

'Yes. Her was all smashed to bits, and dressed in fuckin' man's clothes as well. Her own kin wouldn't have known her!'

'But surely someone has identified her?'

'I've just told you, haven't I! Nobody could say who her was! Her was too smashed up!'

'But is it known who killed her?'

'Oh, yes. It was the Devil's Monk.'

The young man returned to the wagon and clambered on to his seat.

'What's happening then?' the driver asked.

The young man frowned thoughtfully. 'Only a pauper burial.'

The crowd had quietened and begun moving aside to clear the way for the handcart.

Then a woman shouted: 'Come on, Girls, let's take the poor wench down to her grave. Let's see her buried proper, wi' our prayers to help her get to heaven.'

Immediately women ran to help push and pull the handcart while others followed in procession behind it. As they passed the wagon the young man averted his gaze and his white teeth clamped hard on his lower lip. Then he abruptly told the driver: 'I need to do an errand. You go on and I'll follow later.'

He got down on to the roadway and waited while the wagon trundled onwards and its high bulk concealed him from the driver's view. Then he turned and followed the funeral procession.

NINE

'The grace of our Lord Jesus Christ, and the love of God, and the fellowship of the Holy Ghost, be with us all evermore. Amen.' John Clayton intoned the final words of the burial ceremony.

'Amen,' the encircling crowd echoed.

There followed brief seconds of silence, and then a hubbub of chatter and laughter erupted as the crowd dissolved into segments channelling through the gated entrance of the graveyard.

'I must leave, Tom. Else the funeral party at Tardebigge will be wondering where I've got to,' Clayton said.

As they shook hands in parting, Hector Smout came to the graveside and started shovelling the earth down upon the coffins. The clods thumped hollowly upon the thin wooden planks and Smout winked broadly at George Maffey.

'I'll bet if you was a'laying down in that box now, with them noises banging in your ear'oles, you'd be fearing it was Old Boney's cannon balls trying to blow you to bits, 'udden't you, Soldier Boy?'

Maffey's jagged stubs of blackened teeth bared in a savage grin. 'Bloody hell, no! I'd be thinking how bloody lucky I was to have such a comfortable bed to lie in! All my mates that was killed in action or died o' fevers was stripped jack-naked and slung into shit pits wi' not even a scrap o' rag wrapped round their bollocks. It's only the officers who had nice coffins like this 'un to lay in, not the likes of us silly buggers.'

Smout cackled with appreciative laughter. 'Well said, Soldier Boy. Youm a man after me own heart!'

Tom heard the exchange and recognized the underlying tones of bitter resentment against the social system which so grossly favoured those who were born into the higher social strata of his country. 'I sometimes share that resentment,' he conceded wryly.

George Maffey saluted him. 'Shall we get on the march now, Sir?'

'Indeed we will, Corporal Maffey. I'll bid you Good Day, Master Smout, and say thank you once more for your help. I owe you a favour.'

'Ahr, you does, Master Potts.' Smout cackled with laughter. 'And be sure I'll bloody well claim it from you some day. Tarrah to you both.'

Tom and Maffey took a shaft each and trundled the handcart down the cottage-lined lane towards the turnpike road.

'And how have you been faring since I saw you last, Corporal Maffey?' Tom was genuinely interested to know.

'Pretty well, Sir. Me and Mother Readman gets on like a house on fire, and I've been travelling around the Needle villages. There's a fair few blokes hereabouts that took the King's Shilling and saw some service and, although they aren't got much themselves, they don't begrudge an old comrade a bit o' charity.'

'Have you heard much talk about our woman?' Tom enquired casually.

'Oh, yes. I'm well known now as the bloke who found her, and it's done me a power o' good, I'll tell you. It's kept me well supplied wi' food, drink and bacca.'

'I don't doubt that there are those who claim to know who she is, and who murdered her,' Tom observed.

'Oh, yes.' Maffey grinned. 'There's been a few such.'

Tom grinned ruefully. 'I've met more than a few of such, but none who could prove what they claimed.'

They returned the handcart to the Red House stables and parted.

Tom rang the bell of the house and the manservant opened the door to announce: 'My Master is not here, Constable Potts. I don't expect his return until late tonight or perhaps tomorrow morning.'

'Very well,' Tom accepted. 'Would you please inform him on his return that the dead woman from the Lock-Up has been interred in the Old Monks Graveyard.'

The man nodded, the door closed and Tom walked across the Green towards the Lock-Up. He could not stop himself from staring towards the Fox and Goose in the desperate hope that he might see Amy outside its door or leaning from an open window. But as always that hope was again in vain, and the now-familiar desolation of loss swept over him, depressing his spirits.

Inside the Lock-Up, Tom's desolation deepened and, desperate to distract himself from his own thoughts, he fetched buckets of water from the pump, took a brush and rags and began to scrub the floors, starting up in the garret and working his way downwards.

The hard physical labour gradually achieved its purpose, and by the time he had finished the ground floor his spirits had lightened and the hope that he would one day be reconciled with Amy was again on the ascendant.

It was mid-afternoon when a hand tugged on the long, thin iron bell pull outside the front door and the bells on the ground and upper floors jangled furiously.

Tom went to the front door and opened it to be confronted by Hector Smout, who declared, 'You'd best come along wi' me this instant, Master Potts.'

'What?' Tom exclaimed.

Smout scowled impatiently. 'Just come along wi' me, will you.'

'Where to?' Tom demanded.

'The Abbey meadows.' Smout walked away, shouting back over his shoulder. 'Come on, for Christ's sake!'

'Why should I?' Tom demanded.

'Because it looks like the bloody Devil's Monk's been up to his tricks again!'

'Clear the way, you gawpin' buggers, and let the dog see the rabbit!' Hector Smout bellowed as he and Tom walked up to the small crowd clustered at the side of the hedge-bordered ditch.

'Clear the way, will you!'

Muttering and scowling resentfully, men, women and children shuffled to make a passage for the newcomers to pass through.

Tom drew a sharp breath when he saw the body of Methuselah Leeson splayed face downwards on the bottom of the dry shallow ditch, a rusty hatchet cleaving the back of his skull. Tom scanned the faces around him, and questioned aloud, 'Where is his wife?'

'In her cottage being looked after by her neighbours,' a woman answered. 'Her's gone mad wi' grief. Bawling and shrieking and wailing that it was the Devil's Monk what's done this.'

'It could be Nellie Leeson herself who did it! Her's tried to do it enough times afore when her bloody temper's up. Like a bloody mad thing sometimes, so her is,' a grossly obese woman snapped.

'Who found him here?' Tom asked.

'It was Nellie herself,' Hector Smout informed. 'Her come skreeking to me just when I was shaping the last bits on that fresh grave.'

'Did any one of you see Master Leeson coming into this meadow, or meet with him anywhere earlier today?'

The replies were negatives, and there was the shaking of heads.

Tom stepped down into the ditch and bent over the dead man. He felt the body which still held a degree of warmth, and noted that blood was still seeping from the cloven skull and oozing down into the pooled blood Leeson's face was pressing into.

He was unhappy about the presence of these unwelcome sightseers, knowing that they could well begin to assume that the killer of Leeson was the same individual who had murdered the haystack woman. If this happened he knew from past experience that they would then turn on him for his failure to catch that killer, and blame that failure for the death of Methuselah Leeson.

He thoughts raced, then he clambered from the ditch and addressed the crowd. 'If you please, I would request you all, in the King's Name, to spread out and search the ground for any traces of blood leading in this direction. By doing so you will be aiding this investigation to discover the perpetrator of this wicked crime, and bring that evil villain to justice.'

A hubbub of voices erupted as the more literate explained to the illiterate the meaning of words such as 'request, investigation, perpetrator'. Tom waited tensely for some seconds, then a sudden tumult of excitement erupted and the crowd dissolved into individuals spreading out across the short-cropped grasses of the meadow.

Hector Smout winked broadly at Tom. 'Youm a cunning 'un, aren't you, Master Potts. You've got 'um all eating out o' your hand, instead o' wanting to tear out your innards and feed 'um to the dogs for not catching the Devil's Monk.'

Tom smiled wryly. 'Well then, Master Smout, could I cunningly persuade you to go up to the Red House, and ask leave on my behalf to borrow the handcart and a tarpaulin sheet. The sooner I get Master Leeson safely secured in the Lock-Up the better it will be for all.'

Hector Smout winked and grinned. 'I'll go up there directly, Master Potts.'

'And you go with my very grateful thanks, Master Smout,' Tom told him sincerely. 'Once he is secure, I shall then call upon the Widow Leeson. I'm not relishing intruding upon her grief, but I've no choice in the matter.'

'Would you be wanting us to go together and call on her, Master Potts? Only I've been a good neighbour o' both of 'um for a good many years, and Nellie 'ull be easier for you to talk to from me being there wi' you.'

'I'll be very grateful indeed if you will be so kind as to accompany me, Master Smout.' Tom accepted instantly.

As Smout left, Tom got back down into the ditch and carefully searched through Leeson's pockets but found them to be empty, with none of the varied oddments that all men usually carried about. I'll need to ask his wife what he normally carried about with him, he thought, because empty pockets could mean this is just a case of opportunistic foot-padding.

There was also no crutch to be seen, but Tom remembered how the man had appeared to walk very well without it. He also noted that Leeson's distinctive tasselled cap was missing and thought dismissively: It could be anywhere. No self-respecting footpad would bother to take a greasy old cap?

Next, Tom closely examined the embedded rust-corrugated hatchet. For several years he had been experimenting with the esoteric art of identification of hand and fingerprints, and had achieved some success. But he knew that the corrugations would prevent any identifiable prints being left on the handle of this tool.

Could this be the same one that Nellie Leeson was waving in my face? He made a mental note to ask the Widow Leeson to produce her own hatchet.

The searchers were now returning to report that they had found no signs of blood, and to ask Tom, 'What's you going to do with him?'

'I'm going to take him up to the Lock-Up when Master Smout returns with a handcart.'

'I'll help you take him, and I don't want nothing for it,' one man offered, and others followed suit.

The thought of the long and very steep Fish Hill impelled Tom to immediately accept these second uncommon offers of willing assistance in the space of one day.

When Hector Smout returned, many hands helped to lift Methuselah Leeson out of the ditch, place him face downwards on the handcart and cover him with the tarpaulin sheet.

But the return journey to the Lock-Up quickly became an unpleasant running of the gauntlet for Tom. As always, gossip had spread like wildfire throughout the town and as the handcart group neared and passed Needle Mills and workshops the workers flocked out to line the route. Men doffed their hats and caps, women prayerfully clasped their hands, excited boys and girls were cuffed to respectful silence and hostile accusatory glares centred on Tom, who, in company with Hector Smout, was pulling on the cart's front shafts.

'I reckon a good few of this lot am blaming you for what happened to Methuselah, Master Potts. If looks could kill it'ud be you under this tarpaulin,' Hector Smout muttered, and even as he mouthed the words a man shouted angrily: 'If you'd done what youm paid to do, you lanky bleeder, and catched the Devil's Monk, then the evil bugger couldn't have murdered poor old Methuselah!'

.   Some bawled in agreement, then were shouted at by others to keep silent and show respect for the dead.

Tom gritted his teeth, kept his eyes to the front and doggedly struggled on up the steep incline of the Fish Hill and along the Green, every step of the way lined with spectators.

By the time they reached the Lock-Up all of the handcart party were feeling the effects of their work. So after the dead man was securely locked into a cell, Tom thanked his helpers and refreshed them with jugs of ale from the cask in the kitchen alcove.

Hector Smout drew him away from the group and queried, 'Does you still intend to question Nellie Leeson tonight? Only the poor old soul is in such a terrible state, I don't reckon her 'ull be able to answer you wi' any sense.'

Tom was torn between the lust of his aroused hunting instinct, which made him want to question the old woman without any further delay, and his natural pity for her present grief over her tragic loss. After brief seconds his pity won the day.

'No, Master Smout, I'll not be questioning the Widow Leeson tonight. Tomorrow afternoon will be soon enough. But I hope that you will still be able to keep company with me when I call on her?'

'O' course I shall. If I aren't in the graveyard then I'll be in me cottage waiting for you.'

The men finally left as night shadows were deepening. Tom locked and barred the door and took rueful stock of what that day had brought.

Depression once more overwhelmed him. 'I've had enough bad news, and faced sufficient hostility and blame for one day.' He climbed up the stairs to the garret, opened the iron-barred chest and took from it a long-kept bottle of brandy.

'This will put me to sleep for a few hours, and be damned to the sore head and sick stomach when I wake.'

TEN

Tuesday morning, 21 July, 1829

Sitting hunch-shouldered on a low stool in the single-storied cottage, Nellie Leeson was telling her story to Tom Potts and Hector Smout.

'Last thing Sunday night I was in our privy emptying me bowels afore going to bed, like I always does, and when I'd finished and come back in here he was nowhere to be seen.'

The old crone's withered features suddenly twisted in fury and she screeched, 'He'd gone off by hisself again! I told the bugger time and time again that he'd got to wait for me and not go gallivanting off by his'self on this business! But he would keep on sneaking off like a slithering snake. We was rowing day and night about it, so we was.'

'About what, Mistress Leeson? What business were you arguing about?' Tom asked.

'About what he'd found somewhere down the meadows. He reckoned it was something that the Devil's Monk had left behind when he went back to Hell after killing that wench on Parkman's farm. The barmy old bugger said it was something that 'ud put gold in his pockets once he'd got it ready to sell. But he 'udden't tell me what it was.'

'So what did you do after you had found that he'd gone out, Mistress Leeson?'

'Well, I went to me bed, because I warn't going to go out in the dark. You never knows what evil spirits might be roaming about in the dark, does you. Then when I woke up again it was next day. So I went looking all over for him, and I found him a-laying in that ditch wi' our own chopper in his yed. He always took our chopper out wi' him since that poor wench was killed. He said that he'd smash the Monk's yed with it if the evil bugger tried to stop him taking the treasure. He said he'd show the evil bugger that Methuselah Leeson was more than a match for him.'

Her voice choked. 'But the Devil's Monk was more than a match for my Methuselah, warn't he! And I found the barmy old bugger laying there dead wi' our own chopper in his yed, and I couldn't do nothing to help him.' She buried her face in her hands as harsh sobs shook her body.

Pity for her grief coursed through Tom. 'I'm truly sorry for your grievous loss, Mistress Leeson,' he told her quietly. 'And I give you my word that I shall do my utmost to catch your husband's murderer.'

Her body rocking from side to side, she shrieked piercingly, 'Don't talk so bloody daft! There's no mortal man can ever catch the Devil's Monk!'

Hector Smout tapped Tom's shoulder and hissed into his ear. 'It's best if you leave her be for now, Master Potts. I'll stay here wi' her and see that she's all right.'

Tom nodded agreement and quietly left.

'No mortal man can ever catch the Devil's Monk,' Joseph Blackwell grimaced contemptuously. 'In this modern scientific age when intellectual reason should be totally dominant, why are so many of our lower orders still afflicted with the disease of superstitious cretinism?'

'Perhaps, Sir, it is because the lower orders' general condition of poverty impels them to be forced into grinding menial labour from virtual infancy, so they have never had the necessary leisure time and the financial means of their so-called "betters" to pay for any scholastic instruction and so gain intellectual advancement,' Tom could not help retorting, then waited with an involuntary unease for the heated counterblast.

But Joseph Blackwell's thin lips curved in a bleak smile. 'Bravo, Constable Potts. I would have been very disappointed in you if you had not presented me with that unchallengeable fact. Will you now kindly go and do what you're paid to do. Firstly, inform your friend, Laylor, that he is nominated to carry out the post-mortem on Leeson, with yourself assisting him. Then go and continue hunting down that supposed Devil's Monk!'

As he walked away from the Red House, Tom considered how best to begin the hunt for the Devil's Monk. He chided himself: I forgot to ask about anything Methuselah might be carrying in his pockets. But I can rectify that easily enough.

He turned and headed down the Fish Hill.

Two hours later he walked back up its steep gradient, pondering over the list of personal possessions that Nellie Leeson had vehemently insisted her husband always carried with him.

A very valuable engraved silver snuffbox which had been his father's; a costly Hunter pocket watch; silver and copper coins; a tobacco pouch and a silver-banded meerschaum pipe with an engraved bowl. A pocket flint, steel and tinder set, and at least three new cambric handkerchiefs.

Since he knew that the couple had been receiving the very meagre Parish Pauper Outdoor Relief for the last twenty years or so, he doubted the accuracy of the Widow Leeson's inventory.

'I fear this loss has sorely affected the poor old soul's memory, God help her! And God help me as well! Because by this time tomorrow the whole of the district will be buzzing with the nonsense that as well as the treasure trove, Methuselah's personal possessions were also worth a small fortune.'

ELEVEN

Friday, early evening, 24 July, 1829

Tom's empty stomach rumbled uncomfortably as he placed the hunk of stale bread and remnants of even staler cheese on the table of the kitchen alcove, then took a jug and drained the last of the ale from the cask.

He sat down on the wooden bench, picked up the bread and a sliver of cheese, telling himself wryly, 'Well, this supper may not be what a gourmet would appreciate, but it's my own fault for failing to restock my larder.'

He took a bite of the bread, slipped a sliver of cheese into his mouth and, as he doggedly chewed the sour-tasting combination, mentally reviewed the progress of his investigations into the double killings of the 'Haystack Woman' and Methuselah Leeson.

He and Hugh Laylor had performed Leeson's post-mortem on Wednesday and concluded that his death had resulted from the

single injury inflicted by the hatchet embedded in his skull. Tom
was still considering why there were no other injuries or marks
on the corpse which might indicate that the old man had put up
a struggle against his assailant. Even though, according to his
wife's account, he had gone out armed with the hatchet and was
more than ready to use it against any potential attacker.

On Wednesday evening Nellie Leeson and a large party of her
immediate neighbours had come to claim Methuselah Leeson's
corpse and the rusty hatchet, both of which were now on show in
Nellie Leeson's cottage, where, in accordance with the traditional
local custom of the poorer inhabitants, anyone who wished could
view the corpse after paying an entrance fee of a few pence.

Tom had then spent the whole of Thursday and this present
day making fruitless enquiries resulting in no investigative
progress whatsoever. Those enquiries, however, had brought him
full cognisance of the low regard a sizeable number of the parish
population held him in, many of them openly upbraiding him
for his failure to arrest the perpetrator of the crimes.

No matter how farcically unjust, their hostile criticisms still had
a depressive effect on Tom which, added to his ongoing estrange-
ment from Amy, had brought his spirits to a very low ebb.

He tried to console himself: Ah well, tomorrow's Market Day.
I'll restock my larder with the freshest food I can find, and maybe
hear something useful about who the Devil's Monk might be.

TWELVE

Saturday, 25 July, 1829

Since dawn, stall-holders horses and carts, pack-loaded donkeys
and pack- and basket-loaded men and women had been
creating a tumult of noise as they set up their pitches along
the stretch of roadway bordering the southern side of the Green.

Tom had spent a very leisurely day checking the licenses to
trade of the men and women vendors, and ascertaining that they
were up to date with the pitch-rental dues to the Parish Vestry.

For long hours throughout the day there were not many buyers. But now it was five o'clock in the afternoon and the mills and factories had released their work-grimed, sweat-smelling hordes of men, women and children. The crowded market place was a seething hubbub of wares being shouted and bargained for. The inns, taverns and alehouses were thick with tobacco smoke and resounded with loud talk, laughter, snuff snorting, hacking coughs and spat-out phlegm hitting brass spittoons.

Halfway down the Unicorn Hill which ran westwards from the crossroads, rat-featured, fang-toothed Judas Benton was standing beneath the tripled brass balls which overhung the door of his pawnshop.

Outside the Unicorn Hotel and Inn some distance further up the hill, where the steep slope evened out before joining the crossroads, a burly white-smocked countryman was glaring threateningly at a shabbily clad young girl whose thin features bore visible bruising. He lifted his clenched fist in front of her eyes. 'Get down there now, or I'll be giving you another fuckin' leathering.'

White-faced with fear, she pleaded, 'But what shall I tell him if he starts askin' me lots o' questions about where I got it from? What if he asks me what me name is, and where I lives? What if he says I've pinched it?'

'This is the last time I'm telling you, you thick-yedded cow. You tells him that it was your dad's, and your name's Smith, and youm Brummagem born and bred. But your dad's just died, so youm looking for work and lodgings hereabouts. Now get going!' He grabbed the scruff of her neck and shoved her violently towards the downward slope of the roadway.

She stumbled and almost lost her footing, but attracted only momentary attention from the passers-by who were accustomed to witnessing squabbling couples on market days.

Judas Benton, however, had been surreptitiously observing the couple since they had appeared at the top of the slope, and had seen the man take something from his smock pocket and press it into the girl's hands. The pawnbroker's interest had been heightened by her companion's subsequent threatening posture and her fearful reaction. Now, as with head bent she came slowly down the hill, he decided: I reckon I'm going to be offered something by this one, and judging from what's passed between 'um, it could well be something that they aren't got any rights to have. He went inside his shop to await her entrance.

The girl halted outside the door for several seconds, her hands clasped tightly, her expression anxious. A distant shout sounded, and she jerked her head to stare back the way she had come, then hastily stepped into the shop.

'Now then, me duck, you've no need to look so fritted o' me. I aren't going to eat you.' Standing behind the shop counter, Judas Benton greeted her jovially and beckoned, 'Come over here and show me what you've brought me.'

'This!' She gasped nervously. 'It's me dad's!'

Benton spread his arms wide and chuckled. 'Well, me duck, whatever this thing of your dad's is, you'll need to show it me, won't you?'

'Oh! Yes! I got it here!' She stepped jerkily forwards and opened her tightly clenched fist to disclose a silver snuffbox.

He leaned over the counter, took the box from her open palm, briefly scrutinized its ornate engravings, then put the box on the counter and, keeping his hand on it, queried, 'What did you say your dad's name was, me duck?'

'S-S-Smith – his name's S-Smith,' she stuttered.

'Local bloke, is he?' Benton smiled.

'No, no!' She shook her head in vigorous denial. 'He's Brummagem born and bred, like me! I'm come here looking for work and lodgings!'

'Ohhh, are you now. Well, I reckon a pretty little wench like you 'ull easy find both o' them around here. Now, there's just a couple o' things we needs to settle before we can finish this bit o' business.'

He paused and deliberately stayed silent, noting her nervousness heightening with every passing second until her hands were visibly trembling.

'We needs to settle on how much you wants me to give you on your dad's snuffbox, and how much you has to pay me when you wants it back, me duck.'

Her body sagged and she gusted a long breath of relief. 'Ohhh, all right, Master.'

'Does you want to ask your dad how much he wants me to lend him?' Benton smiled.

Immediately she tensed and blurted. 'I can't! He's dead!'

'Oh, I'm very sorry to hear, that, me duck.' Benton oozed sympathy. 'I naturally thought the Gentleman you're with was your dad.'

'Oh, no! No! He aren't! He's me friend!' She was gabbling now. 'He just come wi' me to make sure nobody robbed me of me dad's snuffbox!'

Benton grinned and interrupted her. 'He must be a very good man to do that, me duck. As I'm sure your dad was; and I'll bet your dad's looking down from heaven this very minute and telling you that this day you've met another good-living, honest man here in Redditch. And that honest man is me, Master Judas Benton, the sole proprietor of this establishment.'

She gaped at him in utter bemusement, her lips still moving, but only unintelligible mutterings coming from them, as he went on: 'Now, because I got a kind heart I'm going to lend you four whole shillings on this box, me duck, at sixpence interest for the first week and eight pence interest for each following week.'

He immediately opened the cash drawer, extracted coins and came around the counter.

'What's your name, me duck? I needs to know because when you comes to get your box back I has to tick you off my list together with the box. That's how business is done, you see. What's your name, me duck . . .'

'It's Carrie,' she muttered.

'Carrie who, me duck?' Benton asked, rattling the coins in his hand.

'Uhrrrrr . . . Smith! It's Smith! Like me dad's,' she mumbled.

He pressed the coins into her hand and gently pushed her towards the door.

'Off you go, me duck. And if you've got other things you wants to pawn, or perhaps even sell to me, I'll give you a really good deal on them, like I have with this one. Because I knows that you're a good, honest wench, me duck.'

Still looking bemused, she exited the shop and ran as fast as she could up the hill.

Smiling with satisfaction, Benton took up a magnifying glass and re-examined the ornately engraved snuffbox.

'It's worth a good few bob, this is. Wonder who they pinched it from?'

He opened it and noted tiny indentations on its inner lid, which after a closer study through the magnifying glass he made out to be lettering.

He mouthed the letters that made the name, 'Matthias Leeson.' And gasped. 'Fuckin' hell! That was Methuselah Leeson's dad's name!'

Benton had heard all the wild rumours about the valuable personal possessions Methuselah Leeson had been robbed of and the mysterious treasure he had discovered. Can it be true then? Was the old bugger really robbed of a bloody fortune? And could that bloke in the smock and that half-witted wench be the ones who did it?

He hurried to the front door, but the girl had already gone from sight.

He returned to stand by the counter, angrily berating himself. Bloody fool that I am! If I'd have given that half-wit cow a fair advance on the box it's more than likely that her bloke would have sent her here with the rest of the stuff he robbed. Then I'd have found a way of stripping him of all of it, and having him sent to the gallows as well.

He turned the snuffbox over and over in his hands, and as his initial self-directed anger cooled, told himself: Hold on now, just calm down. If it was them then there must still be a way to get me hands on what they've got. His thoughts turned to the young girl's vocal accent. She's no more Brummagem than I am. She's been bred and born in these parts. But whereabouts, exactly?

Throughout the kingdom, regional accents, speech patterns, vocal inflexions and even vocabulary meanings and usage differed in varying degrees. Here in the Needle District, even with separations of just a few miles, certain phrases and pronunciations differed noticeably.

Benton stood concentrating hard on his memories of the girl's speech. After a short while his decayed fangs bared in a savage grin.

'If she aren't been born and bred down Alcester way, then I'm a fuckin' Dutchman. I reckon I'll close the shop and have a mooch round for a few hours.'

Up in the midst of the market crowds, Tom Potts was paying the price of failing to discover any leads concerning the killings of the Haystack Woman and Methuselah Leeson. Throughout the day as the numbers of people thronging the market had increased, so had the gibes and jeers directed at him for his failure to arrest any perpetrators of either crime.

'Constable Potts?'

Tom steeled himself for yet another hostile gibe and turned to face whoever had called his name.

It was Joseph Blackwell's manservant. 'My Master wishes you to come immediately to him, Constable Potts. He said I was to tell you that he had something of great importance to inform you of.'

Tom instantly experienced a surge of hope that Blackwell had received information about either the Haystack Woman's or Methuselah Leeson's deaths.

Spirits buoyed by this hope, Tom was smiling as he entered Blackwell's study. But his smile disappeared as he saw sitting by the fireside a grossly fat-bellied, purpled-faced man dressed in black clerical garb, white tie-wig and tasselled top hat. The Right Honourable and Reverend Walter Hutchinson, the Lord Aston, Vicar of Tardebigge Parish, Justice of the Peace, Senior Magistrate of the County of Worcestershire and second only to the Earl of Plymouth in the power and influence he exercised over the Needle District.

'Thank you for attending on me so promptly, Constable Potts.' From behind his desk, Joseph Blackwell greeted him pleasantly. 'My Lord Aston and myself wish to hear what progress you have made in the investigations into the deaths of the Haystack Woman and Methuselah Leeson?'

Tom had too much respect for his questioner to attempt to dissemble or obfuscate, and admitted frankly, 'As of yet, virtually none. But I am confident that perseverance will eventually lead to success . . . And I most certainly will persevere, Sir.'

'Persevere, he says!' Aston's bulbous bloodshot eyes glared with fury. 'There now, Blackwell! Have I not been telling you that this damned investigation is nothing more than a damned waste of parish money? We now have the truth of it from this fellow's own damned lips, have we not!'

Anger exploded in Tom's brain and he lusted with all his being to smash his fist into the fat, sweating face of the other man. But he knew that if he did so Aston would use his powers to ruin not only Tom's life but also the lives of those he held dear: Amy and her family.

Aston flung a piece of folded paper on to the floor at Tom's feet. 'Take a look at this, Potts, and then tell me why you have allowed this curse to come upon my parish.'

Tom took up the paper, unfolded it and read with instant unease.

'CAPTAIN SWING WARNS THAT ANY FARMER OR CONTRACTOR WHO THIS YEAR USES A MACHINE TO THRESH THE GRAIN HARVESTS WILL REAP HIS OWN RUINATION. BEWARE THE DAGGER.'

'Last evening I dined with my friend, the Lord Goodericke, and he informed me that this filth was plastered all over Studley Parish days since! Why have you not reported this outrage to me, Potts?' Aston challenged furiously.

Tom chose his words with care. 'Because, My Lord, I've had no reports of any such notices as this one being discovered in the Tardebigge Parish. Personally, I think it unlikely that there will be any "Threshing Machine" wrecking or other such related offences committed in this parish. Should there be, then of course I'll do my utmost to bring the perpetrators to justice.'

Aston slowly shook his head and gritted between clenched lips. 'Oh, no, there's no "should there be" about it. What you will do at this very moment is to abandon any further investigation into the death of this tramper woman and the old pauper and devote all your time and energies into working with the Warwickshire Constables to capture this "Captain Swing" and his fellow ruffians, and bring them before us.'

Loudly grunting, he struggled to his feet then turned his back on Tom and requested Joseph Blackwell. 'Will you please inform the Gentlemen of the Vestry that I and the Lord Goodericke have jointly authorized the constables of both counties to have powers of arrest across both counties.' He bowed. 'I bid you Good Day, Blackwell.'

Blackwell stood up and returned the bow. 'Good Day, My Lord. Be assured that your instructions will be followed to the letter.'

Knowing from past experience the futility of protest, Tom stayed silent as Aston stamped out.

Blackwell swung to face Tom and a wintry smile briefly curved his thin lips.

'As the owner of several tenanted farms, and a fervent advocate of the use of these threshing machines, His Lordship naturally has cause for alarm about "Captain Swing". But until "Captain Swing" actually breaks a threshing machine in this parish, just concentrate on investigating your current cases. I will deal with My Lord Aston's fears for his farming profits.'

Before Tom could react, Blackwell waved his hands in dismissal and ordered sharply, 'Not a word, Constable! Go away! I have urgent work to catch up on. Go away!'

He pulled on his spectacles and bent his head to study the open ledger on the desk before him.

Tom exited the Red House suffused, as on many previous occasions, with an intense warmth of personal appreciation and liking for Joseph Blackwell. For whose powers of intellect and worldly wise shrewdness he held great respect.

As he walked back towards the market, Tom considered the implications of Lord Aston's present actions and what it would mean for his present ongoing investigations. His confidence of success suddenly soared, he smiled grimly and thought: You have unwittingly done me a good service after all, My Lord Aston, to gain me Powers of Arrest throughout Warwickshire. It will save me a deal of difficulties in investigating across the border.

THIRTEEN

It was ten o'clock and the market crowd was rapidly diminishing. Tom was making a patrol of the dark streets and alleys around the Green. The inns, taverns and alehouses were filled with payday revellers, but the day and evening had passed peaceably and Tom had encountered no excessive noise or disturbance.

Then a sudden cry of pain caused him to look about and see some distance away, dimly lit by the lamplight from a tavern window, a man in a white smock and broad-brimmed slouch hat punching a woman in her face as passers-by made no effort to intervene.

She cried out again and fell back against the tavern wall, crouching and covering her face with both hands as the man turned and walked away.

Tom hurried towards them, shouting at the retreating man. 'You there, in the white smock, hold fast!'

The man kept on walking and Tom shouted again. 'I'm the constable, and I'm ordering you to stop there in the King's Name!'

The man halted and half-turned to face Tom, who beckoned and shouted, 'Get back here to me.'

The man slowly raised the forked fingers of his right hand in the ancient archers taunt of contemptuous defiance. He then turned and ran; none of the onlookers moved to stop him.

Tom reached the sobbing woman and told her, 'You needn't be fearful of me. I'm the constable and I'm here to protect you from that man. Are you badly hurt?'

With her hands still covering her face, the woman abruptly collapsed at his feet.

'Oh, Jesus!' Tom gasped in dismay, and for brief seconds was torn between pursuing the assailant or aiding the woman. The dark blood oozing out between her clutching fingers decided his quandary. She could be sorely hurt. He'd have to go after that bastard later.

He went down on his knees beside the woman, laid his staff aside and pulled at her wrists, telling her gently, 'You must let me see your wounds, my dear.'

He drew her hands away from her face and gouts of blood came out of her smashed nose. Tom took a handkerchief from his pocket and she cried out in agony as he pressed it against the wound. 'I'm sorry, my dear, but I must staunch the blood.'

She sagged limply into semi-consciousness. Keeping the pressure on the handkerchief with one hand, Tom lifted his staff from the ground and rapped its crowned head against the framework of the tavern window from where lamp-light shone and sounds of voices and laughter came.

He kept rapping several times until a man he recognized as the tavern keeper came out from the door, shouting angrily, 'What the fuck's going on here? Who's trying to smash me fuckin' windows?'

Then he recognized Tom and noticed the woman. 'Oh, it's you, Master Potts. What's amiss with the wench?'

'A man's just beaten her badly,' Tom told him. 'Was she drinking with him in your house?'

'Well, this wench and man, whoever they might be, warn't in my house!' the keeper declared indignantly. 'I don't never allow any rows or knocking about o' wenches. I keeps a respectable establishment, I does!'

'I know you do, Master Worrell,' Tom snapped impatiently. 'Now, please! Can you get me some help to carry this poor woman to Doctor Laylor's house?'

'Well, if you'd had the sense to ask me that in the first place I'd have already got help for her.' Worrell snorted irately, hurried back into the tavern and reappeared brief moments later with a group of men who were carrying a long table.

'This 'ull serve to carry her on.' Worrell took command, issuing curt orders: 'Lift her gently, lads! That's it! Lay her down gentle now. That's it! Timmo, you keep this towel pressed down on her nose. Now take a corner each, and you and you take the sides! Lift careful now! Head for Doctor Laylor's house! Quick march! Keep the bloody step, will you, Gerry! Youm causing the bloody table to rock too much.'

Tom had been taken aback by the tavern keeper's instant assumption of command and was standing motionless as the men stepped off.

'Am you coming with us, Constable Potts? Or am you going to just stand there bloody gawping while we does all your bloody work for you?' Worrell shouted back over his shoulder.

'I'm coming with you, Master Worrell,' Tom hastily replied, and hurried after the small cortège, whose numbers were rapidly increasing as the onlookers hastened to follow it – one of whom was Judas Benton.

FOURTEEN

'Tom? What's this I find? Sleeping on sentry duty is a serious offence, and you could well be shot for it!' Hugh Laylor laughed accusingly.

'Oh my God!' Tom cried out in shock, propelled himself from the wooden armchair in which he had passed a very uncomfortable night and rushed to the side of the blanket-shrouded girl laid on the dissecting table in Hugh Laylor's dispensary.

Relief flooded through him to see her chest rising and falling, and hear the throaty breaths coming from her open mouth.

'Oh, Hugh, I can't have been asleep for more than a few minutes,' he claimed shamefacedly. 'I could see the dawning through the window and was telling myself that in a few more minutes there'd be daylight enough to enable me to douse the lamp.'

'As there is now.' His friend grinned and moved to extinguish the oil-lamp. 'Don't berate yourself, Tom. It's not yet six o'clock so you can only have dropped off for a minute or so.'

He came to bend over the girl and fingered the thick plaster cast which bisected her badly swollen face. 'Though I say it myself, Tom – I've done a very neat piece of work here. With any luck her nose won't be too grotesquely deformed.'

She groaned and stirred and Laylor nodded with satisfaction. 'See that, Tom. I also judged the opium measure exactly. She'll be wide awake very shortly and you'll be able to question her.'

As he spoke his middle-aged housekeeper entered, carrying a tray which was laden with a steaming mug of coffee, freshly baked rolls and a large platter of ham and eggs.

'Good Morning, Master Tom.' She greeted him with a motherly smile. 'Now you get this lot down you afore it gets cold.'

'Thank you very much, Mistress Blakely, this is most kind of you.' Tom smiled.

She set the tray down on the small table against one of the

walls and pulled a stool before it. 'Come on, now. Sit down this very second and start eating.'

'You'd best do as she says, Tom.' Laylor frowned in mock-warning. 'Or she'll blame me for keeping you from your breakfast.' He assumed an air of self-pity and bemoaned, 'And to think that I used to be her favourite Gentleman until you came into my life and she switched her affections to you.'

The woman laughed fondly as she bustled out. 'You're still my favourite, Master Hugh, but you'll just have to get used to Master Tom being my other equal favourite, won't you.'

When Tom sat down at the table the scents of the food filled his nostrils and kindled a sharp appetite for what would be the best meal he had eaten for days. Within scant time he had devoured all of its components and was savouring the final taste of the coffee.

'You enjoyed that, didn't you?' Hugh Laylor grinned.

Tom nodded. 'I certainly did. It's the best meal I've eaten since Amy . . .' Without warning, the impact of losing her suddenly overwhelmed him afresh and he fell silent, his head bent.

Laylor grimaced sympathetically and, realizing the futility of mouthing comforting platitudes to ease his friend's sadness, said instead, 'I have to go without delay and treat a patient who needs my attention, Tom, so I'll leave this young woman with you. She'll be wide awake and in her full senses any moment now, and then you'll be able to question her to your heart's content.'

As Laylor had hoped, Tom thankfully seized on this distraction from his own bleak thoughts and stood up. 'It'll be fine, Hugh. You get along now.'

Shortly after Laylor's departure the girl moved restlessly and groaned.

Tom went to her side and saw that her badly swollen eyes had opened into narrow slits.

'Be easy, my dear,' he told her gently. 'You're safe here and your injuries are not life-threatening. Your nose has been broken, but the doctor has reset it and the swelling will soon subside.'

She pushed her covering blanket down, lifted her hands to her face and questioned hoarsely, 'What's this on me head?'

'It's the protective plaster over your nose. Don't try to move it because it will ensure that as your nose heals it will retain its shape.'

'What's this place? How did I come here?' she wanted to know.

He explained fully, and then asked her, 'What's your name, my dear, and where do you live?'

'Ermmm . . . erm . . . ermmm.' She seemed confused, before blurting, 'Smith! That's me name! Smith! I'm Brummagem born and bred, and I'm looking for work and lodgings!'

'And your first name, your Christian name, what's that?' Tom pressed.

'Carrie,' she answered immediately.

'Well, Miss Carrie Smith, if you'll tell me your parents' address I can take the necessary steps to inform them of what has happened to you,' Tom offered.

'No! I won't!'

Her blurted refusal shocked Tom. 'Why not?'

'Me dad's dead! He's from Brummagem, born and bred, and he's dead!'

'And the name of the man who hurt you?' Tom countered.

'Ermmmm . . . ermmmm.' Again her reaction was seemingly confusion. Then she suddenly cried out and, casting the blanket aside, levered herself off the dissecting table, wailing desperately, 'I needs to shit! I needs to go to the privy right now! Where's the privy, Master? I'm shitting meself! I can feel it coming!'

Reacting automatically, Tom pointed at the door set in the outer wall of the room. 'That door opens on to the garden, and the privy is down at the far end of it.'

'Ohhh, I'm shitting meself. It's coming out o' me arse!' she wailed frantically, and before Tom could say anything more she had gone through the door and was running down the garden path.

Tom went to Mrs Blakely, who was in the kitchen. 'The young woman has had to rush to the privy, Mrs Blakely.' He hesitated a moment after informing her of this before adding delicately, 'From what she was saying, I think that she may have need to cleanse her nether regions after using it. I need to supply her with the means to do so.'

'Don't you moither about supplying her with what she might be needing, Master Tom. That's no task for a fine Gentleman like yourself. I'll take her down the necessaries.' The housekeeper grimaced disparagingly. 'But truth to tell, from what I've seen and smelled of her since she's been in this house, I don't think she's come from a family that bothers much with any cleansing after they've been to the privy.'

She collected a bucket of water, a piece of rag and a strip of towelling, while Tom returned to the dissecting room.

Some time elapsed before Mrs Blakely came to tell him: 'There's no sign of that young wench, Master Tom. She wasn't in the privy and I've looked all over the garden and around the house, but nothing. She's scarpered!'

'Ohh, Jesus!' Tom exclaimed in dismay and, snatching up his tall top hat and staff, hurried out, telling the housekeeper, 'I'm going to search for her, Mrs Blakely. I think she must have gone over the rear fence, because I would have noticed if she'd come back this way.'

Mrs Blakely called after him: 'If she's gone through the Rough then you're wasting your time looking for her, Master Tom. She could have gone in any direction and you won't be able to see which.'

He went to the end of the garden and climbed over the fence. Even as his feet touched down on the steeply sloping, thickly bushed wasteland, Tom accepted the truth of the housekeeper's words. She's right! he thought. There's no way of telling if the girl has gone uphill, downhill or straight ahead.

The fact that it was so early on a Sabbath morning meant that it was unlikely there would be anyone out on the Rough who might have seen the runaway. No urchins playing or adults walking. No pig-keepers bringing their swine to root for food, no owners exercising their pets or working animals.

He stood deep in thought, carefully evaluating the verbal exchanges he had had with the young girl. Her accent was that of a girl born and bred in the Needle District, not a native of Birmingham, he thought, but why should she lie about her origins, and then run away from me? What mischief has she been up to, perhaps in company with the man who beat her so brutally? Well, there's one way to find that out, isn't there!

He climbed back over the fence, went into the house and requested Mrs Blakely.

'Please tell Master Hugh what's happened, Ma'am, and that I'll speak with him later this week.'

Then he went to seek out an old acquaintance.

*   *   *

Tom walked quickly up the Silver Street, ignoring the hostile stares and gibes that greeted his passing and taking care to avoid treading through the worst of the thickly strewn fetid filth and rancid puddles of sewage. At its southern end the alley terminated in a rectangular square surrounded by ramshackle hovels and a few equally ramshackle larger buildings, the most dominant of which was an ancient, four-storied, one-time residence of a wealthy Gentleman. Now it was known far and wide as Mother Readman's Lodging House, and for a wide variety of unprivileged humankind served either as transient or permanent lodgings.

As Tom walked towards its portico entrance, Mother Readman, six feet tall, raw-boned and hatchet-faced, clad in a man's caped greatcoat and wide-brimmed slouch hat, was standing there smoking a long churchwarden pipe.

'Good Morning, Constable Potts. I hope you aren't come here to lock up any o' my regular lodgers?'

'Indeed no, Mother Readman.' Tom smiled warmly. He had both respect and liking for this tough, formidable woman who ruled her house with an actual rod of iron, as many a trouble-maker had found out to their painful cost . . .

'I'm seeking Corporal George Maffey, late of the Thirty-second Foot.'

'And I'm waiting here for that very same bloke. He's gone to fetch me a drop o' fresh milk from Taffy Morgan's dairy. What does you want with him?'

'The very same that I will be asking from yourself, Ma'am.'

She grinned, displaying widely gapped, decayed teeth. 'That'll be information then.'

'Indeed it will, Ma'am.' He grinned back.

'So tell me and then bugger off, because having you here aren't good for my trade.'

He quickly told her about the assault on the young girl. 'She'll be easy to spot by the plaster on her face. I want to know her name and where she might be living. I'd also like to know the same about the animal who served her so brutally. Incidentally, her Christian name may be Carrie, which was the only thing she told me without any hesitation. I'll pay you, of course, and you know full well that no one will ever find out my source of that information.'

Mother Readman suddenly winked, scowled and raised her voice. 'Just fuck off, will you, you lanky streak o' piss! I got nothing to say to you!'

Tom instantly turned and walked away, meeting as he did so a couple of shabbily clad men approaching the lodging house, who hissed at him as they passed.

'You'll find no informers in this neck o' the woods!'

'You're lucky Mother Readman didn't break your fuckin' jaw for you!'

Tom silently walked on, confident that in the persons of Mother Readman and George Maffey he possessed two very valuable sources of information.

FIFTEEN

Monday, 3 August, 1829

It was not yet dawn when Tom rose naked from his bed and went to the open window of the garret. He stared out across the moonlit buildings, enjoying the warm, still air, and marvelling that the abnormally intense heatwave which had descended upon the English Midlands some days previously was apparently going to continue through this day also.

The Lock-Up bells suddenly jangled loudly and Tom hurried down to the first floor and opened the casement window which overlooked the front of the building. A shadowed figure was tugging at the iron bell rod and Tom challenged, 'Who are you, and what's your business here?'

'It's me, Sir,' George Maffey called huskily.

'All right.' Naked and barefoot, Tom hastened to the front door and admitted his visitor.

'Sorry to get you from your bed, Sir, but I can't risk anybody spotting me coming here, can I? It wouldn't be good for me trade,' George Maffey apologised.

'Of course you can't, Corporal Maffey. Now, what do you have for me?'

'The girl's name is Carrie Perks and she was birthed in the Alcester Parish, but her was orphaned as a babby and raised in the Alcester Poorhouse. The man's name is Jared Styler. He's Studley born, but he's got no living family or settlement in the Needle District now. From all accounts he moves around these parts a lot, and sleeps wherever he finds work to do.'

'What's said about his personal character?' Tom queried.

'Well, he's got the reputation of being a very busy poacher, who's been fly enough to get away wi' it. But folks say that he's a man who can turn his hand to all sorts o' different tasks, so he has no trouble in finding folks who'll employ him. At least, that's when he troubles himself to look for work, which aren't often. He don't have any trouble picking up women, either. But apparently he turns nasty and knocks them about when he's in drink, so they never stays with him for long. Folks says that he's nigh on crippled some women, he battered them so hard, and done the same to a fair number o' blokes as well.'

'I didn't get a very good look at him,' Tom explained. 'So has he got any distinguishing marks that I might be able to identify him by?'

'Well, I did hear that a couple o' months past a woman bit a big piece out of one of his ears. That's one sweetheart he's wishing he'd never used his fist on, I'll be bound.' Maffey chuckled hoarsely. 'So if you spots a bloke with part of his right ear missing, it could well be him. That's all I've been able to find out for you, and now I'd best go before folks are getting up and about and I'm seen here.'

'If you wait a moment I'll go and get your payment for this information, Corporal Maffey,' Tom told him.

Again, Maffey shook his head. 'No, Constable Potts, I don't want any money from you. You did me a real favour by fixing me up with Mother Readman, so this bit of information is my way of returning a favour. I just hope it serves its purpose for you.'

With that he opened the door and was gone.

Nearly two hours had passed, day had dawned and Tom was still sitting at his breakfast table trying to formulate a plan of action. He accepted that it would serve no purpose to raise a 'hue and cry' for Jared Styler. He could arrest him for the assault on Carrie Perks, but he was almost certain that she would deny it was Jared Styler who had been her assailant.

The ringing of the 'Waking Bells' broke Tom's train of thought and brought the remembrance that within hours he had official duties to perform. Today in Redditch the rare event of an Emergency Hiring Market was being staged.

The unusual intensity and duration of the heatwave which was gripping the Midland counties was proving to be a very mixed blessing for the farmers. All across the broad farmlands the fields of grain were ripening with unexpected simultaneous rapidity instead of the normal varied progression, and therefore the entire crops were in danger of becoming overripe, which meant that as the crops were mown the cutting impact of scythes or sickles would shake the over-hardened seeds from the dried-out corn ears and scatter them across the ground, resulting in heavy losses of grain and the subsequent financial income.

Faced with this serious threat, the farmers were forced to search for and temporarily employ large numbers of casual workers to harvest the crops before they reached this dangerous stage of over-ripeness. To enable them to obtain these 'casuals', the local magistrates authorized Emergency Hiring Markets to be held in the nearest towns to the affected areas.

To attract sufficient numbers of temporary harvesters, the individual farmers were forced to pay unusually high wages, and the prospect of such rare largesse attracted swarms of wayfarers, tramps, gypsies and the destitute, plus many unsavoury characters.

Today would be Tom's first experience of personally policing such a market, and he was not looking forward to this virtual invasion, which invariably resulted in increased levels of drunken disorder, violent fights and assorted crimes.

Ah, well, he consoled himself. At least I'll have Will Shayler and Ritchie with me. Thank God!

SIXTEEN

Monday, morning, 3 August, 1829

Although it was only just past eight o'clock, every hitching ring on the front wall of the Fox and Goose secured the reins of several horses and, inside the Select Parlour, Tommy Fowkes, Amy Potts and Maisie Lock were hard-pressed to satisfy the clamorous demands of this influx of landowners and farmers, while in the Tap Room Gertie and Lily Fowkes were equally hard-pressed serving the lower-ranking comers to the Hiring Market.

Outside on the broad triangular sward of the Green, down-at-heel, unwashed men, women and children were constantly arriving to swell the ranks of those who had slept on the ground overnight.

In the Lock-Up, Tom Potts, Will Shayler and Ritchie Bint were facing a group of visitors, but these were not opulently dressed farmers or raggedly clad paupers. These men were plainly dressed Workhouse Masters, Parish Overseers to the Poor and Constables from several of the neighbouring parishes.

Portly, pompous-mannered Edmund Scambler, Overseer to the Poor of the Alcester Parish, was the spokesman of the group, and it was he who explained the purpose of their being here to Tom.

'Now, Master Potts, the constables are here to look out for and arrest any scoundrels who have committed, or are suspected of committing crimes in their respective parishes. As, no doubt, is the reason for Master Shayler being here also.'

'It's partly so, Master Scambler,' Will Shayler agreed. 'But unlike your other visitors, I'm also here on the instructions of Sir Francis Goodericke to aid the Tardebigge Parish Constables in any way they might ask of me.'

'I'm sure there are many present who are prepared to do that, Master Shayler,' Scambler retorted huffily, then continued, 'Now, Master Potts, I will explain the purpose of we who are not constables being here today. Our respective Vestries have instructed us Overseers and Workhouse Masters to identify any of our own parish paupers who find gainful employment in the harvesting gangs. If, on their return to their parishes, they do not inform us that they have pockets full of harvesting money, and instead try to continue to claim relief, then the necessary steps will be taken to punish them.'

This information was greeted with sustained loud applause.

Tom instantly found himself silently sympathizing with any pauper who seized upon this rare opportunity to toil for long gruelling hours to supplement the pitifully small Parish Pauper Allowance.

Scambler noticed that Tom was not applauding and, as the noise died down, he challenged aggressively, 'How now, Constable Potts! Why do you not show your agreement with what we are going to do to stop these parasitical paupers robbing we who pay our rates and tithes and taxes?'

'Because, Master Scambler, not all paupers are parasites robbing us by choice. All too many have been driven to apply for "Poor Relief" by sickness and ageing and cruel Masters. I don't believe that I would notify the Vestry either if I'd slaved night and day at the harvesting for a few shillings extra to buy food for my children.'

Scambler reddened with anger and retorted, 'It seems that you lack both commonsense and true understanding of your lawful duty, Constable Potts.'

He turned to address the gathering again. 'Now, Gentlemen, I shall not presume to advise the constables on their modes of action. However, I'm sure that I speak for all of us when I say that should the rabble become offensive and violent, the constables may be fully confident that they shall instantly receive whatever assistance we can render to them.'

Cheers and shouted affirmations greeted this statement, and Scambler flushed with gratification and bowed repeatedly.

Tom couldn't help but hope that these affirmations would indeed be backed up by physical action should violence erupt and he and his friends be in need of such assistance.

When the noise lessened, Scambler clapped his hands and announced, 'The time has come, Gentlemen. We go about our business now. Leave these premises discreetly, one at a time, and remember that we must observe our paupers from a distance and ensure that they are not aware of our presence. All that is needful is to discover and make note of the farmer who employs them, but do not approach him at this time.'

The group moved to the front door and began to exit one at a time.

Joseph Blackwell emerged from the kitchen alcove where he had been observing the proceedings and beckoned Tom and his two friends.

When they came to him he told them, 'You'll take notice that Edmund Scambler's strictures will not apply to any of our own Tardebigge paupers who manage to find employment at this market. We shall let the poor devils earn a few honest shillings if they can without being penalized for doing so. Your only purpose here is to arrest anyone who commits a criminal act, or breaks the King's Peace.'

The trio murmured their confirmations.

'Good!' Blackwell smiled bleakly. 'And I now request you, Constable Potts, to draw me a flagon of your ale and permit me to sit here in your kitchen to sup it until all these people have vacated these premises.'

'You're most welcome, Sir.' Tom grinned. 'And I trust that you will not object to we three also supping flagons of ale in your company, until our visitors have all left.'

Blackwell emitted a reedy chuckle. 'I shall thoroughly enjoy having your company, Gentlemen.'

In the Fox and Goose the crush of customers were rapidly lessening as farmers went out to look over the applicants for work. One fashionably dressed, darkly handsome man, however, seemed to be in no hurry to leave. He beckoned Maisie Lock to come to his table, and asked her, 'What's your name, my Pretty?'

Maisie smiled archly. 'I don't give my name to any stranger.'

He returned her smile, displaying white, even teeth. 'Well, I'll tell you mine and then we won't be strangers, will we? My friends call me Vincent.'

'And mine call me Maisie. Now where are you from?' she queried. 'You don't sound as if youm from these parts.'

'I'm from London, my pretty Maisie.'

'Oh, am you one o' them Cockerneys.'

He laughed. 'We're not Cockerneys, we're Cockneys. And yes, I'm a true Cockney because I was born within the sound of Bow Bells.'

'Have you seen the King and Queen?'

'Many's the time, and I've shook His Majesty's hand more than once, and been a guest in his palace as well.'

Maisie shook her head disbelievingly, and called to Amy, 'Come here a minute, Amy, and listen to the stories o' this Cockerney.'

When Amy joined her at the table, Maisie urged the man, 'Go on. Tell my mate what you've just told me.'

'Well, what a very pretty one you are, Amy,' he greeted her. 'In fact, it's hard to pick who's the most beautiful of the pair of you.'

Maisie frowned and snapped, 'Just tell her what you told me.'

He smiled at Amy. 'I'm a true Cockney, Amy. Born within the sound of Bow Bells. And I've seen the King and Queen lots of times, and I've been a guest in His Majesty's palace and shaken his hand more than once.'

Lily Fowkes came into the room and instantly joined their company, but the man ignored her and kept his gaze fixed on Amy. 'Well, Amy, do you think I'm telling the truth?'

She shrugged and told him, 'I neither know nor care, Master Cockney. But I'm telling you the truth when I say that we might be country girls but we're not stupid bumpkins to be taken in by any tall stories.'

She turned away, telling Maisie, 'Come on, we've got work to do.'

Another fashionably dressed stranger came through the door and called, 'Come, Vincent, the wagon's here and we need to get going straight away.'

The Cockney instantly rose and bowed to the girls. 'I'll have to love and leave you, Amy and Maisie. But the next time I call in I'll have the proof of my tall stories with me.' He swaggered out of the room.

'Does you think he'll be able to prove what he says?' Maisie wondered aloud.

Amy shrugged dismissively. 'Oh, yes, and it'll be at that same time when he proves pigs can fly.'

*   *   *

On the Green, Tom and his two friends were marshalling the would-be harvest hands into long, stationary lines for the prospective employers to pass along and inspect.

Large numbers of curious spectators encircled the Green and mingled with them were the Overseers to the Poor, the Workhouse Masters and the Parish Constables.

The farmers and landowners clustered together in a sizeable group until the marshalling of the lines was completed. Then they split up and began their individual inspections and selections.

Tom met up briefly with his two friends before they started their separate patrolling of the serried lines and asked them if they knew Jared Styler or Carrie Perks.

Ritchie Bint shook his head, but Will Shayler nodded and smiled grimly. 'Oh, yes, Styler was born and raised in Studley. He's a bloody nuisance of a poacher, and when he's drunk he'll use his fists on anybody who crosses him, man or woman. Trouble is he's been too fly for me to catch him at his poaching, and I've never been able to persuade anybody he's beaten up to lay charges against him.'

'Well, that's why I'm after him myself,' Tom explained. 'His current woman is named Carrie Perks, and he smashed her nose on Saturday night, but I'm sure she'll deny it was him. If she's here she'll be easy to recognize. Hugh Laylor dressed the wound, and the plaster covers the entire middle of her face and extends round her head.' He turned to Ritchie Bint. 'Because it was dusk I could only see that Styler was wearing a white smock and slouched wide-awake hat. He looked to be nigh on six feet tall and strongly built, and I've been told that there's been a piece bitten out of one ear.'

'Yes, his right ear,' Shayler confirmed. 'And he's six foot and got thick black hair worn longish. He's still remarkably young looking considering he must be over forty. His face is clear-skinned and he still had all his teeth the last time I saw him.'

'D'you want me to grab him if I comes across him?' Ritchie Bint asked.

Tom shook his head. 'No, just come and tell me where he is and who he's with. If it's Carrie Perks and they look to be friendly then I don't think there'll be the slightest chance of her laying charges against him.'

SEVENTEEN

Monday, mid-morning, 3 August, 1829

His temper seething, Judas Benton was pacing up and down outside the front door of his shop. Monday mornings were normally busy times for his business. In the aftermath of their husbands' weekend carousing, many housewives would be bringing articles to pawn so that they had money to buy food to feed their families until the next payday.

Today, however, the possibility of obtaining temporary well-paid work meant that the vast majority of his regular Monday customers were up on the Green, standing in the lines of would-be harvest hands.

'Fuck it! I'm just wasting me time down here!' he cursed, and then came to an abrupt halt. 'Maybe that bloke and wench who pawned the snuffbox might be up there looking for work?'

He locked the door of his shop and hurried up the hill.

Farmer Andrew Parkman halted and stared in surprised recognition at the burly, white-smocked man standing in the line in front of him.

'Bloody hell, Jared! I didn't expect to find you here!'

'Oh, I just thought I'd see what was on offer, Master Parkman,' Styler answered.

'Have you had any offers yet?'

'O' course I have, Master Parkman. More than half a dozen already.' Jared Styler grinned. 'But you knows I'm very choosy about what work I does and who I does it for. So I've been waiting to see if you was to come past.'

'And I'm bloody glad you did wait! If I'd known you was here I'd have come straight to you. You're my Harvest Steward as of this very second.' Parkman's ruddy features were radiating satisfaction. 'Now listen – my own people have made a start wi' the scythe mowing, so I'll get back to them straight away and leave you to do the business here. We'll need to use sickles to cut the ripest ridges, so bring me half-a-dozen Sickle Reapers. That'll be two blokes who are experienced Bandsters and four women. Then we can split them into a bloke to reap and bind and pair o' women reapers per ridge. We'll need another experienced bloke for the stooking and to help with some binding as well if needs be. Oh, and you can recruit an extra wench to do the odd jobs, so that's a gang of eight all together.'

'That'll be no problem for me, Master Parkman. I knows how to pick 'um and how to drive 'um,' Styler affirmed confidently. 'Usual offer, I take it. Top wages, with a fair bit extra if they works really well; plus we give them plenty o' food, drink and a dry place to sleep in.'

Parkman grinned and winked broadly. 'That's it, Jared – promise the buggers the earth if needs be. We can settle any misunderstandings about their wages after the harvest is got in.'

Styler grinned and nodded. 'That we can, Master Parkman, and I'm certain that we'll win any arguments we might get into with any of 'um.'

'Right then, that's settled.' Parkman handed Styler some coins. 'Here's some sweetener for you to use, and I'll see you and the new gang at the farm tonight.'

The actual hiring was now steadily progressing, palms being spat on and loudly slapped between bargainers to seal agreements. The general atmosphere was becoming increasingly festive. As always at such gatherings, traders, pedlars and hucksters were displaying their assorted goods and artefacts. Food, drink and sweetmeat sellers were offering their refreshments. Fiddlers and drummers were playing. Balladeers were singing their songs of love and heartbreak. Broadsheet vendors were bawling dramatic news headlines.

'DREADFUL MURDERS IN REDDITCH TOWN! THE DEVIL'S MONK RISEN FROM THE DEAD. A BEAUTIFUL YOUNG MAIDEN AND A FINE OLD GENTLEMAN SLAIN BY THE FIEND FROM HELL! READ ALL ABOUT IT FOR ONLY THREEPENCE!'

Tom was patrolling his allotted area of the lines when this hoarse bellowing sounded loudly in his ears. He turned, saw the vendor only yards distant and on impulse beckoned the man to him and purchased a broadsheet.

The front page of the flimsy doubled sheet of paper was covered in a crudely etched, black-and-white picture of a horned Devil, clad in in a monk's habit, holding a woman's dismembered head in his hands, which he was tearing the flesh from with his fanged teeth. The woman's body was sprawled at his feet, entwined with the body of a man.

The other sides of the sheet were filled with the bloodcurdling testimonies of anonymous witnesses to the actual murders, who had themselves been pursued by the Devil's Monk. These same witnesses also gave harrowing accounts of the terror which gripped the entire Needle District, and virulently criticized the failure of the Tardebigge Parish Constables and Magistrates to track down and capture the Devil's Monk.

Tom, noting the printers were Solomons Bros., Birmingham, accepted that this nonsensical fabrication was standard practice in the production of broadsheets, and was resigned to the fact that he could expect a great many jeers and insults from its readers.

At the end of the line where Tom was standing, a young girl, her head covered and her features concealed by a voluminous shawl, came to an abrupt standstill as she sighted Tom's motionless figure. Then she turned and walked rapidly away.

Dogging her progress, Judas Benton also sighted Tom and congratulated himself.

'I'm bloody well right about this wench, aren't I? She's got something to hide all right, or else why should she shy away from bloody Potts like that?'

By noontime Jared Styler had recruited all but one of the Sickle Gang. He was very confident that his recruits would satisfy the needs of Andrew Parkman, but the single remaining recruit he now sought for was meant to satisfy his own personal needs rather than his employer's.

'Now then, Girl, what can you offer me in return for the very good wages I can offer you?' Jared Styler smiled at the pretty young girl in the line before him.

'What sort of work does you want me for?' she questioned pertly.

'Oh, just easy little odd jobs that might need doing, and I'll show you how to do them if needs be.'

'How many hours do I have to work a day?'

'Five in the morning till sun down. An hour off for breakfast from eight till nine. Another hour off for dinner from one till two, and a fifteen-minute rest to drink your beer at four o'clock. Then work till dusk.'

'And how much will a fine Gentleman like you be paying me for that?' She smiled flirtatiously.

'Whatever you proves to be worth.' He chuckled. 'And for a wench wi' your good looks and spirit, I reckon it could be as much as a half-crown a day, plus plenty o' good food and drink and a clean place to sleep.'

'And whose harvest shall I be helping to get in?'

'Master Andrew Parkman's at Upper Bordesley Farm. I'm his Harvest Steward.'

'And what's your name?'

'Jared Styler. But you must address me as Master.'

'Oh, must I?' She pouted coquettishly. 'Why can't I just call you Jared?'

He grinned. 'Because I can't have the other women thinking that I'm favouring you because youm pretty and I wants to be your friend. Now you tell me your name, if you wants to earn all that money I'm going to pay you. Plus whatever other reward I might give you, which the rest of the gang won't know about, because it'll be our secret.'

'I'm Jenny Tolley.' She bobbed a curtsey and giggled. 'Your humble servant, Master Styler.'

He became brisk and businesslike. 'If you wants the work, go into the Crown tavern at the top of the Fish Hill and you'll find my reaping gang there. Tell the landlord that you're one of my harvest hands and he'll give you a free drink and a bite to eat. I'll be coming to take you all to the farm as soon as I've finished my business here.'

He walked away, leaving her frowning in pique at this casual dismissal.

But on Jared Styler's face there was a satisfied smile. Young Jenny Tolley was exactly the sort of girl he had been hoping to find that day, and he was confident that within a very brief time he'd be bedding her.

Savouring this prospect, he was threading through the encircling crowd when his name was called. He halted and turned as Carrie Perks ran to face him, pulling back her shawl to disclose her features.

'Jared! where've you been? I've been looking all over the place for you ever since Sunday morning! Why did you take your stuff and leave our lodging?'

His gaze flicked around to see if she was attracting any undue attention from the people nearest them, as he demanded, 'Now keep your voice down and tell me what's that on your face?'

'It's the plaster the doctor put on it to mend me nose. You broke it, Jared! You broke me nose! But no matter how many times they asked me, I never told 'um it was you. I said I never knew who did it. I said I never saw the bloke before.'

Her voice faltered and her eyes filled with tears.

'Oh, Carrie, I never wanted to hurt you like that.' He sighed heavily and shook his head. 'You knows very well that I feels terrible whenever I has to slap you to make you behave proper. But it's your own fault for behaving so bad and driving me half-mad with your fuckin' lies and whinging. I left the lodging because I've been worried sick and looking all over the place for you! Yesterday I went to Headless Cross and to Crabbs Cross, and Astwood Bank and Feckenham as well. Now I've only just this morning come back from searching Studley and Sambourne and Spernal Ash.'

Sobbing with relief she threw her arms around him, choking out brokenly, 'Oh sweetheart, I been worried to death that you'd left me! I'll be a better girl. I'll behave meself, I swear.'

'Youm the love o' me life, and I'll never leave you!' he hissed fervently as he rearranged her shawl to conceal her features, then led her quickly away from the thronged Green.

Concealed in that throng, Judas Benton was a very intent viewer of this lovers' reunion.

Ritchie Bint had been discreetly relieving his overstretched bladder against a wall of a hovel in a winding, narrow alleyway near to the Green, and was returning to his patrol area when a man and woman came walking quickly towards him.

Despite the closely drawn shawl around her head, he spotted the plaster dressing bisecting the woman's face and noted that her companion's appearance fitted the general description of Jared

Styler. The woman was clinging to the man's arm and pressing her body as close to him as their quick pace allowed, and as they passed Ritchie Bint she reached up, pulled her companion's head down and kissed his face. His long black hair fell forwards and disclosed his mutilated right ear.

'That's him, that's Jared Styler,' Bint realized but, mindful of Tom's instructions, he made no attempt to stop them as they went on and entered the alleyway.

Then Judas Benton came past him, also walking quickly towards the entrance of the same alleyway. But when Benton reached it, he pressed close to the adjoining wall and appeared to peep cautiously down the alleyway. He withdrew his head, waited for a brief instant then peeped again, and this time stepped into the alleyway and disappeared from view.

'He's bloody stalking them!' Ritchie Bint realized. 'But what for? Is he hoping to "Peeping Tom" them having a shag or what?' He shook his head and chuckled. 'Well, whatever it is the sly bastard 'ull be up to no good, that's for sure. I reckon Tom 'ull be real interested when I tells him.'

As soon as Tom heard the name Judas Benton, excitement pulsed through him. A couple of years previously Benton's brother, Ishmael, had been involved in child trafficking until his own accomplices had murdered him. Tom was convinced that Judas Benton had been involved with Ishmael Benton in that same vile trade, but he had not been able to obtain enough legal proof to charge the pawnbroker.

Ritchie Bint finished his report and grinned. 'What d'you think, Tom? Why was the bastard following them two? Is he up to no good again?'

'I bloody well hope so!' Tom stated emphatically. 'Believe me, Ritchie, I'm going to go and have a little chat with Benton in the very near future.'

The isolated single-storied, mud-walled thatched cottage to which Jared Styler and Carrie Perks had journeyed stood surrounded by wasteland and patches of bushy undergrowth on the outskirts of Ipsley hamlet, some two miles south-east of Redditch Town.

When the couple entered it, sweat-soaked Judas Benton breathed a heartfelt wish. 'I hope this is as far as theym going!'

Inside the tumbledown walls, Carrie Perks told her lover, 'I'll only be a tick getting me stuff, Jared. I've hid it up under the thatch. But you aren't told me yet where we're going to for the harvesting?'

He nodded. 'That's right, my wench. I aren't told you, have I.' Grinning savagely, he grabbed her and pulled her hard against him, using one hand to crush her face into his chest, ignoring her shriek of pain and hissing into her ear. 'I aren't told you where we're going to for the harvesting because you won't be coming with me!'

Judas Benton heard the shriek, and the other shrieks that followed, and leered spitefully. 'Bloody hell! Her's getting it good and hard, aren't her just!'

He had been hiding in the thick undergrowth for more than an hour when Jared Styler came out alone from the small cottage and walked back along the rutted lane.

Benton frowned in surprise. 'Why aren't the wench with him?'

When Styler passed the ditch and went on in the direction of Redditch, Benton hesitated in a quandary. Should he go into the cottage and check on the girl or follow the man?

Styler disappeared from view.

'I can always come back here later to talk to the wench.' Benton exited his hiding place and hurried in pursuit.

Once again, Benton was sweating heavily long before Jared Styler reached and entered the Crown tavern on the top of the Fish Hill. The pawnbroker halted some distance away, mopping his brow while he debated whether to go into the building.

While he hesitated, Jared Styler reappeared, followed by a group of men and women carrying bags and sacks, some of them with sickles slung on ropes upon their backs. Styler led them down the Fish Hill. Benton smiled with satisfaction and made no move to follow. He was a regular customer at the Crown and knew that he could obtain all the necessary information he needed from its landlord.

EIGHTEEN

Tuesday, dawn, 4 August, 1829

'Wake up! Wake up!' Tom and Ritchie Bint shouted repeatedly as they hammered on the cell doors to rouse the overnight occupants, who for the most part reacted with groans, curses and shouts of complaint.

The jangling of the bells added to the cacophony, and when Tom opened the front door Maisie Lock greeted him with a further complaint.

'Bloody hell, Tom Potts! This place stinks worse than a bloody pig sty!'

'Don't I know it,' Tom agreed ruefully.

'Tommy Fowkes wants to know how many breakfasts for the constables? And if you wants any grub sent across for the prisoners?'

'Six of ham and eggs for we constables, bread and cheese enough for eight prisoners, and a small keg of Porter, please, Maisie,' Tom informed her. Then asked, 'How's Amy this morning?'

Maisie's eyes gleamed provocatively. 'Her's singing as sweet and merry as a lark, Tom Potts. Like her's been doing ever since her left this stinking hole.'

Tom controlled the impulse to make a sharp reply and answered quietly, 'I'm very happy to hear that she's in good spirits. Now can you please tell Master Fowkes to have the food and drink sent over here as quickly as possible because this Sessions will be starting at eight o'clock. Remind him that My Lord Aston is to preside, and will be very displeased if the constables and prisoners have not received their lawful rights when he arrives.'

Annoyed by Tom's calm reaction to her barb, Maisie Lock tossed her head and snapped, 'Tommy Fowkes knows very well how to conduct his business, and he'll have everything done in plenty o' time before the bloody Sessions starts. You should do your own job proper and catch that Devil's Monk who's running round killing decent folks.'

Before he could reply she was hurrying away, and Tom could only shake his head resignedly. He turned and shouted to Ritchie Bint, 'I'm going to have that chat with Benton. I'll not be long.'

But when he reached the pawnbroker's shop there were no lights glowing in its windows, and his knocking on its door brought no reply.

Tom walked away, wondering, Where's he gone, and what is he up to?

On Andrew Parkman's farm the harvest gangs had been roused before dawn, and as the sun rose above the horizon they were already hard at work.

Judas Benton had also risen before dawn and at sunrise he was walking along the river bank path. From a distance Benton saw moving figures on the higher section of a sloping field which ran upwards from the river. He halted, took a small telescope from his pocket and trained it on the activity, switching from one figure to another and grinning with satisfaction to find that they were the Sickle Gang, and he was able to identify the stationary horseman overlooking them as Jared Styler.

Benton considered his next move. The landlord of the Crown had known Jared Styler for some time, and had talked freely about Styler's violent temperament and voracious appetite for young girls. He had also described the man as being a gambler and spendthrift, in constant need for money.

Benton touched the hard outline of the pistol in his capacious coat pocket. 'This'll make the bugger think twice about getting rough with me.'

Benton felt the lump of the purse in his waistcoat pocket. 'And he'll be only too eager to take this bait, won't he?'

He put his telescope away and walked onwards.

NINETEEN

The Select Parlour of the Fox and Goose was the designated venue for the Court of Petty Sessions of the Parish of Tardebigge. This morning's 'Special Sessions' was an extracurricular court being held solely to deal with any arrests made during the Hiring Fair, and Reverend the Lord Aston was presiding as magistrate by himself.

As always, the room's furnishings had been rearranged for the Sessions. Lord Aston was now sitting in a capacious, sumptuously padded armchair facing tightly spaced rows of stools, chairs and tables. At Aston's right-hand side was a small table bearing a selection of glasses and bottles of wines and spirits. From the moment of his arrival an hour previously to take breakfast at the Fox and Goose, Aston had been freely partaking of the selection on offer, and these libations, coupled with the after-effects of his previous night's debauchery, had rendered him intoxicated. But his long years of heavy drinking had conditioned him to present a facade of sobriety.

To Aston's left side, Magistrates' Clerk Joseph Blackwell was sitting at a desk strewn with ledgers, sheaves of paper, quill pens, inkwells and a very large leather-bound Bible.

Tom Potts was standing beside the desk, his yard-long constable's staff shouldered like a musket.

Tommy and Lily Fowkes were behind the counter feverishly filling tankards and glasses with drinks which Amy and Maisie were carrying to the noisy men and women cramming the room.

In the wide entrance corridor of the inn, Ritchie Bint, William Shayler and the three visiting constables guarded the manacled prisoners.

As the wall clock struck the hour of eight o'clock, Tom stepped forward and shouted, 'Order! Order! This court is now in session! Silence in the King's Name! Bring in the first prisoners.'

One of the visiting constables entered, carrying a small bulging sack bag in one hand and leading three heavily manacled, ragged, barefoot men who were chained together by their necks, and whose heads and faces were visibly bruised and bloodied.

'What's your name and parish, Constable? And who are these rogues?' Aston demanded.

'I am William Seymour, Constable of Alcester, Warwickshire, My Lord. These rogues are refusing to give me their names. But I have good reason to believe that they are the culprits who robbed a cobbler's workplace in Alcester two nights since.'

'What is that reason?' Aston queried.

The constable tipped the sack he carried and six shiny, new-looking boots fell on to the floor. 'They were wearing these, My Lord, and could give me no proof that they had come by them honestly. May I respectfully bring to your attention, My Lord, the invaluable assistance I received from Deputy Constable Bint to secure these rogues when they violently resisted arrest. With your permission, My Lord, I wish to take these rogues back to Alcester and have the cobbler identify these boots as his property.

'Also, My Lord, may I respectfully request that you permit Deputy Constable Bint to help me escort them back to Alcester.'

Aston leered. 'Permission granted, Constable, and you and Bint also have my permission to boot these scum up their arses all the way back to Alcester, and after their committal, then all the way to the Warwick Gaol.'

An outburst of jeering laughter and applause erupted from the audience as the constable led the trio out of the room. Lord Aston allowed it to continue as he poured himself another glass of wine and gulped it with patent satisfaction.

At the hour of eight o'clock down on Lower Bordesley Farm, Jenny Tolley led a donkey pulling a small cart along the river bank path and through the open gate of the field where the Sickle Gang were working. As she passed through the gate she aggressively challenged Judas Benton, who was leaning against the gatepost grinning lasciviously at her.

'You needs to pack in gawping at me like that. My friend up there on the horse is the boss here, and he'll learn you some manners double quick if I says the word to him.'

'Oh, you're a friend of Master Jared Styler are you, me duck. Well, that being the case I'm honoured to make your acquaintance, and I'm truly sorry if I've angered you in any way.' Benton lifted his tall hat and bowed apologetically. Then asked politely, 'Could you please do me a favour and ask Master Styler if he could spare a little time to have a private word with me. You can say that I promise him it'll be very much to his pecuniary advantage to do so.'

'What's that word, pecunn-whatever?' She shook her head. 'I don't know what that means.'

'No matter, me duck.' He waved his hand in casual dismissal. 'If you just say it'll be worth money to him, I reckon that'll serve just as well.'

She walked on and he resumed leaning against the gate-post.

'Here's your breakfast coming,' Jared Styler told the workers. 'Finish the stooks you're cutting and then knock off.'

He turned his horse and walked it down the slope to meet the oncoming donkey cart, and when he neared it shouted: 'What's you brought us, Jenny?'

'Freshly baked bread, cheese, onions, a big bucket of mutton and turnip stew, and a keg of ale,' the girl shouted back and smiled mischievously. 'And a chance to make your fortune.'

He reached her and, as they both halted, queried curiously, 'What was that last thing you said?'

She giggled and turned to point at the gate. 'That bloke down there says that if you'll have a word with him he'll make you your fortune.'

'Did he now.' Jared Styler peered hard at the top-hatted figure leaning against the gatepost. 'And did he tell you what I must do to earn it?'

'No, he never.' Jenny Tolley shook her head, then preened flirtatiously. 'But I've always said that if a man with a fortune came a'courting me, he'd have a lot more chance of winning my hand than if he hadn't got one.'

'Well, if that's the case, I'd best go and have that word with him straight away.' Styler chuckled and kicked his horse into a fast trot down the slope.

Now that the moment of confrontation with this violent man was here, Judas Benton's heart began to beat rapidly. His right

hand moved into his coat pocket to grip the butt of the pistol
and he moved away from the gateway to stand on the river bank
pathway.

As Jared Styler reined in, recognition came to him with the
memory of the day he had sent Carrie Perks to pawn the snuffbox,
and he demanded, 'Why d'you want to speak with me, Master
Pawnbroker?'

Benton coughed to ease the nervous constriction in his throat.
'I wants to speak with you, Master Styler, about something which
could be very profitable for both of us.'

'And what might that be?'

'The treasure that Methuselah Leeson found. I know you've
got it hid away somewhere.'

For a few seconds Styler stared impassively into Benton's eyes,
then his head went back, his mouth gaped wide and he roared
with laughter.

Benton's own jaw dropped and he could only stare at the other
man in totally shocked bewilderment.

Still roaring with laughter, Styler kicked his horse into sudden
movement and its weight smashed into Benton, sending him
staggering backwards and toppling into the river.

The combined effects of heatwave and drought had made the
river levels low, and Benton landed on his side in thick mud and
water less than a foot high. Frantically scrabbling with hands
and feet, he managed to eventually struggle back up the steep
bank and on to the pathway, where he collapsed face down,
dragging in wheezy gasps of air.

Jared Styler didn't wait to watch what Benton was doing, but
rode back up the field to where his gang were sitting eating and
drinking. As he dismounted, Jenny Tolley hastened to bring him
a platter of food and a tankard of ale.

'Here you are, Master Styler. You sit yourself down and have
some breakfast. I've tried to pick the best bits for you. When are
you going to make your fortune then?'

He took her offerings and grinned. 'Not today, my wench,
that's for sure.'

TWENTY

Tuesday, noon, 4 August, 1829

The Special Sessions proceedings were drawing to a close. The Constable of Bromsgrove had presented a prisoner who had deserted his wife and children, leaving them to be supported by Parish Relief, and Lord Aston had given permission for the man to be taken back to be dealt with by the Bromsgrove Magistrates.

Lord Aston's permission was also given to William Shayler, Constable of Studley, who had apprehended two suspected horse thieves, whom he would escort to appear before the Warwick bench, and to the Constable of Henley in Arden, who had arrested a deserter from the army, who would also be taken before the Warwick bench.

All of the constables had immediately departed with their prisoners after receiving their permissions.

The last remaining prisoner, escorted by Tom, was now standing before Lord Aston. He was heavily bearded, clothed in filthy rags and skeletally gaunt.

'Hold on for a moment, Constable Potts,' Joseph Blackwell requested, and then informed Lord Aston. 'This final prisoner, My Lord, was found by Constable Potts lying on a grave in the chapel yard in the early hours of this morning. The man appears to be wandering in his senses, and could give no account of himself to Constable Potts, who then took him into custody for the man's own protection. Constable Potts has brought him before you to request that you will commit the unfortunate creature to be secured in safety in our Poorhouse. To remain confined there until such time as the Parish Vestry can meet to determine what should best be done to help him.'

Aston scowled and drawled sneeringly, 'How blessed the people of this parish are to have such a benevolent soul as Thomas Potts protecting them in his post as Constable of Tardebigge

Parish. This morning five constables have appeared before this bench who have done their lawful duty and arrested violent, thieving rogues. A duty which protected we, the loyal, law-abiding subjects of His Majesty from the depredations of law-less scum. Constable Thomas Potts, however, afforded none of those constables any physical assistance in arresting these dangerous rogues. Constable Thomas Potts obviously had other fish to fry. Such as holding in his personal custody a helpless, harmless simpleton.'

Aston paused and, taking a folded broadsheet from his pocket, made a great show of opening the paper out and smoothing across his knees.

The roomful of people were silent, avidly intent. Behind the serving counter the faces of Tommy Fowkes and his three female helpers displayed varying emotions.

Tommy and Lily Fowkes were smiling maliciously. Amy Potts was staring anxiously at her husband, while Maisie Lock, after glancing at her friend's troubled expression, directed an angry glare at Tom Potts.

Aston held the broadsheet up, displaying the crude picture of the Devil's Monk to his audience. Slowly shaking his head from side to side, his pendulous swollen jowls wobbled in concert as he proclaimed in a tone of despairing sadness, 'Ladies and Gentlemen, I expect many of you have already perused this account of these foul, evil murders which have struck dread and fear throughout the length and breadth of our beloved parish. I have no doubt that all of you share my own fervent wish, that rather than wasting his time arresting helpless, harmless simpletons, Constable Thomas Potts should instead devote himself solely to the pursuit and arrest of the Devil's Monk! The vile fiend who slaughtered these poor, helpless victims. The same vile fiend who remains free to slaughter any one of us or our families. This Devil's Monk!'

After an instant of silence the room erupted with foot-stamping and hand-clapping. There were bellowed cheers and plaudits for Lord Aston and jeers and insults directed at Tom, who could only grit his teeth and struggle to keep his face impassive, while in his mind a furious loathing for Lord Aston was raging.

Amy covered her face with her hands and ran out of the room, and Maisie went after her.

Grim-faced, Joseph Blackwell rose from his desk, came to

Tom and ordered, 'Go immediately and take this fellow to the Poorhouse, Constable Potts. Tell the Master that I've authorized the committal and will have the documentation delivered to him tomorrow.'

Lord Aston, grinning broadly, poured himself another glass of wine and lifted it in a congratulatory toast to the crowd before gulping it down.

As Tom led the vagrant out from the hostile tumult he looked for Amy, and felt relief that she was no longer in the room. Yet at the same time he was racked with bitter shame that she had witnessed this public humiliation.

TWENTY-ONE

Tuesday, dusk, 4 August, 1829

When the Lock-Up bells jangled Tom's only desire was to ignore the summons and remain in the darkly shadowed kitchen alcove. The shame of the humiliation he had endured that morning in the Fox and Goose still tormented him, and his anger against Lord Aston and the hostile, jeering crowd still burned.

But the ruthless self-honesty which was an integral part of his character also impelled him to acknowledge that if he had been spectator instead of target that morning, he would have accepted that the hostile reaction of the crowd was understandable: 'This killer might strike again at any moment, and I'm failing to find a single clue as to identity. Of course, the locals are fearful and angry.'

The bells jangled again and Tom sighed ruefully. 'Ah, well, duty calls.'

He used flint, steel and tinder to light a lamp and went with it to open the front door.

'Don't shine that bloody lamp in me face!' Judas Benton snapped. 'Let me in, for God's sake!'

He pushed past Tom and urged, 'Close the bloody door, will you! I don't want anybody to see me here!'

Tom closed it and again shone the lamp beams on to the other man, noting the caked dried mud on his clothing, hands and face. But only queried, 'Where's your hat, Master Benton?'

'Drowned in the bloody river, where I'd have bloody drowned as well if that murdering bastard, Jared Styler, had had his way.'

Tom's heart rate quickened and excitement kindled. 'You'd best come and sit down, Master Benton, and tell me exactly what's happened to you.' He led the other man to the alcove, and seated him before asking, 'What has Jared Styler done to you, Master Benton? And why has he done it?'

'The bastard's tried to murder me, like he murdered Methuselah Leeson!' Benton shouted agitatedly.

Tom's heart thudded violently, and he was forced to draw a deep breath before he could ask: 'Have you proof that Styler murdered Methuselah Leeson?'

'Oh, yes! Oh, yes! Oh, yes! Oh, yes!' Benton's head nodded jerky affirmation with each repetition of the words.

'And what is that proof?' Tom interrupted the constant repetitions.

'This for starters!' Benton pulled a silver snuffbox from his pocket and thrust it into Tom's hands. 'Just open it and look hard underneath the lid.'

Tom did so, holding the box close to the lamp, squinting his eyes to centre on the tiny letters. He then drew his breath sharply as he deciphered the name. 'Matthias Leeson.'

'How did you come by this box?' he questioned Benton.

'It was the Saturday before last, and the Finish Bells had been rung a few minutes afore, so the work folks were coming to do their shopping. I was outside me shop and I noticed a couple further up the hill who looked to be having a row. I saw the bloke hand the wench this box, and then I went back into the shop. Then the wench come in and wanted to pawn this box. I asked her the usual questions, and she told me her name was Smith and that she was born and bred in Brummagem. She said this was her dad's box, and her dad was Brummagem born and bred as well.

'Then I asked her if the bloke I'd seen her with was her dad, and she said no, it was her friend. Then why had he got the box in his pocket? I asked her. She said he was keeping it for her in case she might be robbed by somebody . . . And the reason she was now in Redditch was to look for work and lodgings. O' course, by that time I'd already twigged that she was telling me a pack o' lies about her being Brummagem born and bred. I knew from her speech she was most likely born and bred down Alcester way.' Benton paused, and asked, 'Can you give me a drink? Me throat's that dry and sore it's paining me to speak.'

As Tom selected a tankard from the cupboards and filled it with ale from the trestle-borne keg, he deliberately slowed the process to give himself time to calm his own excitement and to marshal his thoughts.

Up to this point he judged that Benton's story bore the ring of truth, and from what he had been told about Styler's character the man was capable of violence which could prove to be lethal. But although this lead looked very promising, Tom bore in mind that it was still only a promising lead.

While Benton was taking his first mouthfuls from the tankard, Tom asked, 'Why did it take you so long to discover that this box was inscribed with Matthias Leeson's name?'

Benton swallowed, belched, then stated bluntly, 'It didn't! I found the name on it the very same day when I had the time to check it carefully.'

Tom was taken aback and could only exclaim, 'Then why in Hell's name didn't you come and tell me that you'd taken pawn of a snuffbox which Methuselah Leeson's wife said had been stolen from him?'

The other man scowled and snarled, 'Because I saw the opportunity to restore my good name in this parish, after what me cursed brother did to drag it into the mud. I know what you thinks of me, Potts, and I wanted to show you how wrong you am about me. So I decided to bring to justice whoever had killed Methuselah Leeson by myself. And I've fuckin' well done it, aren't I!' He grinned triumphantly. 'While you've been buzzing around like a blue-arsed fly and getting nowhere, I've tracked down and discovered who the fuckin' killer is. So that's fucked you up your arse, aren't it! And after Styler's been hung I shall demand you to make a public apology to me for bad-mouthing me like you've done these past couple of years!'

'If Styler is guilty then I most certainly will give you all the credit you deserve for bringing him to justice, Master Benton.'

Tom meant what he said. 'But tell me why Styler attacked you today? Did you accuse him of killing Leeson?'

The other man bared his rat-like fangs in a sneering grin and scoffed, 'To ask me that shows why you're no fuckin' use as a constable.' His tone became boastful. 'O' course I never accused him. I'm too bloody sharp-witted to do that. What I did was to let him know that I knew he'd got Methuselah Leeson's treasure hidden away, and then I told him that if he wanted to make good money from it he should let me deal with the business side o' things.'

'And what did he say to your offer?' Tom queried.

'He looked fritted to death, and he shouted at me to tell him how I'd found out what he'd done to Leeson,' Benton declared. 'And the next second he went fuckin' mad and did his best to kill me. He knocked me into the river to drown me, but I landed on the mud in the shallows. He was going to come down the bank at me, but I pulled this out and it fritted him off.'

Benton took the muddied pistol from his pocket and brandished it. 'If I hadn't had this with me I'd be a dead man now.'

'Was his sweetheart with him when all this was going on?' Tom questioned.

Benton shook his head. 'He never took her with him to Parkman's farm. But I know where they've been lodging because I followed them both there on the day of the Hiring Fair. That's if he aren't killed and buried her to keep her silent about the murder he's done, because when I was hiding and watching the cottage they'd gone into, I could hear her screaming and begging him to stop battering her.'

For brief moments Tom mulled over what action he should take, and the memory of his morning's humiliation impelled his reaction. 'Take me to that cottage, Master Benton. I need to speak with her this very night.'

'Bloody hell! Give me the chance to finish me drink and have a bit of a rest, will you!' Benton protested.

'You'll rest all the easier when Jared Styler is locked in one of my cells, Master Benton. Because if you have told me the truth, Styler will already be planning how he'll shut your mouth for good.'

Benton instantly gulped the tankard empty and stood up.

TWENTY-TWO

Tuesday, 4 August, 1829

I t was nearing midnight, and no light or sound was coming from the small, single-storied cottage as the two men approached. Tom led his companion into the undergrowth then loaded and primed the brace of pistols slung in separate holsters across his chest. Next he checked that the low-turned wick in his shielded bullseye lantern was still alight.

'You stay here, Master Benton, and keep still and silent,' he whispered.

'If Styler's there, make sure you shoots the bastard afore he grabs you,' Benton hissed in reply.

A cocked pistol in his right hand, the shielded lantern in his left, Tom trod cautiously as he moved slowly through the undergrowth. His heart was pounding and his breathing rapid and shallow from mingled excitement and fear.

When he reached the wall of the cottage he stepped to the side of the door, which to his surprise was slightly ajar. He stood holding his breath, his ear close to the gap between the door and doorpost, listening hard. All was silent within. He hesitated for long seconds, mentally castigating himself for his fearful reluctance to burst into the room and face whatever peril might be lurking within.

He opened the shutter of the lamp, dragged in a strained breath and burst into the room, swinging the lamp beam around the malodorous interior, shouting aloud, 'Stand fast in the King's Name or I shoot!'

On the earthen floor of the room was a large straw mattress with a coarse blanket and light-coloured sheets strewn across it. The only other furnishings were a broken-backed wooden chair and two three-legged stools. Skeletal remnants of what had been a plank partition divided the interior into two cramped compartments.

Slowly, the pounding of Tom's heart began to lessen and his

breathing eased as he swept the lamp beam slowly across the floor and walls.

Built into one wall was a small brick hearth, fire grate and chimney with a built-in iron grid and hooks for cooking pots to sit on or hang from. By the side of the hearth there were two iron cooking pots, some small earthenware bowls, wooden spoons and a large reed basket covered with a cloth.

Tom bent over the basket and lifted the cloth to disclose half a loaf of mouldy bread. He straightened and thought hard before returning to where Judas Benton was waiting.

'Why was you so long in there?' Benton demanded pettishly. 'I was starting to think fuckin' Styler had done for you!'

'Well, he hasn't,' Tom snapped curtly as his intense dislike for this man momentarily came to the fore. 'The place is deserted, but I need to make a thorough examination of it, so I'm going to wait here until daylight. You can go back home now.'

Benton scowled suspiciously. 'Has you found some valuables in there that you don't want me to know about?'

Tom's temper fired, but he only shook his head and replied, 'No! But if I do they'll be brought before the court as evidence. Now just go, and I'll come and speak with you when I've finished here.' He waved his hand in dismissal, turned his back on the other man and walked away.

Benton bared his fangs in a vicious snarl, shook his fist at Tom's retreating figure and, hissing foul abuse, also walked away.

In case Carrie Perks or Jared Styler might return, Tom could seek no respite in sleep, and the long hours waiting for daylight were a seemingly endless journey through the torments of his separation from Amy.

When Wednesday dawned, Tom felt intense relief that he could now begin physically investigating his surroundings and escape from his memories. He rose stiffly from the broken-backed chair and, after making sure that there was no one outside the door, went out himself.

He made a cautious circuit of the cottage, but found no signs and heard no sounds of human nearness. Impelled by urgent physical necessity he went into a dense thicket of bushes, pulled down his pantaloons and squatted to empty his bladder and bowels.

By the time he had wiped his backside with leaves pulled from the bushes, and cleansed his hands by rubbing them through dew-wet grass, the sun had cleared the horizon.

Tom stood for some time savouring its strengthening rays and the full daylight they were bringing to his surroundings. He also relished the increasingly powerful thrill of the hunt that any exploration of fresh aspects of an investigation aroused in him. Now he was able to thrust away the melancholy of loss and centre his emotions on the task awaiting him within the cottage. He returned to its door whistling a jaunty marching tune he had learned as a boy in the military establishments where his beloved father had served.

As Tom stepped into the room it was immediately the makeshift bed on the floor that caught and held his attention. A slender ray of sunlight lancing through a small ragged gap in the thatched roof was striking the bedding upon the straw mattress and where it impacted, creating a luminous white shimmer of reflection.

Tom went to the mattress and knelt down, handling the stained white sheeting material.

'It's silk!' The recognition surprised him. 'How in Hell's name does such costly fabric come to be used as sheeting for a pair of trampers?'

He separated two pieces of silk from the blanket and took them outside where there was space to spread them out on the ground. He judged that they both measured two yards long and one yard wide, and noted that they were composed of smaller pieces crudely sewn together. He lifted one, stared closely at it, then used his tongue to moisten and taste a patch of dark reddish-brown staining, drawing a sharp breath as he identified it to be blood. After careful scrutiny he found several more patches of dried blood on both pieces of sheeting.

He went back into the cottage, knelt to study the sack cover of the mattress itself and discovered another patch of dried blood. He then lifted the mattress and saw beneath it the now cracked and distorted plaster cast which had covered the broken nose of Carrie Perks.

He sighed regretfully, as this discovery could well confirm what he had suspected since finding the dried bloodstains: that Jared Styler had killed her!

Next, he spent a long time scrutinizing all parts of the walls and floor, pushing his hands into the gaps of the thatch above his head, feeling with his fingers for anything which might be hidden there, but they found nothing.

He went outside and began a search of the area surrounding the building moving in ever-widening circles, hunting for either the girl's body or signs of disturbed earth where a burial might have been made.

An hour later, after finding several sizeable areas where the ground had been disturbed, Tom accepted that he'd best postpone this search until he had more available time and help.

He returned to the cottage, pocketed the cracked nose plaster, made a bundle of the silk pieces and the sack mattress cover and carried it back to the Lock-Up.

It was nearing midday and he was feeling the effects of a lack of sleep and food. But his lust for the hunt would not let him rest or eat, and as soon as the bundle and plaster cast were locked away he went immediately to the Red House.

When the manservant ushered Tom into the study, Joseph Blackwell's lipless mouth quirked in a knowing smile, and his eyes sparked in shrewd recognition of the reason for this unarranged visit.

'May I take it that you have identified a suspect for the Devil's Monk murders, Constable Potts?'

'Indeed you may, Sir,' Tom confirmed quietly. 'I request that you issue me with a warrant for Jared Styler's arrest on suspicion of committing two murders and one attempted murder.'

Blackwell blinked in surprise. 'How so, Constable?'

'Well, Sir, I want to arrest Jared Styler on suspicion of the murders of Methuselah Leeson, and the girl, Carrie Perks, and for the attempted murder of the pawnbroker, Judas Benton. I've found nothing material as yet to tie him to the Haystack Woman's murder. But Methuselah Leeson claimed to me that he had met the killer of the Haystack Woman on the night of her death. Could that killer be Jared Styler? Who, to ensure Leeson would never be able to identify him at some future chance meeting, came back and murdered and robbed the old man.'

Blackwell pursed his mouth and appeared deep in thought for a brief while. Then he pointed to one of the fireside chairs and told

Tom, 'Place that chair before my desk, but before you sit on it you'll find in that cupboard there . . .' he pointed to the wall cabinet, '. . . two bottles of claret, a jar of the finest American tobacco, some pipes and glasses and a box of Lucifer Friction Lights.'

'Lucifer Friction Lights?' Tom was impressed. 'I've heard that they are all the rage right across the country, even though costly to use.'

'They will render flint, steel and tinder obsolete within a very few years,' Blackwell stated positively. 'And no doubt the ease of instantaneously striking a flame from a small thin stick of wood will send the rates of criminal arson attacks soaring to the heavens.'

Tom fetched the various articles and placed them on the desk.

Blackwell immediately filled the glasses with wine, stuffed the bowls of the churchwarden pipes with tobacco, and invited, 'Now please sit down, Thomas Potts, and we shall drink, smoke and be comfortable while we discuss what justifiable evidence there is for my issuing you with these warrants.'

They were drinking the second bottle of claret and smoking their second pipes of tobacco when Blackwell signalled for a pause in their discussion, and Tom waited tensely.

Blackwell's initial words came as a shock to Tom. 'If I issue all these warrants, Constable, the first reaction of the generality of people will be that because of My Lord Aston's public humili-ation of you yesterday, you are now desperately clutching at straws to salvage your pride.'

'Indeed I am not!' Tom riposted indignantly. 'Of course I'm greatly angered by what he did. But I swear upon my honour that my anger against him is not the reason I've come here to ask for these warrants. I truly do believe that there are sufficient grounds for arresting Styler on suspicion of committing these two murders, and also the attempted murder of Judas Benton.'

Blackwell smiled bleakly, and held up his palm in a gesture of mollification.

'Well answered, Thomas Potts. Unhappily however, anonym-ous bloodstains and a discarded plaster cast for a nose are not proof enough to hang him for the murder of Carrie Perks. We need her corpse, or a witness, or his own confession. The snuffbox that was Methuselah Leeson's property, and the fact that Judas Benton has kept record of the circumstances of his coming into its possession is promising for us. As is the alleged attempted murder of Benton by Styler.'

Blackwell abruptly closed his eyes, bent his head and rested his chin upon the points of his clasped and steepled fingers.

Tom fell silent, knowing from experience that any further words he spoke would be superfluous and he must restrain his impatience and wait for Blackwell to come to a decision.

After a short pause, Blackwell's eyes opened, his head lifted and he said, 'At this particular time I shan't be able to obtain either of our magistrates' signatures upon the warrants. The Reverend Timmins is travelling on the continent and My Lord Aston is at the Malvern Spa.'

Blackwell's almost lipless mouth quirked in a sarcastic smile, 'Taking the "Waters" to ease his gout! Or at least that is what he wants the world to believe. I happen to know he is taking treatment for another type of ailment altogether, which is an unhappy memento of his brief encounter with a fair damsel the last time he went on his travels. You say that Styler is currently employed as a Harvest Steward by Andrew Parkman. Well, now, Thomas Potts, that will most assuredly be of considerable interest to My Lord Aston. Therefore, you have my permission to arrest and hold in custody Jared Styler on suspicion of the robbery and murder of Methuselah Leeson and the attempted murder of Judas Benton. He can be formally charged when Lord Aston returns to the parish.'

Tom gusted a sigh of relief and nodded. 'I'll go to Parkman's farm and arrest Styler immediately.' He rose to his feet. 'Many thanks for your hospitality, Sir. The claret and tobacco were as always of most superb quality.'

'No! You will not go to Parkman's immediately!' Blackwell chopped his hand down in negation. 'Jared Styler is a violent and dangerous man, and I will not unnecessarily risk your bodily safety. So you will go there tonight accompanied by Deputy Constable Bint, and make the arrest when Styler is sleeping and you can achieve complete surprise. That is an order, Constable Potts, and you will not question it.'

Tom couldn't help but grin wryly and admit, 'Yes, Sir, I do accept I would empty both my pistols into Styler if he attacked me and still be doubtful of overcoming him. So truth to tell, it's an order I've no ardent wish to question.'

A wave of weariness washed over him and he couldn't restrain a wide yawn, for which he immediately apologised. 'Pray forgive my ill manners, Sir.'

'Go and get some sleep, Constable Potts.' Blackwell smiled. 'You'll need to be fresh for the fray tonight.'

TWENTY-THREE

Wednesday, early evening, 5 August, 1829

'He's back again!' Maisie Lock announced excitedly as she came into the back parlour of the Fox and Goose, where Gertie Fowkes, her daughter Lily and Amy Potts were sitting at the table.

'Who's he?' Amy Potts queried without much interest.

'That good-looking Cockerney who was asking me all about meself the last time he come in!' Maisie's face was flushed with excitement. 'You remember him, Amy – he said he was from London.'

'Oh, you means that flash-dressed Cockney who was making sheeps' eyes at Amy. Which he warn't making at you, Maisie Lock,' Lily Fowkes sneered.

'He fancied both me and Amy,' Maisie riposted huffily. 'You was the one he warn't taking any notice of, warn't you, Lily. But that's how it always is for you, aren't it. No bloke even notices you when us two am around.'

'That's enough squabbling, you pair!' Gertie Fowkes snapped curtly. 'You acts like daft kids, you both does. Why can't you be like Amy. She don't act like a silly kid no matter how many blokes makes eyes at her. And anyway, what's you doing in here, Maisie? Who's looking after the Select Parlour?'

'Master Tommy, and he's sent me in here to tell you that Samuel Thomas is here with that Cockerney and another bloke.'

'So, Sam Thomas is here, and he's brought company.' Gertie Fowkes smiled broadly. 'We'll be earning well tonight then. You'd best get in there a bit sharpish, Amy, because Old Sam likes pretty faces around him.'

Samuel Thomas, who had begun his working life as a mason's labourer, had risen by his own efforts to become a very rich and successful Needle Master, and sole owner of the large modern mill at the base of the Fish Hill. Unlike his fellow Masters he had no interest in, nor any ambition for social advancement and 'gentility'. His manners and speech were still that of a common labourer, his dress simple and unpretentious. But he was noted for his kindness to his workforce and his liberal spending when he entertained others.

Maisie Lock shook her head doubtfully. 'You'd best hold here, Amy, because Sam Thomas has sent word for your husband to join him. So Master Tommy says that if you aren't happy about your husband being there, and if Mrs Fowkes is agreeable to it, you can work in the Tap Room tonight.'

Amy instantly shook her head. 'No, Mrs Fowkes, I don't mind working in the Select. I've no bad feeling towards Tom, and I'm sure he's none towards me.' She grimaced with a hint of chagrin. 'He always looks to be happy enough anyway, whenever I accidentally catches any glimpse of him.'

'Accidentally catches any glimpse of him, do you say?' Lily Fowkes challenged with greatly exaggerated surprise. 'When you spends bloody hours at your bedroom window looking out for him to pass, and then makes any old excuse to run out into the road so he can see you!'

'That's enough from all o' you!' Gertie Fowkes snapped. 'Now you get your glad rags on and work in the Select if that's what you want to do, Amy, and you set about that bit o' sewing I wants you to do, Lily.'

Tom was dozing fully dressed on his garret cot when the jangling bells roused him and brought him down to open the front door.

'Master Samuel Thomas wants you to join him straight away over at the Fox and Goose. He says it's very important,' the messenger said, and immediately walked away from the door of the Lock-Up.

'Did he say why he wanted me?' Tom shouted after the retreating figure, only to be answered by a silent wave of negation.

Tom donned his coat and hat and walked across the Green. As he came through the door of the Select Parlour of the Fox and Goose, Samuel Thomas pointed to the empty chair at the table where he was sitting with two companions, and then at the bottles and glasses on the tabletop.

'Set your arse there, Tom Potts, and tell me what you wants to drink.'

'Nothing as yet, I thank you,' Tom politely declined as he sat down. 'If you have urgent work for me to do then I'd best keep a clear head.'

'There's naught urgent, so you'll have a drink wi' me or I'll be sore offended.' The Needle Master mock-scowled threateningly.

'Very well, to avoid giving you offence, I'll have a glass of whatever is in this bottle.' Tom accepted the invitation with a smile.

'That's better!' Samuel Thomas grinned broadly and filled a glass with brandy which he placed in front of Tom, who immediately picked it up and took a drink.

His host applauded loudly and told his two companions: 'There now, what did I tell you! This chap might look like a long, soft streak o' piss, but I knows that he's got the heart of a British lion and the brains to match, which he's proved more than a few times since he's been the constable o' this parish.

'Any bugger who causes any upset when we has our Grand Opening 'ull find themselves banged up in a bloody cell in two shakes of a mare's tail. Because there won't only be Constable Potts keeping watch. Constable Will Shayler from Studley, Deputy Constable Ritchie Bint and plenty o' me own mill hands am going to be sworn in as Special Constables for the day as well.'

'What is this Grand Opening, Master Thomas, and when is it to be?' Tom queried.

'It's the opening of me own gasworks at me own mill.' Samuel Thomas indicated the middle-aged man on his left hand. 'Master Clegg has been building it for me and it'll be up and running within the next couple o' months. Aren't that so, Master Clegg?'

'It is indeed so, Master Thomas,' Clegg confirmed positively.

'A gasworks!' Tom was simultaneously shocked and greatly impressed. 'Here in this town! My God, Master Thomas, I've heard that you were building something at your mill, but assumed it was merely new workshops and furnace facilities. There was nothing said about a gasworks.'

'No, because Master Clegg and his workmen was all sworn to secrecy, and the works site was fenced off and covered so that nobody could see what was being built. My people was told it was going to be new workshops. But now with the gas pipes having to be run all over me mill and me house, the secret is out. I told me people before I come up here this morning that theym going to be working under the brightest lamps that's ever been seen in this town. Lamps that'll turn the darkest nights into sunny days.'

From behind the serving counter Tommy Fowkes had been listening intently, and now he came up to the group and exclaimed in fervid admiration, 'I've known you ever since we was raggedy-arsed nippers going scrumping apples, Sam Thomas, and I got to say that I reckon youm bloody well amazing! There's gasworks in London, there's gasworks in Brummagem, and now you've brought a gasworks to the Needle District! Your mill 'ull look like a bloody great bonfire burning day and night down the bottom o' the Fish Hill! There'll be bloody thousands coming to gawk.'

'That's so.' Samuel Thomas grinned broadly. 'But I think that there'll be tens o' thousands coming to gawk when the word spreads about what's going to mark the opening of my gasworks.'

'And what might that be?' Tommy Fowkes asked.

The Needle Master grinned at the handsome, black-haired, dandily dressed man at his right hand. 'You can tell him yourself, Master Sorenty.'

Vincent Sorenty visibly preened and announced boastfully, 'I am the foremost Aeronaut in the world, and I have designed and constructed the most modern and powerful balloon that the world has ever seen. I can guarantee that when it soars heavenwards it will have every country bumpkin in these backward parts rubbing their eyes and yelling their thick heads off.'

Maisie Lock and Amy had come into the Select Parlour and had been listening intently to the conversation. As Vincent Sorenty boasted they reacted with excited exclamations.

Tom turned his head towards them, and his stomach lurched sickeningly when he saw Amy's eyes were shining admiringly upon the handsome Dandy.

'And it's my very own coal gas from my very own gasworks that going to be filling that balloon and carrying Vincent Sorenty up into the skies.' Samuel Thomas beamed proudly. 'And it's going to be displaying a great big poster saying the name of the man paying for this flight! Samuel Thomas of Redditch! Who's the foremost Needle Master in the world, and owns the most modern Needle Mill in the world.'

Although Tom disliked Sorenty's arrogance and his contemptuous attitude towards the people of the Needle District, he still could not help but be impressed by the man's claims, and asked, 'Tell me, Master Sorenty, do you know the famous Aeronaut, Charles Green? My father had, and I have, a great interest in Aerostation, and my father was a close friend of Charles Green. He took me to meet and talk with that Gentleman many times.'

'Of course I know Green. When he made his ascent last year from the Eagle Tavern in the City Road, seated on the back of a horse suspended by harness from the basket, I piloted his balloon.'

He expelled a hiss of derision. 'Of course I sent him packing when he first asked me to fly it for him. Because his balloon was a crude, old-fashioned thing. But he begged and begged me because he does not trust any other Aeronaut to have the skills to carry him safely. So in the end I gave way to his pleading and agreed to help him.'

Sorenty paused, then with a smile that bordered upon a sneer, added: 'Of course, poor old Charles must be aged forty-five years by now, and is well past his prime. His advancing years are weighing very heavily upon him.'

'Not like you then, Master Sorenty,' Maisie Lock gushed admiringly. 'It's plain to see that your years don't number enough to weigh you down.'

'That's enough o' your sauce, Maisie Lock! Youm offending Master Sorenty!' Tommy Fowkes reprimanded.

'No, indeed she is not, Master Fowkes,' Sorenty contradicted. 'In fact, I have to congratulate you on your great good fortune in having two such beautiful and spirited Young Ladies as Amy and Maisie in your service. They would be a great attraction to the public if they were serving as my Aeronaut Maidens, I do assure you.'

'What does they do, them Maidens?' Maisie questioned eagerly.

'Oh, I train them to do a great many breathtaking artistic feats,

which have the crowds cheering them till the heavens resound.'
Sorenty smiled across at Amy, who blushed and smiled back. 'When
I am next here, I will tell you, my lovely Amy, and you also, Maisie,
all about my Aeronaut Maidens and the riches they earn.'

'Will you give over now, Maisie, and take these Gentlemen's
orders for whatever they wants in the way of refreshments,'
Tommy Fowkes ordered sharply.

'That's right, you pretty minx, take our orders and put 'um
all on my slate,' Samuel Thomas chortled heartily, and told his
companions, 'And you'd all best eat and drink until youm filled
to bursting, Gentlemen. I'll be sorely offended if you don't.'

Tom's stomach had lurched sickeningly when he'd seen Amy
blushing and smiling at the Aeronaut, and now one single impulse
dominated him: the overwhelming need to escape from this room
before he erupted with angry jealousy.

He rose and, exerting all his self-control, managed to bow to
the Needle Master and tell him politely, 'Unfortunately I must
ask your pardon, Master Thomas, for being unable to accept your
kind invitation. I have a very urgent task to fulfil which regrettably I cannot delay.'

'Is it to do wi' them Devil's Monk murders?' Samuel Thomas
asked.

'It is indeed, Sir. So I must bid you all farewell, Gentlemen.'
He bowed, turned away and, unable to risk looking at Amy,
hastened from the room and out of the inn.

In the sky the quarter moon was beginning to show, and Tom
welcomed its coming because it was bringing the night and forcing
him to put Amy from the forefront of his thoughts and concentrate
on the task ahead instead.

TWENTY-FOUR

I t was midnight and in the cloudless, moonlit sky the air was
still, while the remnants of the day's intense heat were continuing to emanate from the hard-baked ground. There was no
visible movement among the huddled buildings of Andrew

Parkman's farm. No glimmers of lamp or candlelight showing from the windows of the house, the arrow-slits of the barn or the pierced shutters of the varied storage sheds.

At their vantage point on the high ground, some forty yards distant to the south of the farm, the two men were crouched low, staring down at the buildings.

'How the fuckin' hell are we going to find where the bastard's sleeping?' Ritchie Bint hissed in frustration.

'I'm sorry! This is my fault! I should have found out that fact before we came here!' Tom apologised, guiltily accepting that his troubled thoughts had been too jealously distracted by Amy smiling and blushing at the Aeronaut.

The ghostly pale shape of a predatory barn owl swooped low over their heads and circled over the buildings below, moving ever lower towards the ground. Then suddenly it emitted a harsh cry and soared upwards.

'Something's scared it off!' Bint declared. 'Barn owls am always silent hunters, and that's its warning cry.'

Even as he spoke he grabbed Tom's arm and pointed to the barn. 'Theym down there! They looks to be a bloke and wench!'

Tom peered hard at the black-etched figures. The much taller of the two appeared to be wearing breeches and the smaller what looked like a long skirt. They came to a halt and then the male figure suddenly grabbed the female figure, lifting her bodily from the ground and carrying her towards a small shed which was some distance from the remainder of the buildings.

'Am you thinking what I'm thinking?' Bint queried excitedly.

Tom smiled grimly and nodded. 'I think I am, Ritchie. That could be Styler getting up to his usual tricks with a woman.'

'Well, we can find out about that in very short order. Let 'um get settled somewhere and then we'll make our move.' Bint grinned happily as he momentarily peeped inside the shield of the bullseye lamp to check that its flame still burned. 'I'm looking forwards to seeing what this 'un throws a light on.'

'Nooo! Noo! I don't want you to do that! I don't like it! Nooo! Youm hurting me! Stop it! Stop it! Nooo!'

As Tom and Ritchie Bint neared the shed the girl's frantic protests grew shriller and then were abruptly cut short. Both of them broke into run and burst through the door. Ritchie Bint swung the lamp's beam on to the writhing figures sprawled on the low mound of hay.

'What the fuck!' Jared Styler shouted as he rolled off the girl and tried to get to his feet, then grunted and collapsed as the brass-weighted pistol butt cracked into the side of his head.

'Nice one, Tom!' Ritchie Bint laughingly congratulated.

'Don't be afraid, my dear. We're constables. We'll not harm you!' Tom tried to reassure the girl who was keening and shaking with terror. 'You're safe now. We're constables. You're safe!'

'Quick! Get his hands behind his back and shove these on the bugger!' Bint urged as he took manacles from his canvas knapsack and handed them to Tom.

Tom wrenched Styler's hands rearwards and locked the close-chained iron rings around both wrists.

Bint proffered another set of longer-chained manacles. 'Do his legs as well. Else he might try to kick us in the balls.'

By the time this second set was secured Styler was rapidly recovering his senses. Now crouching on hands and knees, blinking repeatedly against the beam of the lamp, as Tom told him, 'Jared Styler, we are Constables, and I'm arresting you, in the King's Name, for the murder and robbery of Methuselah Leeson and the attempted murder of Judas Benton.'

Styler shook his head and shouted, 'Youm talking bollocks!' He then urged the now-whimpering girl, 'Run quick to Master Parkman, Jenny, and tell him what these stupid bleeders am doing to me!'

'You've no need to, my dear,' Tom told her, 'because we're going to take him directly to the house and speak to Master Parkman ourselves.'

Ritchie Bint thudded his boot into the manacled man's bare buttocks and jeered. 'On your feet, Styler, and I'll pull your britches up for you. Else you'll be mocked at by everybody who catches sight of your prick. Your new wench must be as tight as a flea's arsehole if that miserable little worm o' yours was hurting her.'

'Hold your tongue, Ritchie, and show some decency towards the girl!' Tom ordered sharply. Then said gently to Jenny Tolley, 'If you want, my dear, you may remain here until you are calmer.

I shall be keeping your friend in the Redditch Lock-Up for some time to come, and you may visit him there if you so wish.'

After continuous hammering on its panels the front door of the farmhouse opened and Andrew Parkman, wearing a long-tasselled nightcap and voluminous nightshirt, appeared in the narrow doorway. While behind him in the passage, a covey of candle-bearing, mob-capped, blanket-swathed women were straining their necks, bending and crouching in their efforts to see through the gaps in the doorway unfilled by the farmer's bulk.

Tom hastily explained the reason for his being there, and Parkman exploded in furious protest.

'You can't take my Harvest Steward to the Lock-Up when we're in the middle of the bloody harvesting. Where the bloody hell did you get the bloody stupid notion that he's murdered bloody Methuselah Leeson? Who's been filling your bloody thick head wi' such a bloody cock and bull tale? I'll break their bloody heads for 'um when I finds out who they are!'

'All will be revealed when Styler comes to trial, Master Parkman. Suffice to say that I have sufficient evidence to arrest him at this time,' Tom informed quietly.

'And what if I don't intend to let you take my Harvest Steward from me?' Parkman scowled threateningly. 'What if I takes them bloody chains off him and wraps the buggers round your scrawny neck?'

As always when faced with raging hostility and the threat of violence, Tom's heart pounded sickeningly and nervous tension enveloped him. But by sheer willpower he betrayed none of this and managed to counterfeit a calm confidence.

'Should you make any such attempt, then Deputy Constable Bint and myself will arrest you also, Master Parkman. So I would strongly advise you against impeding officers of the King's Law who are fulfilling their lawful duties in the King's Name.'

Parkman stood drawing in long, rasping breaths, his head sporadically jerking. Then, to Tom's shock, the farmer bared his broken, tobacco-browned teeth in a snarling grin and hissed, 'Oh yes, youm an officer of the King's Law right enough, Constable Potts. But I'm very close to another officer of the King's Law, who's a bloody sight higher in rank than you.'

He paused to give emphasis to his next words before announcing triumphantly, 'I'm a tenant of My Lord Aston, and he's very caring of me because this farm pays him one o' the highest rents in the county. He looks after me like I was his kinsman.'

There instantly sprang into Tom's mind the words of Joseph Blackwell when he had spoken about Andrew Parkman employing Styler . . . 'Upon my word, Thomas Potts, that will most assuredly be of considerable interest to My Lord Aston.'

Tom hadn't known until this moment that this farm was owned by Lord Aston, and now he couldn't help but smile with ironic amusement and mentally acknowledge: You cunning old bugger, Blackwell. You were savouring the fact that what I'm now doing will give both you and I the great satisfaction of annoying that arrogant bastard!

Parkman saw Tom's smile and erupted again. 'You'll be grinning on the other side of your bloody face when I tells My Lord Aston what you're doing to ruin my harvesting!'

Tom immediately apologised. 'I am truly regretful if my actions here are hindering your harvesting, Master Parkman, but I am carrying out my lawful duty in arresting this man. Now I must also request that you hand over to me whatever personal possessions he has here on your property.'

Parkman shook his head and declared, 'His personal possessions are in the bedroom he uses in my house. And until you gets a magistrates' warrant to enter my house and take 'um, his personal possessions stays in my safekeeping.'

Knowing he hadn't sufficient legal grounds to force entry, Tom shrugged and turned away from the other man. 'Let's take our new guest to his new quarters, shall we, Deputy Constable Bint.'

'You'll find no girl in them quarters, my Bucko.' Ritchie Bint laughed and, jerking on Jared Styler's wrist manacles, led him away.

'Don't you be worrying, Jared,' Andrew Parkman shouted after the trio. 'When Lord Aston hears about this you'll be out of the bloody cell and them two stupid bastards 'ull be inside it.'

From the moment he had been led out of the shed, Jared Styer had not uttered a single word, and during the long walk to the Lock-Up he remained silent.

While putting his prisoner into a cell, Tom said, 'Are you thirsty? I'm prepared to give you a cup of ale.'

'I want no ale from you, Potts. Just take these off me.' Styler shook his wrist manacles.

'All right,' Tom agreed. 'Turn round and get down on your knees.'

'And if you makes one wrong move, I'll bust your bloody jaw,' Ritchie Bint added warningly.

Styler turned and went down on to his knees. Tom unlocked the wrist manacles, left the cell and bolted and padlocked its door.

Jared Styler shouted threateningly, 'I knows your face, Bint. And when Lord Aston gets me out of here we'll see whose jaw gets bust, won't we?'

Later, as Tom and his friend parted at the front door of the Lock-Up, Ritchie Bint asked, 'What's your next move, Matey?'

'Well, I want to inform Judas Benton about Styler's arrest. Then take this snuffbox to Nellie Leeson for her to identify it. After that, resume the search for Carrie Perks's body. But I can't do anything until I have somebody to keep watch on Styler.'

'Well, I can't afford to help you do any o' that search.' Bint grinned. 'But I'll kip for a few hours then come back and watch over Styler while you finds somebody else to act as Turnkey here. As soon as you gets one, I'll have to get on me saddle double-quick and point an awful lot o' needles to make up me loss o' wages. Now you go to bed yourself, Tom, and I'll see you tomorrow morning.'

As Tom watched the other man walk away, he yet again acknowledged his great good fortune in having this loyal, tough, fearless Needle Pointer as his deputy.

TWENTY-FIVE

Thursday, 6 August, 1829

Tom stirred into wakefulness at the ringing of the early 'Waking Bells' and, for the first time since Amy had let him, welcomed the advent of a new day.

'I've got the Devil's Monk in a cell, and he's going to pay the price for what he's done. Surely this will soften Amy towards me.'

He followed his customary toilette routine, washing, shaving and cleaning his teeth at the pump, and when fully dressed and booted went to Jared Styler's cell and opened the foot-square door hatch.

Styler stood up from the raised stone sleeping slab and stepped to the hatch, demanding, 'Come to your senses, have you, Potts? Come to let me go free, have you?'

'No!' Tom replied flatly. 'I've come to take you to the privy if you have need of it.'

'I does.'

'Then turn round, put your hands behind you and poke them through the hatch.'

'Listen, Potts, I aren't got any thought o' trying to harm you and then doing a runner. And me legs am already chained, arn't they. So you've no need to chain me hands behind me. All I'm wanting is for you to let me take a shit and be able to wipe me own arse afterwards.'

Tom hesitated for a brief moment, then acted upon his own instincts. He unlocked the padlock and drew the door bolts back. 'Come on out.'

When they returned to the cell, Tom locked the other man in and told him, 'You'll get food and drink later, and some bedding and a bucket for pissing in. Later this week you'll be formally charged with the robbery and murder of Methuselah Leeson, and the attempted murder of Judas Benton.'

Tom tensed for an angry outburst, but to his surprise, Jared Styler only shook his head and sneered contemptuously, 'Oh, Potts! Youm making a bloody fool of yourself if you reckons that I killed Leeson, or that I'se ever tried to murder that piece o' shit, Judas Benton. You really am a proper prize prick if you thinks I'm the Devil's Monk!'

Tom was stung into countering sharply, 'Are you going to tell me next that you only murder women, such as Carrie Perks?'

Styler's jaw dropped in shocked stupefaction, and Tom slammed the hatch shut and instantly walked away, angrily berating himself for having reacted to that goading by momentarily losing his own self-control.

'I've put him on his guard about her now, damned fool that I am!'

As soon as Ritchie Bint came, Tom told him, 'I'll report to Blackwell straight away and tell him I've urgent need to get a temporary Turnkey.'

As Tom exited the Lock-Up there were men, women and children making their various ways to the mills, factories and workshops, and to his dismay one man shouted, 'Ritchie Bint says that you and him has catched the Devil's Monk!'

Instantly a loud clamouring of voices came from all directions.

'About time you did it, as well!'

'You ought to have catched him sooner!'

'It's your fault he was still free to kill poor old Methuselah!'

Tom clenched his teeth and walked on towards the Red House in dogged silence, knowing that the news of the Devil's Monk arrest was even now spreading rapidly throughout the entire Needle District, and he would face similar reactions to these wherever he went.

'Well now, Constable, I was watching your progress across the Green, and it appears you were met with a somewhat harsh reception.' Joseph Blackwell grimaced sympathetically as he greeted Tom's at the door of the study and pointed to the fireside chairs. 'Come, let us be seated comfortably while you make your report.'

When Tom had completed that process and fallen silent, Blackwell frowned thoughtfully. 'Doubtless My Lord Aston will be most irate when Parkman tells him that your arrest of Styler has hindered the harvesting. However, Aston has told only myself the address where he will be lodging in Malvern. He doesn't want any visitors calling upon him while he is receiving his particular mode of treatment. So I don't believe Parkman will succeed in finding him and then returning here within less than a week. I don't doubt that you will make very good use of that time, Constable, and if I can be of any help in your continuing investigations you need only ask it of me.'

Tom instantly requested, 'Ritchie Bint needs to get back to his needle-pointing and earn some decent wages. So while Styler remains in our custody, I'd like your permission to employ a temporary Turnkey to lodge in the Lock-Up, because I fear I shall be spending most of my waking time away from there.'

'You have it,' Blackwell agreed without hesitation, and they made their goodbyes.

The door and window of Judas Benton's shop was shuttered and barred and Tom hammered loudly on the door with his staff several times before a voice from above shouted, 'If you've damaged my door you'll be paying for it!'

Tom stepped back and looked up to see Judas Benton's scowling face poking out from the upstairs window.

'Good Morning, Master Benton. I'm come to inform you that Jared Styler is now being held in custody at the Lock-Up.'

'About bloody time! It's been costing me money waiting for you to get off your lazy arse and put that murdering bastard where he belongs!'

'How so?' Tom couldn't resist challenging.

'Because if I hadn't stayed hid in here behind locked doors that bastard would have come into my shop and bloody well finished what he'd started.'

Tom repressed the strong urge to tell Benton that Styler would have undoubtedly garnered many plaudits for fulfilling that particular task. Instead he merely nodded and said quietly, 'Within the next few days I shall require a written statement from you concerning your dealings with Styler. Good Day to you, Master Benton.'

Tom then went back up the hill to face what he expected to be another hostile reception. To his great surprise, however, his reception in the Fox and Goose was cordial and congratulatory from all its staff. Tommy Fowkes offered his hand and praises while the four women hastened to excitedly flutter around him.

'All those buggers who was in here jeering and mocking you the other day, Tom Potts, 'ull be having to ate their words now, won't they just! Youm a hero, so you am!' Gertie Fowkes declared. 'Now what does you fancy to drink, my dear? Brandy? Wine? Gin?'

'Whatever it is, it's on the house,' her husband announced grandly, 'no matter if it's the most expensive beer that we stocks.'

Amy took both his hands in hers, and with shining eyes told him, 'I'm ever so glad for you, Tom. Really and truly I am.'

Tom's heart thudded as hope flooded through him that this might be the moment of their reconciliation.

But then she said, 'You take good care of yourself now.'

And with that she was gone, and Tom's hope disappeared with her.

He swallowed hard and forced himself to smile at the two Fowkes. 'I thank you both very much for your kind offer of hospitality, but I fear I have very pressing tasks to fulfil. I'm only come here to tell you that I shall be requiring food and drink daily, sufficient for three men, to be sent over to the Lock-Up for the next week, at least. On the usual terms, of course, and the Vestry will, as customary, settle the bills.'

TWENTY-SIX

Thursday, midday, 6 August, 1829

The burning heat intensified the myriad foul smells perco-lating the air in the near vicinity of the Big Pool – the large, fetid, rubbish-strewn pond on the eastern edge of the town which served as the water supply to the inhabitants of the rows of decrepit housing which surrounded it.

Tom halted on its northern bank and beckoned to a solitary small, ragged girl. 'I'll give you a penny if you take a message to Mother Readman who lives in that big house in Silver Square.'

'Yeah, I 'ull. I knows where it is, and I knows Mother Readman as well. Her's me auntie!' The child accepted eagerly.

Tom spoke briefly, asked her to repeat the message, then sent her off, promising, 'If you're really quick to bring me an answer then I'll give you not one but two pennies.'

The child whooped with excitement and ran off, returning in a surprisingly brief time. 'Me auntie says to tell you, the corporal 'ull come to the Lock-Up after dark tonight.'

'Thank you very much, my dear.' Tom gave her the two coins and, whooping again with delight, she ran off to disappear into the nearest row of houses.

Thankful to distance himself from the Big Pool, Tom set off on his next errand.

*   *   *

He was passing the Old Monks Graveyard when a man shouted, 'Hold hard there, Master Potts!'

Tom halted and Hector Smout, his features grimed with sweaty dust, came out from the Graveyard, declaring, 'Well done for catching the Devil's Monk, Master Potts. Is it right that he's that Jared Styler who used to live down Studley?'

'That's so.'

'Ahhhr well, I've always said that the bugger 'ud end on the gallows. His dad and his grandad afore him was nasty tempered bastards as well. But anyways, never mind that for now. You'se saved me a walk, Master Potts. I was coming up to see you tonight.'

'How can I be of service to you, Master Smout?'

'You can make Nellie Leeson have Methuselah buried as quick as can be. This bloody heat has caused him to rot in double-quick time. He's naught but a cesspit now, and there's more bloody flies buzzing in and out of our houses than there is around a butcher's slaughterhouse. He's stinking the whole bloody lane up, and the neighbours am playing up merry hell about it!'

'I assume she already knows that we've arrested her husband's murderer?'

'Oh, yes, I told her the very minute I heard it meself this morning.'

'How did she react?' Tom was curious.

'Shouted at me to piss off, and slammed the bloody door in me face! Truth to tell, her's going down the same road as Methuselah. I often hears her shouting and swearing at him like he's alive.' He sighed sadly and shook his head. 'Her's losing her marbles, and it's a bloody shame because her used to be a real nice girl. So nice that when her was young, I once asked her to marry me. But her chose to wed Methuselah.'

'Well, I'd best go and speak with her, Master Smout. I need her to identify this as being her husband's property.' Tom pulled the snuffbox from his pocket and displayed it to the other man. 'Will you come with me?'

'Ohhh no!' Smout shook his head. 'These days the less I has to do with her the better. I hates seeing what's becoming of her.'

Tom walked on down the lane, and as he neared the row of cottages the foul smell wafted to meet him.

He walked up to the Leeson cottage and was several paces

from it when the door opened. The reeking stench of rotting flesh struck so overpoweringly into Tom's mouth and nostrils that he involuntarily halted and took a backward step, waving his hand before his face.

'It'll cost you a fourpence to see him, and the chopper that killed him.' Nellie Leeson's cracked voice sounded from within the dark-shadowed interior of the cottage.

'I'm Constable Potts, Mistress Leeson. I'm here to see you, not your husband's corpse.'

She burst out of the doorway, brandishing a rusty hatchet, spitting furious recriminations. 'It's you who's stopping folks coming to see Methuselah! Why am you tormenting me? Why am you stopping folks coming?'

Trying to breathe as shallowly as possible, Tom told her, 'Mistress Leeson, I haven't stopped anyone from coming to your house. I'm here to inform you that the man suspected of causing your husband's death has been arrested and is being held in custody. And to . . .'

He reached into his pocket for the snuffbox, but she shook the hatchet at him and screeched, 'I already knows that, so just bugger off and leave folks free to come here when they wants to.'

Now Tom realized that she was wearing what looked to be the tasselled schoolboy's cap that had been her husband's. He also surmised that the hatchet she brandished was the same one that he had removed from her husband's skull. He put the thought from his mind and said gently, 'Mistress Leeson, I can't help but smell what is happening to your husband's body. Do you not think that the time has come to lay him to rest? If you lack funeral money, then the Vestry will pay the costs of your husband's burial.'

Her red-rimmed, bloodshot eyes narrowed to slits as she hissed menacingly, 'The Vestry can piss off! And if you knows what's good for you, you'd best piss off right now!'

Unnoticed by Tom, interested onlookers had come out from the nearer cottages to cluster close by, and a grossly obese woman shouted, 'Do what youm paid to do, Tom Potts, and get poor Methuselah away from her and into his grave.'

'You mind your own bloody business, you stinking fat whore! Me husband's staying where he wants to be. And that's wi' me!' Nellie Leeson screeched.

'Don't you call me a stinking whore, you mad old bitch. The sooner youm in your own bloody grave the better it'll be for everybody else who lives down here!' the obese woman retorted angrily.

'You stinking whore!' Nellie Leeson repeated in a piercing shriek and came hobbling past Tom, whirling the rusty hatchet around her head, howling, 'I'll kill you! I'll kill you! I'll kill you!'

The cluster of onlookers scattered. The obese woman screamed in fright and tried to run with the rest, but stumbled and fell. She lay face downwards, sobbing in terror as she struggled to raise her gross body from the ground.

Despite being taken off guard, Tom reacted quickly enough to catch up and grab Nellie Leeson before she reached the obese woman.

With surprisingly wiry strength the old crone struggled furiously, forcing Tom to exert more force than he would have wished to wrest the hatchet from her and hold her writhing body in his close-wrapped arms.

Then she abruptly collapsed, and dismayed guilt struck through Tom. 'God forgive me, I should have been gentler with her!'

He carefully lowered her on to the ground, and she lay there gibbering incoherently, her body convulsing erratically. Tom was considering his best course of action when Hector Smout's voice sounded.

'Looks like it's a good job I changed me mind and followed you down here, Master Potts. Nellie's had a couple o' these fits lately when her's been out in this bloody sweltering weather. We needs to get her inside. I'll dose her with laudanum to keep her quiet, but for her own good I reckon it's best if she goes into the Poorhouse until Methuselah's buried.'

Tom nodded in agreement. 'I'll go directly and arrange for her admittance, and get transport to carry her there. Also I'll go and see Joseph Blackwell and tell him we need to bury Methuselah as soon as possible.'

'And I'll nail her cottage up, to keep any light-fingered buggers out of it. Not that there's anything worth much, and the bloody stink 'ull most likely keep anybody from even coming near to it.'

'Many thanks to you for your assistance, Master Smout,' Tom told him appreciatively.

Smout shook his head. 'No need to thank me, Master Potts. I'm doing this for old times' sake, for the days when I wanted to wed this little wench. Now all I can feel is pity for what she's become. God have mercy on her!'

He bent, lifted the old woman's convulsing body in his arms and carried her into his cottage while Tom turned and strode hurriedly away.

The sun had long set before Tom returned to the Lock-Up and jerked on its iron bell pull. Metal bars clanked and the door creaked open to reveal Ritchie Bint, who announced, 'Thank Christ it's you. I've been pestered all bloody day by folks wanting to come in and gawk at Styler. But I told 'um all that it warn't permitted. Ohh, and that old Redcoat's waiting to see you. Him that's settled down in Mother Readman's.'

'Well, I'm glad you didn't let anyone in, because if Joseph Blackwell came to hear of it he'd be very displeased indeed. And I'm going to offer Corporal Maffey the job of Turnkey.'

'Well, Mother Readman thinks the sun shines out of his arse.' Ritchie Bint grinned. 'So that's good enough for me, because she's one of the best judges of men I've ever known.'

'I share that opinion.' Tom stepped through the doorway to be faced by the red-coated, shako-topped figure of George Maffey, standing rigidly to attention.

Tom grinned and asked, 'Do you accept the post of temporary Turnkey of the Lock-Up, Corporal Maffey?'

Maffey flashed up a quivering salute. 'I do, Sir.'

'Good! Then you are the Turnkey from this moment.' Tom grinned again. 'And you do not have to call me Sir, or salute me. I'm sure that we're already good friends enough to be addressing each other by our Christian names.'

'Oh, I knew from the first time I met you that we'd be very good friends.' Maffey chuckled. 'And I'm speaking now as a friend when I tell you that I loved being a soldier, and the worst day o' my life was when I got invalided out of the army. All that stretched before me then was being a licensed beggar man for the rest o' me days. For me to be doing this job, and having somebody I can truly respect giving me the orders . . . Well, I loves it! So because you're my good friend, let me salute you and call you Sir. And you call me Corporal, as if you're my officer. It makes me feel like I'm a soldier again, and have the right to respect myself, like I could when I was following the drum.'

Tom laughed and nodded. 'Then it shall be as you wish, Corporal. Now, there's a bed for you upstairs in the front room and food and drink in the kitchen. I have to go out again now, but Ritchie will show you where everything is and explain your duties. Normally we keep the front door locked and barred at all times, but only lock it tonight because I may be very late returning, and I've no wish to wake you merely to let me in. Now I'll bid you both a Good Night.'

Tom left the Lock-Up and went directly to the house of his friend, the Reverend John Clayton, to inform him, 'I've got Nellie Leeson settled in the Poorhouse, and Joseph Blackwell has obtained a coffin. It's on the handcart in his stables. Hector Smout will be opening the grave as soon as all is quiet down there.'

The clergyman nodded. 'I suggest we now drink some coffee and smoke a pipe. It's best that we allow the neighbours plenty of time to be sound asleep before we do the business.'

Tom smiled wearily. 'That's the most beguiling offer I've received all day.'

It was nearing midnight. There was only the slightest whisper of wind and the orb of the moon shed a soft light as Tom and John Clayton pushed the handcart and the empty coffin it bore along the lane leading to the Abbey Meadows.

They halted at the gate of the Old Monks Graveyard and carried the empty coffin to where Hector Smout was just completing the crushing down of decayed coffins and their contents to make space in the grave he had reopened.

When the three of them exited the graveyard, Tom used one of Joseph Blackwell's Lucifer Friction Lights to fire the wick of his shielded lamp. Then, taking the handcart, they walked on until they neared the row of buildings. They halted and Hector Smout held out two small cloth pouches with cords attached.

'Here, these got strong mint and lavender in 'um. You tie 'um round your noses and they'll take the edge off Methuselah's stink.'

The vile odour he referred to was uncomfortably strong even though they were still yards from the Leeson's cottage.

Both men gratefully thanked him as they tied the pouches around their heads.

'Where's your own pouch, Master Smout?' John Clayton enquired.

'Phooo! I've no need.' Smout expelled a dismissive snort. 'I'se been pickled in dead 'uns stink for more years than I cares to remember. Now I'se already took the nails out o' the door, and we needs to get him out as quick and quiet as we can. Because if we wakes any of the neighbours up, we'll have 'um all out here jabbering like loonies and getting in our way.'

Leaving the handcart and moving as quietly as possible they went into the cottage, and were enveloped by a stench that seemed to force its way through their very pores. Tom opened the lamp shield to illuminate the dead man lying face upwards on blanket-draped, boarded trestles. Accustomed as he was to look upon and physically handle corpses, he still drew in a sharply hissing intake of disgust.

Methuselah Leeson's face was hideously bloated and blackish-green in colour, his naked body grotesquely ballooned by gases, its soft tissues in the process of disruption and liquefaction which had created cavities oozing blood and pus over the outer layering of skin.

Being by far the physically strongest of the trio, John Clayton instructed, 'Tom, Master Smout, take a corner each of the feet end of the blanket. I'll take the head.'

Tom extinguished the lamp and they lifted the makeshift stretcher and carried the dead man back to the handcart. Tom and John Clayton wheeled it away while Hector Smout went to secure the cottage door. When he rejoined them at the graveyard gate they carried the corpse to the waiting grave and lowered it down to the lidless coffin which they had placed at the bottom of the shallow shaft.

As they had anticipated, the corpse was so swollen that only parts of it sank into the coffin. As gently as possible they lowered the coffin lid down upon the visible remains and, using the shovels that Hector Smout had brought in readiness, the three of them filled the grave.

John Clayton conducted a burial service and, satisfied that they had given Methuselah Leeson the laying to rest that was his due, the three men shook hands and parted, Hector Smout returning to his cottage and Tom Potts and John Clayton wheeling the handcart back up towards the town.

TWENTY-SEVEN

Friday, 7 August, 1829

At eight o'clock in the morning, Maisie Lock brought over the breakfast of bacon cobs and a large jug of porter. As Tom took the basket and jug from her at the door, she slipped past him and walked down the passage, asking excitedly, 'Which cell is the Devil's Monk in? I wants to have a look at the bloody animal.'

'You'll have to wait until he comes to trial for that,' Tom told her curtly.

'Youm a mean nasty bugger, you am, Tom Potts!' She flared petulantly. 'It's no wonder poor Amy left you. Her ought never to have wed you in the first place.'

'Just go away, Maisie,' he snapped.

She flounced away through the door, shouting, 'That good-looking Cockerney's took a strong fancy to her, and she'll be down in London with him before very long! Living and dressing like a queen! Not like the pauper her was when she was living wi' you, you lanky streak of piss!'

Maisie Lock's personal insults didn't trouble Tom, but the mention of Vincent Sorenty brought back the troubled memory of Amy's blushing cheeks and shining eyes when the Aeronaut had spoken to her.

Dear God, he thought, what will I do if she does go to London with him? I'm only able to bear this situation now because I can still hope that she'll return to me one day. Please God, let her come back to me.

'Potts, will you take me out to the privy?'

Tom felt almost grateful for Jared Styler's shouted request because it distracted him from his troubled thoughts of Amy. He unlocked and opened the rear door, fetched his constable's staff then concentrated his all attention on the prisoner as he unlocked the cell door and ordered, 'Move slowly, Styler, and keep your distance.'

As he exited the cell, Jared Styler questioned, 'Why aren't you lot been making money by letting folks have a gawk at me?'

'Because this is a Lock-Up, not a fairground freak show,' Tom answered curtly. 'Now walk slowly ahead of me.'

The other man obeyed, his leg manacles clanking as he shuffled towards the rear door, turning his head to ask, 'Why did you say what you said to me about Carrie Perks?'

'Because I know that you killed her.'

'What?' Styler halted and, shouting furiously, swung round to face Tom. 'Youm a fuckin' loony, you am, Potts. I aren't killed Carrie Perks, nor Old Leeson, nor any other bugger! Youm a fuckin' loony if you thinks that I'm a fuckin' murderer!'

George Maffey came hurrying down from the upper floor, wielding a lead-weighted cudgel and shouting to Tom, 'Shall I discipline him, Sir?'

Tom shook his head. 'No, let him be for the moment, Corporal. I'm curious to hear what else he might have to say.'

Styler was now dragging in long harsh breaths, baring his teeth like a threatening animal and continually shaking his head in denial.

Tom decided to bait him into further reaction. 'You thought that Carrie Perks's body would never be found, didn't you, Styler? But when I searched that cottage at Ipsley I found her blood on those pieces of silk and the mattress. I also found the plaster that Doctor Laylor had fashioned to cover her broken nose. That broken nose that I myself witnessed you inflicting.'

Styler's head stilled, his jaw dropped in shock and he could only gasp, 'Youm telling me that Carrie's dead? Where is her? Take me to her!'

'The only place you're being taken to is the privy, and then back to your cell,' Tom snapped. 'Now move on.'

He tensed, half-expecting the other man to disobey. But again, shaking his head and now muttering inaudibly, Styler obeyed.

Tom signalled to George Maffey and they walked side by side behind the prisoner.

When Styler was secured back in his cell, Tom placed food and a tankard of porter on the flat surface of the opened door hatch.

'Here's your breakfast. When you've finished drinking put the tankard back on here.'

He received no answer, so went and sat with George Maffey in the kitchen alcove and they took their own breakfasts.

The current behaviour of Jared Styler was giving Tom much thought, and eventually he asked his companion, 'Tell me, Corporal, what do you think about Styler's reaction when I spoke of the girl, Perks, being dead?'

'Well, he did look to be real shocked, Sir. But it could well ha' been shock that you'd found her body when he believed he'd hidden it too well for it ever to be seen again.'

Tom sighed pensively. 'That's the trouble, Corporal. I'm going to need the Devil's own luck to find her, and unless I do I've got no proof of her death.'

He sighed again and stood up. 'Now I'm going to the Poorhouse, and tell Nellie Leeson that we've given her husband a Christian burial. So I'll bid you farewell for the present.'

Some two and a half miles to the west of Redditch Town, the Tardebigge Parish Poorhouse stood isolated beyond the straggling village of Webheath. The large semi derelict building was currently housing more than sixty of the casualties of Fate. Paupers too old or enfeebled to care for themselves. Younger people who were physically crippled or mentally afflicted. Abandoned wives and children, pregnant unmarried girls, orphans and infant foundlings.

Despite the bright afternoon sunshine Tom's spirits, as always, momentarily dipped as he reached its gothic-arched entrance door and, as always, prayed silently. *Dear God, I beg that I don't have to end my days in here.*

He reached for the lion-headed door knocker, but his fingertips had only touched it when the door swung inwards and a female voice commanded, 'Be good enough to step aside, Sir, and let my Young Ladies pass through.'

Tom obeyed, and four small girls emerged, walking in single

file, all wearing grey bonnets and dresses bearing the large letters 'TP' painted in red. The emblem of the Tardebigge Parish Pauper.

They were followed by a short, sturdy-bodied woman wearing a severe black dress and a man's slouched hat and hobnail boots.

'Stay, Girls!' she commanded, and as the small girls halted she smiled at Tom.

'Good Afternoon, Master Potts. Me and these Young Ladies am just off to Lame Ben Mitchell's house to do a bit o' dancing. He normally comes here to play for us, but he's sent word that his legs is bad today, so we're going up to him. Aren't that so, Girls?'

'Yes, Missus,' they chorused in unison.

For Tom, the best features of this Poorhouse were its Master and Mistress, Edwin Lewis and his wife, Hilda, who, in stark contrast to many in their positions countrywide, used the sparse resources the Vestry allowed them to the best advantage for their powerless inmates.

'Good Afternoon, Mistress Lewis.' He smiled. 'Would it be possible for me to speak with Nellie Leeson?'

Hilda Lewis grimaced sympathetically. 'Well, you're more than welcome to speak with the poor soul, Master Potts. But whether you'll get any sense out of her, it's hard to say. None of us here have been able to.'

She turned her head and shouted through the door. 'Will somebody please come here and take Master Potts to see Nellie Leeson.' She then told Tom: 'There'll be somebody here directly, Master Potts, but me and my Young Ladies have got to get on to our dancing. So we all bid you a Good Day. Mind your manners, Girls!'

The girls curtseyed in unison, chorusing, 'Good Day to Your Honour!'

Tom lifted his tall hat and bowed. 'I bid all you Young Ladies a very Good Day, and my hopes that you'll have a most enjoyable time of your dancing.'

The girls walked on in pairs, chattering and giggling excitedly and taking backward glances at Tom.

'You've made their day giving them that Gentlemanly bow, Master Potts.' Hilda Lewis beamed and followed her charges.

It was Edwin Lewis who came in answer to his wife's shout.

A middle-aged, powerfully built man with the upright bearing of the veteran soldier he once was. He and Tom had an amicable relationship.

'I'm glad to have this opportunity to congratulate you on catching the Devil's Monk, Master Potts.' He shook Tom's hand. 'I've met up with Jared Styler meself a couple of times in the past, but to be fair I found him civil spoken enough. I was surprised to hear he's been doing this killing and robbing.'

He led Tom upstairs to the cramped room where Nellie Leeson, dressed in a nightgown and mob cap was sitting upright in a narrow cot, her fingers toying with the blanket, her eyes staring blankly down and her lips moving but only unintelligible mumblings coming from them.

Two old crones were perched side by side on a wooden bench facing her, both of them champing noisily on short-stemmed clay pipes.

'As you brung us firing for our bacca, Master?' one of the crones demanded. 'Me and Jess am bloody well dying for a spit and smoke!'

'Ahrr, that's right, that is! You swore you'd bring us firing for our bacca if we looked after Nellie, didn't you? And you bloody well aren't done it, has you! Youm a bloody vile, cruel Master, you am!' her companion scolded.

'Stop bullying me, will you! I've got your firing with me.' Edwin Lewis grinned good-naturedly and produced flint, steel and tinder box. He quickly struck the sparks which ignited the tinder and used miniature tongs to transfer shards of flaming tinder to light their pipes.

They both greedily sucked in and expelled clouds of strong-smelling smoke, grunting and beaming in toothless satisfaction.

Tom looked closely at Nellie Leeson, who had shown no reaction to the newcomers or the exchanges between the crones and Edwin Lewis.

'Hello, Nellie, do you know me?' he asked her.

Again she showed no reaction, and he repeated his greeting twice more with the same results.

He turned to the crones. 'Tell me, Mistresses, has she said anything at all to either of you?'

It was Jess who answered. 'Not to us, her aren't. But a couple

o' times her shouted out, "I'm real sorry, but it's your own fault
for being such a dirty robbing old bastard!" That's what her shouted.'

'Has she said anything else?' he persisted.

Jess glared at him. 'Will you bloody give over pestering me,
Master! I've told you already, aren't I! That's all her did! So
bloody well bugger off and leave me be!'

Tom accepted defeat. Edwin Lewis escorted him back downstairs and invited: 'Will you have a parting drink, Master Potts?
I've got some ale.'

'No, but thank you for the kind invitation, Master Lewis. I
must get back to the Lock-Up. Will you please let me know how
Nellie progresses? I do need to tell her that her husband has had
a Christian burial.'

'You may be sure that I will, Master Potts.'

As he walked slowly back to Redditch, Tom was overtaken
by a fast-moving gig, and as he recognized its fashionably dressed
driver he experienced a shiver of dread.

Where's Vincent Sorenty going in such a hurry? he thought.
Is it to the Fox and Goose to pay court to Amy? Dear God, I
pray not!

In the depths of his mind a voice jeered, Don't be such a fool
as to believe that it's any of God's concern who pays court to
Amy. If Sorenty can offer her a life of riches and excitement
she'd be a fool not to accept him.

Tom was driven to answer that voice. But she's my lawful
wedded wife! We swore before God that we would love and be
faithful to each other until death parted us!

Well, Death has parted you, hasn't it? the voice stated
solemnly. Death took the boy baby that you planted in her
womb. The baby made from your seed that turned her womb
into a coffin. The dead baby that you fathered, whose memory
constantly torments and grieves her, and yourself also. If Sorenty
can soothe her torment and ease her grief, then how can you,
who claims to love her beyond all other things, begrudge her
this chance of some relief from her terrible sufferings?

Total despondency flooded through Tom, and tears stung his
eyes as the answer was torn from him in strangled whispering,
'I can't begrudge her finding some relief through this man! But
it should be me who brings her that relief!'

TWENTY-EIGHT

Saturday, 8 August, 1829, Market Day

Tom had spent sleepless hours tossing and turning. He left his cot long before dawn to wake the snoring George Maffey and instruct him.

'If anybody comes here to ask why I'm not patrolling the market today, Corporal, you tell them that I went out very early and didn't say where I was going, or when I'd be back.'

'Very good, Sir,' Maffey saluted, pulled the blankets over his head and went back to sleep.

Tom got dressed and left the Lock-Up to walk as quickly as he could to the cottage of Josiah Danks.

'Bloody hell's bells, it's you, Tom! Why's you hammering me door at this hour? What's amiss?' Josiah Danks stepped out of cottage and the moonlight bathed his naked, muscular body and glinted upon the long barrel of the shotgun in his hands.

'I need your help, Josiah,' Tom blurted. 'I've got to find a young woman's body!'

He went on to explain the situation in great detail, and the other man listened intently. Then, when Tom fell silent, he commented, 'I've had dealings with Jared Styler. I know for sure that he's done a good amount o' poaching on our land, but I've never been able to catch the crafty bastard at it. So I'm more than happy to help you get him hung. Now, have you got anything of the girl's that we can get her scent off?'

'Some bedding that she used, and several dried bloodstains on that and her nose plaster.'

'Well, if she's sweated on the bedding, and we dampen and warm the bloodstains that might do the business. I've got a fresh bought young Otterhound in our kennels that looks likely to have the sharpest snout I've ever known. This 'ull be a good tryout for him.

'Now you go back to the Lock-Up and sort out the bedding

and plaster, and wait there for me. I'll go to the Grange and get the hound, shovels and ropes. I'll get a horse and trap as well so we'll make better time o' getting to Ipsley.'

He paused, then added: 'And it'll save us having to hump the poor wench's body back to the Lock-Up on our shoulders.'

The morning sun was high and hot when the two men reached the isolated, derelict building. As Josiah Danks reined in the horse, the large, unusually multicoloured Otterhound, secured by a long leash to the tailboard, emitted deep-pitched baying.

'Bloody hell!' Danks grunted. 'He's belling out because he's young and gets excited easy. I'll take him into the cottage and quieten him, then give him a good sniff and taste of the bedding and bloodstains afore we starts.

'You go lay out the guide ropes for the first cast, Tom. Ten yards width. We'll circle tight round the cottage to start with.'

'But I've already searched the near surrounds of the cottage, Josiah,' Tom objected. 'And found no trace of recently disturbed ground. Shouldn't we rather put the dog to work where there are areas of disturbed ground?'

'Tom, these Otterhounds can follow a scent through running water. If this wench was killed in the cottage and then dragged across the ground away from it, this dog 'ull be able to pick up her scent from off the ground and follow it direct to where she's laying. There's been no rain or strong winds since her went missing, has there, so the scent won't have been much dispersed.'

Josiah took the slender roll of bloodstained cloth and the dog into the building, and Tom lifted the long coils of rope and laid them in a circle around the walls. As he worked he felt the familiar tension of expectation, and the intensifying excitement of the hunt throbbing in his brain.

When Josiah and the dog made the cast around the circle, Tom followed close behind carrying the two long-handled shovels. Nothing was found and Tom repositioned the ropes to create a straight corridor leading outwards from the cottage.

Time passed and the procedure was continually repeated until, on a wide patch of disturbed ground, the dog suddenly halted, frantically scrabbling its front paws against the earth and baying repeatedly.

Josiah dragged the dog back and Tom began digging, his excitement rising as he found the stony soil malleable and easily worked due to previous penetration.

Barely two feet down the shovel blade began to hit what seemed to be wood, and when Tom had cleared a larger area of dirt from it he found a layer of branches from the shrubs. He lifted them away and plunged the shovel blade into the earth again. This time it bit into something soggy, and the stench of rotting flesh rose to his nostrils. The dog's baying became hysterical as it fought against its restraining leash in frantic efforts to reach the hole.

Josiah dragged the dog some yards further away and secured its leash to a shrub, leaving it howling and struggling to break free. Then he took the other shovel and aided Tom in carefully uncovering the find.

It was a rag-wrapped, unevenly rounded bundle, over a foot in diameter and weighing several pounds. The two men exchanged a long look, both instinctively knowing what they were confronting. Tom knelt, carefully unwrapped the rags and sighed pityingly.

'They're both girls. And could have been full-term in the womb judging by their size and weight. Dead not too long since, judging by the degree of rotting. Whoever buried them took care to make sure that animals couldn't dig them out.'

'I'll tell you what I'm wondering, Tom.' Josiah Danks scowled. 'Look how their belly cords are broke, but not knotted. I'm wondering if theym Jared Styler's and Carrie Perks's kids, and if he forced Carrie Perks to let him abort 'um I'm wondering if he killed Carrie Perks because her was threatening to tell folks what he'd done?'

That same explanation had already occurred to Tom, but now he was struggling against the overwhelming temptation to accept it as fact before he had discovered the absolute confirmation of its truth.

'It could well be the case, Josiah. During my medical days I've known men who've done the same to girls they made pregnant, and some to their own lawful wedded wives as well. But until we find Carrie Perks's body and have it examined for any evidence of recent pregnancy, then those charges won't stand muster before a judge. We'd best wrap these poor little mites back in their rags and stow them in the cottage until we're done here.'

The sun was setting when, hungry, thirsty and frustrated, the two men finally decided to abandon their fruitless search. The Otterhound had proven its powers of detection, and they had dug up a wide variety of decayed flesh and bone detritus, none of which were readily identifiable as human remains.

'Thanks to the dog we've certainly covered a very wide area,' Tom observed ruefully.

His companion offered some comfort. 'Well, at least we know that the wench aren't anywhere in this particular stretch o' land, and I can't see him risking burying her on local farmland. Or even in the woods at this time o' year when the bloody poachers and their dogs, and us keepers and our dogs am searching through 'um day and night. So he must have had a horse when he shifted her, and that means her could be buried anywhere within a hundred square miles or more.'

'He'd certainly got access to both horses and wagons after he took the job as Harvest Steward for Andrew Parkman, so you could well be right,' Tom accepted.

Josiah Danks shrugged regretfully. 'Trouble is Tom that I can't take any more time off me work to help you search further afield. So I reckon youm just going to have to hope that somebody comes across her grave and reports it to the local constables, wherever that might be.'

Dusk had fallen when Josiah Danks dropped Tom off at the Lock-Up and bade him farewell. Tom stood motionless watching the horse and trap travel around the Green to avoid the market area where shoppers still flocked about the stalls.

Since finding the dead babies Tom's mind had been tormented by the memory of his own dead child, and a savage anger against whoever had been responsible for the deaths of the two baby girls had been burning within him.

Now, although his body was desperately weary, his mind was alert as he grimly planned his course of action. When he had decided upon it, he rang the bells and silently told God, *Hear me, Lord, I'll not be repenting for what I intend doing to Styler. He's an evil brutal bastard, and I'm going to do whatever is needful to find out the truth.*

The door opened and light from the indoor ceiling lamp spilled across Tom.

George Maffey, dressed in red tunic and black shako, snapped smartly to attention and saluted. 'All present and correct at this post, Sir. The prisoner has behaved well, and has been fed and watered. No reports received of any trouble at the market or in the town, Sir.'

'Thank you, Corporal Massey.' Tom entered and gently placed the rag-wrapped bundle and the slender roll of silk cloth and mattress cover on the floor. 'Come, we'll go to the kitchen and I'll explain what I've in mind to do, for which I shall need your presence.'

Within a very short time Tom and George Maffey, both armed with pistols, were standing at the prisoner's cell door. When Tom unlocked the door and pushed it open, Jared Styler lay snoring on the raised bed block.

George Maffey trained the beam of a bullseye lamp on Styler's face, and Tom stepped into the cell to roughly shake the sleeping man's shoulder, ordering loudly, 'Get to your feet and step out of the cell!'

'Whaa! What!' the man grunted, blinking his eyes, dazed.

'Step out of the cell!' Tom reiterated. 'Step out of the cell!'

He grasped the other man's shirt collar and dragged on it, and Styler, still groggy with sleep, got to his feet and stumbled into the passage.

'Stand fast!' Tom shouted.

Styler stood for several seconds, alternately rubbing his eyes then blinking hard at the two men facing him, who both were pointing a pistol levelled at his face.

'What the fuck's going on here?' Styler appeared to be completely bewildered. 'What's I done?'

'You'll find out in just a moment.' Tom gritted out the words. Facing this man whom he regarded as being nothing more than a cruel, bestial brute, this was one of the extremely rare moments in his life when he was actually lusting to hurt and to kill.

Now he pointed to the rag-wrapped bundle placed on the floor directly in the beams of the hanging ceiling lamp.

'Do you see that bundle there, Styler? You are to go down on your knees and open it with great care.'

'What?' Styler shook his head in bemusement. 'What sort o' fool's game am you playing, Potts?'

With his left hand Tom pulled a second pistol from his shoulder slung holster, levelled it at Styler's cell door and pulled the trigger.

The blast of the report was deafening in the confined space, the acrid smoke of burnt powder swirled round their heads and the impact of the lead ball sent the cell door slamming back on its hinges.

'Do as I say, Styler, or I'll blow your head off.' Tom enunciated the sentence very calmly and clearly as he levelled his right-handed unfired pistol at Styler's face. 'I shall count to three. If you have not obeyed me when I reach that count of three, then you are a dead man.'

He paused for an instant, then enunciated firmly. 'One! Two! Th . . .!'

Styler dropped to his knees and began to tear at the rags.

'Open it very carefully, Styler, or else!' Tom snapped.

Styler snatched his hands back, his breath now coming in quick, harsh pants. 'I'm being careful! Look! I'm being careful!'

His hands were visibly trembling now as he slowly and with exaggerated care began to unwrap the bundle. When he saw its contents, he gasped out: 'What's this?'

'Surely you can recognize your own daughters? The daughters you tore out of Carrie Perks body and slaughtered, you evil scum!' Tom gritted the words out and, stepping forwards, rammed the pistol muzzle against Styler's forehead, breaking the skin and causing blood to spurt. 'I'll save the hangman a job, you murdering bastard!'

Styler's eyes widened in terror and he screamed out: 'No! No! These am naught to do wi' me! I can't have kids! I knows nothing about these!'

'Where have you buried Carrie Perks?' Tom hissed. 'If you don't tell me by the count of three, you're a dead man! One! Two!'

'Noooo!' Styler howled like a terrified animal. 'No, I've not killed her, nor these neither! I don't know nothing about where's her's gone! Or who these belongs to! I knows nothing! Nothing! I'm telling the gospel truth! I aren't never harmed any babby in me life!'

Tom began to physically shake with furious hatred as images flashed through his mind of the tiny pathetic corpse of his own dead son, the bloodied, smashed bodies of the Haystack Woman and the child she carried, the broken bleeding face of Carrie Perks and the filthy ragged shroud of her dead babies.

A red mist veiled his sight, and his finger was tightening on the pistol trigger when suddenly George Maffey's hand clamped and pushed down the pistol barrel. George Maffey's fingers rammed into the narrow gap at the rear of the trigger so that it could not be pressed far enough to fire the weapon. George Maffey's voice was shouting into his ear, 'Listen to me, Tom Potts! I'm not letting you get into trouble for shooting this bastard. We'll find that wench's body and then go together to watch him dangling from a rope. A ball in his head 'ull give him too quick and easy a death. He'll suffer far more when he's sitting nights and days in the Death Cell waiting for the hangman to come for him! Believe me, I knows this from experience!'

Maffey's hobnailed boot lifted and thudded into Styler's face, sending him sprawling backwards, blood exploding from his nose and lips. 'Get back in there, you fuckin' piece o' shit,' Maffey bellowed and, like a terrified wounded beast, Styler scrabbled on his hands and knees back into the cell.

Tom stood motionless, dragging in gulps of air as the red mist slowly cleared from his sight and the lust to kill slowly ebbed from his mind.

At last, he said quietly, 'You may release me now, Corporal. My fit of madness has passed. And I give you sincere thanks for saving me from the possible consequences of it. I can only hope and pray that I never again lose control as I just did.'

Maffey instantly released his grip, quickly locked and barred the cell door, then told Tom, 'You don't owe me any thanks, Sir. The only reason I stepped in was what I told you. A ball in the head is too quick and easy a death for the bugger. Now I've saved us our rations, so I reckon we should ate and drink our fill and then get a good night's sleep.' He grinned and added: 'But I wants to hear all the details about what you've been doing today before you goes to your bed.'

Tom was now relaxed enough to smile. 'And so you shall, Corporal. That Otterhound we used is a most remarkable beast. I've never seen the like of its skills before. But first, I'm going to wash these poor mites, wrap them in clean cloth and lay them peacefully in the end cell.

'I'll be honoured to help you do that, Sir.' Maffey patted Tom's shoulder. 'You'd have made a fine officer, you know, because you're one of the "Come on, men! I'll lead!", and not one of the, "Go on, men! I'll follow!"'

TWENTY-NINE

Sunday, 9 August, 1829

At seven o'clock in the morning, Tom rose from his cot and came down to the ground floor of the Lock-Up to answer the ringing of the bells. He found that unexpectedly it was Lily Fowkes delivering the breakfast keg of porter, small pail of porridge and platter of bread and beef-suet sandwiches.

'Good Morning, Lily, it's most unusual to have you doing this job,' he remarked casually as he took the porter keg and porridge, placed them on the floor just inside the door and reached for the platter.

'Pfft!' Her fat cheeks swelled as she expelled an indignant snort. 'It aren't fair, Tom Potts! This is our skivvies' job, not mine. But theym both swanking about like Lady Mucks and getting all primped up in their finery, just because the Flash Cockerney is coming in his fine gig later on to take 'um up to Brummagem with him. It aren't fair!'

She thrust the platter into his hands and flounced away.

Why would Vincent Sorenty be taking Amy and Maisie to Birmingham on a Sabbath morning? Tom wondered. I wouldn't think it would be to hear a preacher? . . .

'Sir!' George Maffey shouted.

Tom turned to see Maffey peering through the opened hatch of Jared Styler's cell.

'What is it, Corporal?'

'This bugger looks like he might be needing a bit of attention. It could be that I might have booted him a bit harder than I intended.'

'I'm in fuckin' agony, you Redcoat bastard! You'se busted all the front o' me face! I needs a doctor! I'm bleeding to death, so I am!' The hoarse cries of Jared Styler sounded from the cell.

Tom closed and barred the front door and went to the cell to peer through the hatch.

Styler was sitting hunched on the edge of the raised slab, his grotesquely swollen face and clothing seemingly plastered in blood, which was also liberally splashed upon the bedding and floor.

Tom felt no twinges of guilt or remorse – his pity was only for Styler's victims.

'Of course I'll have a doctor brought here to see you, Styler. Just as soon as you tell me where you've buried Carrie Perks.'

'Dear God, save me!' Styler howled like a wounded dog. 'How many times must I tell you? I aren't killed Carrie Perks! I left her alive in that fuckin' cottage! Her was skreeking and blarting at me, but her was living! I aren't killed nobody at all! Never in me life has I killed anybody! Not man, nor woman, nor fuckin' child . . . Neverrrrr! Neverrrrr! Neverrrrr!'

Those final words were long-drawn-out bellows of utter desperation.

Tom closed the hatch and stepped back from the door, and as he did questions abruptly forced their way to the forefront of his thoughts.

If he believed that where he buried the two babies would never be discovered, why didn't he bury Carrie Perks in that same place? Why would he risk transporting her corpse for perhaps a distance of miles when so nearby he already had what he believed to be a safe burial area?

A flicker of doubt flashed through his mind. Could it really be possible that Jared Styler was telling the truth? Could Carrie Perks still be alive?

'Can I speak plain about what's in me mind, Sir?' George Maffey requested.

'Of course, Corporal. You are always free to give voice to whatever's in your mind.' Tom was relieved for this distraction from what were becoming somewhat troubling thoughts.

'Well, Sir, I've seen many a tougher bastard than him broken when I was soldiering. And I reckon he's getting very near to breaking point now. We should just leave the evil bugger to stew in his cell, with no word from us, nor food nor drink. I reckon that by tomorrow morning he'll be ready to tell us what we wants to know.'

Tom pondered briefly, then nodded. 'I suppose it's worth a try, Corporal. Now let's have our breakfasts.'

'And after you've ate, Sir, why don't you go and visit a friend and make merry for a while? It'll do you a power o' good,' Maffey suggested.

Tom grimaced ruefully. 'After I've breakfasted I need to go and see Judas Benton and tell him I'll be needing to take a written statement from him in due course.

'There's also a necessity to arrange a Christian burial for those two little mites. So none of these things are conducive to any light-hearted entertainment, and truth to tell, Corporal, I'm not in the mood for merrymaking anyway. But when I come back you must take a few hours' leave and perhaps share a bottle or two with Mother Readman. I'm sure she'll have plenty of interesting gossip to share.'

Maffey grinned broadly. 'Thank you, Sir. I'll enjoy doing just that. Me and Mother Readman am become very good comrades. So much so, that I'm giving up the wandering life, and we're going to get wed. I'm settling down here in Redditch with her for the rest o' me days.'

'Well, I'm very glad to hear so, Corporal, and many congratulations to both of you. Mother Readman is a fine and decent lady, and I'm sure that you'll both be very happy together,' Tom sincerely told him. And at the same time was sincerely hoping, 'And may you have better fortune in your wedded life than I've had, Corporal Maffey.'

When Tom rapped the shop door with the crowned head of his staff, Judas Benton almost instantly opened it and, scowling, demanded, 'What's took you so bloody long in coming? Now how much is the reward? Has you brought it with you?'

'Reward?' Tom was momentarily taken aback. 'What reward?'

Benton's rat-like fangs bared threateningly. Belching loudly, he drunkenly stumbled forward and the reek of gin filled Tom's nostrils.

'Ohhh, I see! That's your game, is it, Potts? Going to try and

cheat me out of what's rightfully mine, are you? Well, youm
barking up the wrong tree, my Bucko! I aren't some thick-yedded
slum rat. I'm a man who's got a sharp brain and some schooling
to go with it. I've give you the Devil's Monk, and now I wants
the reward money, and until I gets it you won't get no bloody
written statement from me. Does you understand me, Potts?'

With an effort Tom suppressed the angry retort which instantly
rose to his lips. Then, slowly shaking his head, said quietly, 'As
of yet there's been no reward offered, Master Benton, so I'll not
trouble you any further at this time.'

He turned and walked away up the hill.

Benton blinked hard and stood as if stupefied for some
moments, then stepped out from the doorway and followed Tom,
shouting, 'Hold on a second, Potts! What's you playing at?'

Tom slowed his pace, turned his head to look back at the other
man and shouted, 'Go back home, Master Benton.' Then
continued slowly on up the hill.

'What the fuckin' hell's the matter wi' you, Potts? Just you
hold there! I wants my money!' Benton bawled furiously and
broke into a shambling trot.

When Tom reached the central crossroads he saw a small group
of respectably dressed men and women talking together outside
the chapel gate. None of their faces were familiar to Tom, but
he assumed they had attended the earlier chapel service.

Benton came up on to the crossroads, panting heavily now but
managing to shout between gasps for air. 'Now what about my
fuckin' reward money? What's you done with it, you thieving
bastard!'

He shook his fists and advanced threateningly towards Tom,
bawling, 'I'm going straight to the magistrates if you don't hand
over my money, Potts! And when I does, you'll be cursing God for
the day you was birthed by your fuckin' fat, nasty cow of a Mam.'

Tom glanced at the talking group, who were staring in horri-
fied disgust at the hatless, shirt-sleeved pawnbroker and told
them, 'Ladies and Gentlemen, I'm the constable of this parish.
I regret that you should have had to be disturbed by this man.
May I most respectfully ask you to bear witness while I arrest
him for the offences of Drunken Behaviour and Profanity on the
Sabbath Day.'

'Indeed you may, Constable.' The spokesman was a burly middle-aged man. 'And if needs be I will aid you in making the arrest.'

'My thanks to you, Sir.' Tom bowed. 'I will be most grateful for your aid, if needs be. However, I am not expecting any physical resistance.' He bowed again. 'I bid you Good Day, Ladies and Gentlemen.'

He turned and strode towards the oncoming Benton, who abruptly halted and demanded uncertainly, 'What's you doing?'

'Judas Benton, I'm arresting you in the King's Name for Drunken Behaviour and Profanity on the Sabbath Day. Come quietly or it will be the worse for you.'

'What?' Benton stared in befuddled shock.

Tom grabbed him by his shirt collar and dragged him towards the Lock-Up. Benton wailed in protest, 'But I aren't done nothing wrong! I only wants me reward money!'

The group at the chapel gate applauded decorously and their spokesman shouted, 'Well done, Constable Thomas Potts. You are indeed a most worthy holder of your Office, and well deserving of your fine reputation.'

Tom was surprised by the plaudits and their use of his name. He lifted his staff in salute to them and upped his pace, causing Benton to stumble and reel and complain vociferously all the way to the Lock-Up.

As always in Redditch when people saw what was happening, they came hurrying from their houses to ask Tom why Benton had been arrested, and to mock and jeer at the unpopular pawnbroker.

Inside the Lock-Up, Tom put the now whiningly complaining Benton into the cell furthest away from that of Jared Styler, then told George Maffey, 'It'll be interesting to see what Styler's reaction will be when he finds out who's his new neighbour. Has he been quiet while I was out?'

'Well, at first he was raving and bawling that he was innocent and he'd never killed anybody. But then he went quieter, and I could hear him praying to God to send Carrie Perks here to the Lock-Up to prove that she wasn't dead. But I've said nothing to him, nor dropped the door hatch, and he's been a lot quieter, but still praying by the sounds of it.'

They moved to stand outside Styler's cell and listen to the broken mumblings coming from inside.

Again the unwelcome question raised itself in Tom's mind: could it be possible that Styler might be telling the truth and that Carrie Perks is still alive? Have I arrested the wrong man? Involuntarily he shook his head as though to physically expel the disturbing thoughts, and told George Maffey, 'I'm just going to go and have a brief talk with Reverend Clayton and make my report to Joseph Blackwell, Corporal. As soon as I return you can go on your furlough and make a full night of it. I'm sure you'll sleep very soundly at Mother Readman's.'

'At your orders, Sir.' Maffey saluted smartly and winked broadly. 'I'm not so sure about the sleeping soundly, though. I might get disturbed at odd times because Mother Readman expects me to do my duty as a true soldier should, you see, Sir.'

Tom winked back. 'And like a true British soldier you will not shirk that duty, Corporal. Of that, I am convinced!'

John Clayton was at home and greeted Tom warmly. 'Come in and have a drink with me, Tom. I've just been presented with a bottle of very good brandy.'

Tom was happy to accept and, as soon as they were seated and had had their first taste of the fragrant spirit, Clayton told him, 'I wish you could have been at chapel this morning, Tom. You are being hailed as the Hero of the Parish for your capture of the Devil's Monk . . . Well, certainly by all our reputable, God-fearing parishioners, though I've no doubt that the majority of our disrepu table inhabitants are equally admiring of what you've done.'

Tom was truly surprised that he had been so lauded, and now realized that was the reason the group by the chapel had recognized his name and given him such compliments. He was quick to answer. 'Well, Ritchie Bint is more than equally worthy of everyone's praises, John. We made the arrest together, and he's a much braver man than I am, I assure you. But what I want to speak to you about now is a rather delicate matter . . .'

He went on to tell his friend about the dead babies and the urgent need to bury them.

John Clayton instantly concurred with that need, then shook his head sadly. 'Do you know, Tom, if I had guineas to match the numbers of abandoned dead babies I've known of, I'd be a wealthy man. This is a damned cruel world for weak, defenceless creatures, is it not.'

Tom could only nod in grim acknowledgement and tell his friend, 'I'll go now and report to Blackwell. I'm sure he'll agree that we must give them a decent Christian burial as soon as possible. But sadly they'll remain nameless, because I've not got any proof who their parents are.'

'Our Gentle Saviour will most certainly love and care for their souls and know their names, Tom,' John Clayton declared with absolute certainty. 'And now I'll go straight to see Hector Smout and have him prepare a grave for them.'

It was Joseph Blackwell himself who opened the Red House door and quickly ushered Tom into the study.

When they were both seated, Blackwell smiled warmly. 'I'm very pleased to see you, Thomas Potts. It seems that you are now the hero of the hour, and the whole parish is ringing with your praises. I sent word of the arrest of Styler to My Lord Aston in Malvern and his reply, which I received on Friday, quite astounded me. It appears that the Devil's Monk murders, and the speedy manner of his subsequent arrest, have created a great deal of interest throughout the entire Midlands.'

Blackwell chuckled sarcastically. 'My Lord Aston is of course claiming all the credit for your appointment as constable of this parish, and is greatly looking forwards to basking in the reflected glory when Styler is brought to trial and hung. So much so that when Andrew Parkman finally managed to bribe his way to Lord Aston's hiding place, my noble lord sent him packing with a very large flea in his ear. Of course, we all have our own individual cross to bear, and My Lord Aston is mine, but now undoubtedly will be poor Farmer Parkman's also. But enough of this drollery! Now, let me hear what progress you are making in your investigation, Thomas Potts. I've heard it rumoured that you have discovered dead babies that Carrie Perks may have birthed. You have my permission to arrange their burial without further delay; the Vestry will meet any costs.'

Tom was forced to battle against the immediate impulse to tell the other man what the other man was hoping to hear, before admitting bluntly, 'I've made no progress in the Haystack Woman's case. I've no evidence that the babies are Styler's or Perks. Neither am I any closer to being able to prove any of the murder charges against Styler. At this time, I'm reduced to hoping that he is near to breaking point, and if he does so break, then he will make confessions. But how long can we continue to hold him, without bringing charges which are backed up by possession of some strong grounds of proof? Surely the Law of Habeas Corpus prevents us from doing so for this length of time without such grounds?'

Joseph Blackwell shrugged his narrow shoulders and smiled bleakly. 'The current practice of Habeas Corpus is that a suspect can be held for up to twenty days. But it is my opinion that True Justice is not always best served or best achieved by a slavish adherence to the Letter of the Law, Thomas Potts. The fact is that it is only those who are poor and powerless who must slavishly adhere to the Letter of the Law. I am not numbered among those individuals. You will keep Styler in custody for a hundred days without charge if I decide that doing so is necessary to achieve True Justice. You should return to the Lock-Up now and release your admirable new Turnkey, Corporal Maffey, to enjoy a few hours of rest from his duties. I bid you Good Day, Constable Potts, and assure you that I am very confident you will achieve the success we both wish for in your ongoing investigations.'

Tom knew that there was nothing to be gained from prolonging this conversation, and answered quietly, 'Thank you for the confidence you display in me, Sir. I bid you Good Day.'

THIRTY

Sunday, 9 August, 1829

The small tented encampment was on open ground adjoining the great Boulton and Watts, Soho Manufactory. It was the boast of Birmingham and the most modern industrial enterprise in the world, with its multitude of workshops, its own coal gas production plant, foundrie and private

hoop of canal giving it access to the myriad tentacles of water
borne transport. Even on this Sabbath Day its chimney stacks
were smoking and there were numbers of operatives carrying
out a wide variety of tasks.

Vincent Sorenty reined in his smart gig, pointed his long
horsewhip at the cluster of tents and told the two women sitting
at his left side on the driving seat, 'That's the encampment of
the Vincent Sorenty Grand Aerostation Company, Ladies. We
pipe the gas for my balloon directly from that gas works there,
close to the tents. Coal gas is more dangerous to use, but has a
much cheaper cost and is much more convenient than hydrogen
gas bags. I can fill the balloon for take-off in a fraction of the
time by being able to pipe the coal gas directly into it.'

'Where's your balloon then? I can't see it!' Maisie Lock
pouted with disappointment. 'You promised you was going to
show it to us. But if it aren't here, then you've brought us all
this way for nothing!'

His dark eyes momentarily hardened with fury. But when he
turned to give answer he betrayed no sign of that emotion, only
smiled broadly and said to the outer passenger, 'Amy, will you
explain to our dear Maisie or shall I?'

'Explain what?' Amy asked.

'The fact that my balloon lies virtually flat on the ground until
it's filled with gas. It's now on the ground on the other side of
the tents, hidden from our view.'

'Well, you never told us that, did you!' Maisie protested huffily.

'And I truly am sorry for not telling you, and I beg you both
to forgive me for my remissness. I shall have my men begin the
inflation the very moment we reach the tents.' He flicked his
whip and the glossy coated horse jerked into motion.

Amy was experiencing flickers of guilt. Her reaction at not
seeing the balloon had been the same as Maisie's. She had immediately thought that Vincent Sorenty had brought them here on a
false promise, and now she mentally reproved herself: I'm
becoming far too ready to think the worst of all men, even though
all too many of them have given me cause enough these last weeks.

She knew only too well that in the world's eyes she was now
again a lowly menial. Uneducated, untravelled, with neither money
nor property. Also a woman of highly suspect morality, because

recently she had willfully separated from her lawful husband. This last fact had lately emboldened some men to make crudely verbal and physical sexual advances to her, all of which she had very firmly repulsed.

But Vincent Sorenty's approaches toward her had been soft-spoken, complimentary words, delicately expressed and always with total courtesy. However, although she acknowledged to herself that she found him to be a very charming, physically attractive man, she harboured strong doubts as to the sincerity of his increasingly frequent professions of having tender feelings towards her.

She frequently castigated herself for even allowing her thoughts to sometimes dwell upon Vincent Sorenty, when in all truth her feelings for Tom Potts were still so powerful as to create a maelstrom of conflicting emotions. There were moments when with all her heart she wanted to rush to him, throw herself into his arms and beg him to take her back as his wife. Then there were other moments when she virulently hated him for impregnating her with a dead child, and all she wished for was to see him suffer for it.

'Look sharp! The Master's back!' a voice shouted as the gig neared the encampment, and when it halted in the centre of the circled tents several men came hurrying to it.

A man took the horse's bridle and Vincent Sorenty jumped from the gig and walked around it to offer his hand firstly to Amy, then to Maisie and help them step down.

A tall, slender bodied youth pushed through the group.

'This is my personal assistant and Second-in-Command, Mario Fassia.' Vincent Sorenty smiled and introduced the women. 'Mario, I present Mistress Amy Potts and Miss Maisie Lock.'

'I'm honoured, Ma'am.' The youth bowed to each in turn.

Amy was amazed by their close physical resemblance and remarked impulsively, 'You look very like each other – you must be close related.'

'Don't tell him that.' Vincent Sorenty smiled at her. 'If he gets the idea that he's my relative he might well begin to question the rightful authority I wield over him as his Master.'

He swung round to face the youth, frowned and ordered curtly, 'Prepare Valkyrie for a Captive Flight. I'm taking her up for these Ladies to view the panorama, so allow a hundred and twenty feet for the winch and tether ropes, and load standard ballast.'

Mario walked away shouting orders and the group of men broke up and hurried off in different directions.

Vincent Sorenty offered his arms to the women. 'Come, my Dears, we'll be seated comfortably and enjoy some refreshments while we watch my wonderful Valkyrie being readied to soar heavenwards.'

One of the men brought three chairs and a small table out of a tent, then fetched bottles of wine, glasses and plates of cakes.

Maisie began to eat and drink heartily, as did Vincent Sorenty, but Amy was so intent on what was happening that she took only a few sips of her wine and ate nothing as she watched the men uncoiling long canvas hosepipes and making the preparations to inflate the balloon, which, now some twenty-five yards distant from their chairs, appeared to be only a wide flat expanse of cord netting and colourful patterned oiled silk with a nine feet long, gaudily painted wickerwork gondola, guy-roped to the thick wooden hoop of the balloon's narrow circular base.

The hosepipe nozzle was pushed into the wooden hoop. A loud hissing ensued as the coal gas flowed and the great silken envelope began to slowly waver and undulate.

Amy's gaze was intently fixed on the spectacle taking place before her. Her heart thudded ever harder, her breathing quickened and excitement gripped her while the silken envelope grew and grew, expanding in all directions, slowly metamorphosing from a shapeless bulbous mass into a vast ever-expanding circular orb, raising higher and higher from its flattened base until it lifted from the ground with its gondola dangling beneath it.

Vincent Sorenty rose from his chair and went towards the balloon, shouting out orders, and men heaved and pressed on winch rods, ropes tautened and strained, and slowly the balloon sank lower until its gondola rested motionless on the earth.

He came back to the table, smiling broadly, and invited, 'Come then, Ladies, let us rise up into the sky like birds.'

Aflame with excitement, Amy jumped to her feet and, lifting her long skirt and petticoats to her knees, ran towards the balloon, Vincent Sorenty running with her. But when they reached the gondola, Maisie was not with them.

Amy turned to see her friend still sitting at the table, and shouted, 'Come on, Maisie! Don't lag!'

Maisie Lock's normally rosy cheeks were pale and she shook her head. 'I'm not coming.'

'What's the matter with you? Why are you being such a scaredy-cat?' Amy was puzzled at this unusual display of timidity from her normally bold-spirited friend.

'I don't want to ride in that thing. If the Lord meant for us to fly, He'd have give us wings!' Maisie was adamant. 'I'm not coming! And that's that!'

'Well, I'm going to fly!' Amy declared and, grasping the guy ropes, lifted her legs over the low side of the gondola.

'Bravo!' Vincent Sorenty applauded. 'I knew the very first moment I saw you, Amy, that you were a woman of exceptional courage and spirit.'

He followed her into the gondola and shouted to his relative. 'Release us, Mario!'

The gondola jerked upwards and Amy gasped and clutched the guy ropes hard. Then the rising smoothed and, as the earth fell away beneath her, Amy was experiencing total exultation and couldn't stop herself crying out over and over again, 'It's wonderful! It's wonderful! It's wonderful!'

Vincent Sorenty roared with laughter and told her, 'It's always wonderful, Amy. It never ceases to be anything less than wonderful. And if you want, you can do this wonderful thing over and over and over again.'

'Oh, yes!' Amy cried out. 'Yes, I want to! I want to do this every day of my life!'

She twisted and turned, looking up, looking down, looking round, marvelling at how different everything now appeared, and when the gondola jerked and stopped rising, she cried out in protest, 'Why can't we go higher? Why can't we?'

'We can someday, Amy. We can rise so high that we are above the clouds, and we can fly over the land and sea like birds, and travel to distant lands like they do.'

'Really?' She gasped out unbelievingly. 'Would you really take me to far-off lands?'

'Of course. We can travel the whole world together, and wherever we go they will receive us like a king and his queen.'

Even now, at the height of her excitement, the term he used disturbed Amy. 'No, Vincent!' She shook her head. 'I can't be your queen. I'm a good living woman, even though I'm presently separated from my husband. I'm not a whore who sleeps with other men.'

He instantly answered, 'Oh, no, Amy! You've sadly misunderstood what I was saying. Of course I respect you as being a wedded lady who would never behave loosely, and so bring shame upon yourself. What I meant was that we would both be received and treated as two individuals who are honourable friends, and who work together like a brother and sister might. Myself, as the Aeronaut Pilot, and you as the Aeronaut Maiden. But I know from experience that we will be also received and feted as though we were of royal blood. When people first meet us Aeronauts, they cannot control themselves, because we are doing things which they have never before witnessed and think to be impossible for mere mortals to perform. We are performing in front of their eyes what they have always believed only the birds of the air, and the angels of heaven can perform. We are flying through the skies! We are the living embodiments of ancient legends!' He paused, watching to see the effect of his words.

Amy had listened in wide-eyed enthrallment, and now, almost timidly, she asked, 'And will you still teach me to become an Aeronaut Maiden? And take me with you on your travels? Even though I won't share your bed?'

'Of course,' he said solemnly. 'We will be as brother and sister.'

Again he paused, for what seemed to Amy to be an interminable time. Then he asked her, 'So, my dear Amy, will you join my team and let me train you to become my new Aeronaut Maiden?'

'Oh, yes! Yes, I will!' she cried out delightedly.

He moved to open a wooden locker fixed to the wickerwork and took from it a bottle of wine and two glasses.

He gripped the cork between his strong white teeth and pulled it free, filled the glasses and handed one of them to Amy. Then, smiling and lifting his glass high, he proclaimed, 'I give you the toast to the new Aeronaut Maiden, and future Queen of the Skies . . . Mistress Amy Potts.'

Tears of excited joy stung Amy's eyes and her heart pounded with the thrill of this marvellous moment, marking the beginning of a personal adventure that never in her wildest fantasies could she have visualized.

THIRTY-ONE

Monday, 10 August, 1829

Tom had spent yet another restless night of broken sleep, long spells of wakefulness and hard thought – much of that thought engendered by something Styler had blurted out when Tom had come so close to shooting him.

George Maffey returned to the Lock-Up at sunrise while the 'Waking Bells' were ringing across the town for the third and final time.

'Have you enjoyed your furlough, Corporal?' Tom asked as he opened the front door.

'Very much, Sir. But I'm well content to be back to duty. Have the prisoners been "Stood To"?'

'Not yet, Corporal. I wanted to wait and discuss matters with you.'

Tom beckoned the other man to follow him and led the way upstairs, where, out of earshot of the cells, they talked for several minutes.

Downstairs again, Tom slightly lowered the door hatch of Judas Benton's cell and peered through the slit.

The pawnbroker was sitting hunched on the edge of the bed slab, hands covering his face, his breeches wet with urine, some of which was pooled on the floor around his boots.

George Maffey took a peek, Tom closed the hatch, they moved to Jared Styler's cell and repeated the sequence.

Styler was on his knees on the floor, his upper body slumped over the bed slab, his head face downwards on his cradled arms, incoherent words coming from him in a continuous mumbling.

Tom and Maffey went back upstairs, and Tom asked, 'What do you think about Styler, Corporal?'

'I reckon he's all but broken, Sir. A couple more hours should finish it,' Maffey stated confidently.

Tom nodded thoughtfully. 'Very well. We'll leave him be until

I come back. I shouldn't be away more than two or three hours if I can get a horse from Blackwell's stable.'

'What do you want me to do with Benton, Sir?' Maffey grinned expectantly. 'I can think of more than a few ways to make the bastard sweat blood.'

'Release him in about an hour. Tell him that I've said that if he delivers the written statements I require I'll drop all charges against him.'

'Don't you reckon that's being far too soft on him?' Maffey queried doubtfully.

It was Tom who now grinned like a mischievous urchin. 'Possibly not, Corporal. I do believe that when he gave chase to me, he left his shop door unlocked. And he lives alone, doesn't he?'

Maffey roared with laughter and spluttered out, 'Bloody hell! I wish you'd told me about that when I went on me furlough! I might now have had very nice betrothal and wedding rings for me wife-to-be!'

Tom found William Shayler sitting alone in the snug bar of the Barley Mow Inn. The Studley Constable mock-scowled and told him, 'You can bugger off back to Redditch this instant, Tom Potts. I'm bloody well sick and tired o' being told by everybody I meets about what a bloody clever constable you am and what a bloody stupid constable I am! And how they wishes you was down here in bloody Studley and I was up there in bloody Redditch.' Then he laughed, got up from his seat and, seizing Tom's hand, shook it hard. 'It's brilliant what you've done, Tom! Brilliant! How did you manage to identify that Styler was the Devil's Monk so bloody quickly?' Shayler abruptly apologised. 'Oh, I'm sorry, my friend. I'm being a very bad host. You sit yourself down, I'll get the drinks and pipes and then you can tell me all about everything.'

When they were seated with tankards of ale before them and long pipes of fragrant tobacco in their hands, Tom said, 'I've come for your help, Will. I need answers to questions.'

'Ask away then, Tom.'

'Have you ever heard any stories about Jared Styler being impotent?'

'Impotent?' Shayler grinned. 'I wish I was as impotent. I've heard that every wench he goes with tells her mates that he's like a bull on heat, and wants it half a dozen times a night.'

'So has he fathered any children that you know of? Because what he said to me was that he couldn't have children.'

Shayler frowned thoughtfully and mused aloud, 'Shooting blank cartridges? Well, come to think of it there were eight kids in the Styler family . . . Three lads and five girls if I remember rightly. Jared was the last-born of them. One lad and three girls died as kids. I know for a fact that the other lad got wed, but hadn't had any kids when he was still living in these parts. Both the girls got wed as well, and neither had had any kids when they died. Now, thinking about Jared, whenever he's been in my neck of the woods he's always had some wench or other hanging on his arm. But I can't remember any of them bringing claims against him for a babby. A lot o' families do become barren and their name dies out. The Stylers could be one of that sort, so it could be Jared's telling the truth and only shoots blank cartridges.'

Tom next spoke about his discovery of the dead babies, and Shayler shrugged.

'It's been common land for centuries, Tom, and lots of trampers, tinkers and gypsies bed down on it for a couple o' nights or so. Those babbies could have been buried there by any of them, or even by locals. When women get driven to desperation they're forced to take desperate measures. God pity them!'

The two friends drank and smoked for another hour as they discussed every aspect of the Devil's Monk murders. When the time of parting came Will Shayler sincerely expressed his absolute conviction that Jared Styler was the perpetrator, and heaped praises on what he what truly believed was Tom's brilliance as an investigator.

But as he rode back to Redditch, Tom was still thinking hard about certain aspects of what he had encountered during the investigation and, deciding his immediate course of action concerning those particular aspects, he returned the horse to Joseph Blackwell's stable and went to the Lock-Up, where George Maffey reported to him.

'The prisoner's snoring like a trooper, Sir, and Benton aren't come back, so it don't look as if his shop was looted. More's the pity! Padre Clayton came round to tell you that the grave for the babbies was ready down in the Old Monks Graveyard, and Hector Smout was readying a nice little box for 'um to be laid in. He suggests that you call for him at his house sometime after sundown when all's quiet, and you and him can take the babbies down there and hold a little service over them.

'Oh, and it was your Missus who brought our rations and said that she wanted to speak with you as soon as possible.'

Tom's heart thumped; rapid alternations of hope and dread coursed through him and all his action decisions were instantly postponed. 'I'll be back as soon as I can, Corporal,' he stammered out and ran to the Fox and Goose.

He burst into the entrance corridor, almost colliding with Tommy Fowkes, who cried out in shock, 'Heigh up! You've nigh on knocked me off me bloody feet!'

'I'm sorry, Master Fowkes,' Tom apologised. 'I'm here to see my wife. She has asked to speak with me without delay.'

'Humphh!' Fowkes grunted sourly. 'It's all your fault, this is!'

'What is?' Alarm struck Tom. 'What's happened to Amy?'

'Nothing's happened to her! It's to me and me Missus it's happened! And it's all your bloody fault!'

'What is?' Tom demanded impatiently.

'Her leaving! That's what is! Our best barmaid is leaving!'

'Master Fowkes, will you leave me and my husband alone to talk, please?'

Amy came hurrying from the back parlour.

Tom swung to face her, demanding elatedly, 'Leaving here? Does that mean you're coming back to live with me, Amy?'

By now the doors of the other rooms along the corridor had opened to reveal avidly staring onlookers.

Amy grabbed Tom's arm and pulled him with her out of the door and across the Green.

He made no effort to resist, and was inwardly laughing with delight. She's coming back to me! She's coming back to me! She's coming back to me!

When they reached the Lock-Up, she ordered, 'Inside! We'll speak inside!'

The door was still unlocked, and as they entered George Maffey came hurrying to meet them. 'It's my fault the door aren't secured, Sir. I wasn't sure if you wanted it locked and barred or not!'

Suffused with happiness, Tom waved him away. 'No matter, Corporal! No matter! Please, will you leave us alone.'

Maffey saluted. 'At your orders, Sir,' and hurried away through the rear door, closing it to a crack behind him. But then pressed his ear to the crack and listened intently.

Tom turned to Amy and started to tell her, 'Amy, you've made me the happiest—'

'No Tom! No!' She reached up and put her fingers over his lips. 'I'm not coming back to live with you, Tom! I'm going to fly on Vincent Sorenty's balloons and travel all over the world.'

He didn't react immediately and she repeated more loudly and forcefully, 'I'm not coming back to live with you! I'm going away from Redditch this very day, Tom! I'm going to be an Aeronaut Maiden! I'm going to travel all over the world as one of Vincent Sorenty's Aeronaut Maidens!'

This time her words penetrated his euphoric elation and their impact struck him like a hammer blow. He could only shake his head and repeat half-dazedly, 'Vincent Sorenty's Aeronaut Maidens? Travel all over the world?' Then question brokenly, 'Amy, what is it I've done that's caused you to hate me so much?'

'Oh, no!' Amy shook her head and sudden tears filled her eyes. 'Of course I don't hate you, Tom. I still love you! But I can never again be a proper wife to you. And you deserve so much better than that. But I can't ever be a wife to you again. Nor to any other man. Goodbye, my Darling!'

She turned and ran out on to the Green.

Tom wanted to follow, but it was as if an invisible force was holding him motionless and the all-powerful voice deep within his mind was re-iterating over and over again, 'Stay here! Stay here! You must let her go free. She must go free! Fate, Tom! Fate!'

Tom remained motionless, losing all track of passing time, his consciousness utterly enveloped by that all-powerful voice.

Abruptly the voice ceased and Tom experienced a sensation of sudden awakening. He shook his head, trying to clear his thoughts, struggling to come to terms with the strange mental dichotomy he was now experiencing, as if one half of his mind was furiously

cursing the uncontrollable haphazardness of the sheer ill luck which
had cost him his beloved Amy, while the other half was quietly
accepting that it had been a pre-ordained and inescapable destiny.

Which, if it was their pre-ordained destiny to be so, would
someday reunite them.

Another voice began talking to him. 'I couldn't help hearing
what's just happened between you and your Missus, Sir. I had
summat like that happen to me when I was a young Johnny Raw.
My old sergeant told me, "Listen, Private Maffey, when life
knocks you flat, a real soldier just bites hard on the bullet, gets
to his feet, shoulders his musket and marches on!" That's the
best bit of advice I ever had in me life, Sir.'

For many, many seconds, Tom stared down into the weathered,
deep-lined features of this tough, battle-hardened old veteran.
Then drew a long breath and said huskily, 'I do believe that it's
the best bit of advice I've ever received in my own life, Corporal
Maffey. And I thank you for it.'

'Do we march on then, Sir?' Maffey questioned.

'Indeed we do, Corporal,' Tom affirmed. 'And we'll step off
by having a talk with the prisoner.'

'Get to your feet, Styler!' George Maffey barked the command
as he opened the cell door.

Jared Styler stayed down on his knees, upper body slumped
on to the bed slab, face in his hands, mumbling incoherently.

Tom pointed to the large bucket in the corner of the cell which
was half filled with excreta and urine and said loudly, 'What do
you think to that, Corporal Maffey? Have you ever known a truly
mad man to take such great care to piss and shit into a bucket
to save his breeches from being soiled?'

'Never, Sir!' Maffey grinned.

Tom stepped into the cell and shook Styler's shoulder. 'Listen
very carefully to what I say, Styler. You are sadly mistaken if you
think you can use insanity as a defence. For that defence, you
must be able to prove that you are so totally deprived of understanding and memory as not to know any more than an infant or
a wild beast what you are doing. And even if it were possible for
you to use that defence at your trial, it is highly unlikely to enable
you to escape the death penalty for just the one murder, let alone

the five you are going be charged with. Also, there are more than two hundred hanging offences in British Law. So your only chance of being granted clemency is if you had accomplices in these murders and you turn King's Evidence against them. So, do you want to eat and drink your fill, and smoke a pipe or two of good tobacco, then follow that by having a sensible talk with me? The only man in England who is willing to try to help you. Or will you continue foodless and thirsty and smokeless on your journey towards the gallows? Shout out when you wish to speak with me.'

Tom exited the cell and George Maffey slammed and locked the door.

The two of them went and sat in the kitchen alcove, and George Maffey asked, 'If he does talk wi' you, Sir, what will you try und do for him?'

Tom shrugged. 'I haven't got the faintest idea, Corporal. I'm of the strong opinion that this world would be a better place without women-beating scum like him in it. But, in all truth, I'm not yet fully convinced of his guilt for any of the murders. The doubts are like tiny worms wriggling in my brain. They don't cause me any physical pain but they constantly remind me that they are there.'

The next few hours passed tortuously slowly for Tom. No shout sounded from Jared Styler and, when at spaced intervals Tom peeped through the slightly cracked open hatch, Styler was still in the same position, still mumbling incoherently.

Finally Tom said to George Maffey as they sat together in the kitchen alcove, 'I have to confess, Corporal, I'm beginning to wonder whether he might really have lost his senses. If nothing else I would have thought he'd be crying out for a drink because he must be suffering terribly with thirst by now.'

Maffey grinned and shook his head. 'No, Sir. I reckon the stupid bugger didn't believe what you told him and thinks if he acts loony he'll just be committed to a madhouse. And I reckon he thinks that whichever madhouse he gets sent to will treat him like a bloody king because of all the money the Turnkeys will earn by using him as a bloody peepshow. Certainly lots o' folks 'ull be clamouring to pay to have a squint at the Devil's Monk.'

He paused for a moment or two, then winked slyly. 'I'm willing

to wager that most of our Vestrymen are thinking that they should
be getting back the money they're spending for our rations and
my wages by turning him into their own peepshow.'

A succession of the Vestrymen's faces paraded through Tom's
mind's eye, and he couldn't help but nod in mock-lugubrious
agreement.

Then the disturbing fact that he still had not the slightest
incontrovertible proof of Styler's guilt pressed upon Tom once
more, and he suddenly thought at a tangent: If Styler were indeed
to be innocent, then the guilty killer is crowing in triumph. Could
it be that if I sought for proofs of Styler's innocence, rather than
his guilt, I might find signposts pointing me towards finding if
that guilty killer actually exists?

Gripped by uncontrollable impulse, he jumped up from the
chair, drew a tankard of ale from the keg and piled a platter with
bread and cheese, which he carried to Styler's cell.

He lowered the hatch and put the tankard and platter on its
surface, then unlocked the door and entered the cell. He used his
hands to lift and turn Styler's head so that the man's puffy, slitted
eyes and swollen features were revealed. He indicated the food
and drink on the hatch. 'You shall have this ale and food, Styler,
and I'll bring you a pipe of tobacco also. But only if you listen
to me very carefully, and without making any interruptions. Will
you agree?'

After a pause, Styler muttered, 'I'll listen.'

'Very well.' Tom accepted. 'I'll be frank with you. I despise
men like yourself, who I believe are nothing more than brutal
beasts. So I make this offer purely to satisfy my own vanity
in my powers of investigation. What I propose to do is to help
you to prove your claim to be innocent of these murders. What
you must do in return is to answer with complete honesty any
question I put to you. I'll leave you now so you can eat and
drink, and later I'll bring you a pipe of tobacco. I shall want
your answer then.'

Tom forced himself to wait for almost an hour before he
returned to the cell with a lighted pipe of tobacco and handed
it to Styler, who immediately began drawing in and expelling
clouds of smoke which wreathed around his head.

'Well? What's it to be?' Tom questioned.

Styler nodded, and now there was no pretence in his manner or in his voice of being mentally broken. 'I'll answer you true whatever you asks of me.'

Tom couldn't help but feel gratified that his plan appeared to be working, and he shouted for George Maffey to come to the cell also.

When Maffey arrived, Tom told him, 'Pay close attention, Corporal, and store what he says to memory.'

'O' course I will, Sir. Orders is orders, and I obey 'um.' Maffey frowned grimly. 'But truth to tell, I don't relish you trying to keep this fuckin' animal from meeting the hangman.'

'I don't relish it myself, Corporal,' Tom replied, then asked Styler in the mild conversational tone he intended using throughout this session of questioning, 'What's the name of the woman who bit the piece out of your ear?'

'Heptiza Lee,' Styler answered without hesitation. 'The bloody Gyppo whore did it nigh on two months since, when I was laying drunk after we had a row. By the time I'd come to me senses, she'd done a runner and had cleaned out me pockets as well. The thieving bitch!'

'Where might she have run to?'

'How the fuck would I know? Her's a bloody Gyppo. Her could be roaming about anywhere! We used to get together for a bit o' fun and devilment whenever she came through these parts. She gets up to all sorts o' dodges to get money.'

'How did you come to kill Methuselah Leeson? Were you having a row with him?'

'I never laid a hand on that old bastard in me life!'

'What have you done with Carrie Perks's body?'

'I've done nothing wi' Carrie Perks's body! She was alive when I left her.'

'Why did you kill her babies?'

'As far as I know, she's never had any kids, and I've never killed any kid in me life! Nor nobody else neither!'

'Is Heptiza Lee the Haystack Woman?'

'Her could be. But I aren't seen the fuckin' whore since she ate me ear.'

'How did you come into possession of Methuselah Leeson's snuffbox?'

'The same way I come into possession of his miserable bits o' money, and his miserable bits o' dirty old silk!'

Both Tom and George Maffey were completely taken aback by this unexpected admission and momentarily stared at each other in shock, before Tom continued, 'You'd best explain just how you got them from him.'

'It was Carrie who got 'um from him, not me. And I didn't know what she'd been doing to get stuff from Leeson until about a month or so since. That's when I come across a pound's worth o' silver and coppers that she'd hid away, and I give her a belting for hiding it from me. It was then she told me what she'd been doing with Leeson to get it.'

His tone became indignant. 'And been doing it for bloody weeks! She'd been meeting up regular wi' him down in the Abbey Meadows, and he'd been giving her money to let him suck on her parts. That's all he could manage, you see, because he was too old to get a hard-on.'

Tension gripped Tom. 'The pieces of silk, and the snuffbox? When did Carrie get those from Leeson?'

Styler didn't hesitate. 'A few nights afore I heard that he was dead. What it was, you see, he'd said that he was having trouble getting the money to pay her. So I told her to tell him that if he hadn't got money she was done with him.

'Well, this particular night he brought them bits o' dirty old silk with him, and said he'd no money and that was all he could get. So she told him to fuck off! Then he got that desperate for a suck, he offered her the snuffbox as well. So she said all right, and they did the usual and parted company. That's the last time her saw him.'

Tom asked next, 'What about that fine Hunter watch he gave her? And the silver-banded meerschaum pipe and leather tobacco pouch? When did he give her the flint and steel pocket set, and the brand-new cambric handkerchiefs?'

'I don't know about any o' that stuff. If he did give her any of 'um, I never set eyes on it. Her was supposed to meet him again on the night after he'd give her the snuffbox and bits o' silk. But she come back and told me that he hadn't turned up. And the next time I heard anything about him was that he'd been found wi' a chopper in his head. For all I know it could have

been bloody Carrie who stuck it there on the night she told me
that he hadn't turned up!'

'When exactly did you finally part from her?'

'The same day I got took on as Harvest Steward by Andrew
Parkman. I parted from her that same afternoon in the old cottage
at Ipsley where we'd been camping out.'

'For what reason did you part from her?'

'Well, I'd had enough of her being such a dirty, lying, cheating
whore. Old Leeson warn't the first old fart she'd whored with,
not by a long chalk. Her was doing the same with another bloke
when I first met her. But she said that now she'd got with me
she didn't want to do anything with him no more. There was a
few times when I hadn't got a penny piece to me name, though,
so I had to send her to go and see him.

'When I told her we was finished she went for me and I had
to fight her off. And when I left the cottage she was blarting and
shouting her was going to kill herself and make it look as though
it was me who'd done it. But I left her living, and I aren't seen
hide nor hair of her since! And that's the God's honest truth, that
is!'

Styler fell silent, and Tom was somewhat disconcerted by his
own instinctive reaction that the story he had just listened to had
indeed held the ring of truth. But then came the rapidly mounting
excitement of having discovered a fresh spoor to follow.

'Tell me the name of the man she was whoring with when
you first met her, and where I might be able to find him?'

Styler's strong, yellowed teeth bared in savage menace. 'That
bastard's been an enemy o' mine ever since I was a nipper, and
he's tried to have me took up by the constables scores o' bloody
times. His name's Edmund Scambler and he's the fuckin'
Overseer to the Poor down at Alcester. And, come to think of it,
her might very well have took up wi' him again, now I've
buggered her off. So the sooner you gets down there, the better!'

Tom managed to keep his excitement hidden and said quietly,
'I'll follow up this information in due course. In the meantime,
if we have any more noise or trouble from you it will go very
hard with you indeed. Come, Corporal Maffey, we must attend
to our other duties.'

When Styler's cell was closed up and secured, the two men

went to the kitchen alcove and Tom asked, 'What are your thoughts on what he's been telling us, Corporal?'

Maffey grimaced. 'Well, I hates to say this, Sir, but it all come across like it could be true. He was real steady-eyed while he was telling it, and I was finding meself giving him the benefit of the doubt.'

'So was I,' Tom readily admitted. 'And if tomorrow I get confirmation that Carrie Perks is alive that will most certainly change the state of affairs.'

'Well, you've still got the other murders to lay at his door, Sir,' Maffey pointed out reassuringly.

Frowning thoughtfully, Tom shook his head. 'This must remain between you and I, Corporal. Truth to tell, I'm now beginning to wonder if indeed Jared Styler is guilty of any murders at all!'

The doorbell suddenly rang out and Maffey jumped to his feet. 'I'll see who that is, Sir.'

He returned very quickly, and when Tom asked who had called, shook his head. 'There was nobody in sight, Sir. But this was laid outside the door.'

He handed a single-page broadsheet to Tom, who read the headlines out aloud.

'"THE TRUE ACCOUNT OF THE CAPTURE OF THE FIENDISH DEVIL'S MONK!"'

At the bottom of the page in small print was the information: 'Printed by Solomons Bros., Birmingham.'

As he quickly scanned the largely fictitious and gory account of the murders and subsequent arrest of Jared Styler, Tom could only shake his head and groan ruefully.

'No doubt by now there'll be hundreds who've read this rubbish, many of them believing it! How will they react towards me if it turns out to be that I've arrested the wrong man? Thus leaving the Devil's Monk still roaming around and free to kill again?'

'Well, with all respect, Sir, I reckon that you'd best go and borrow that nag again and get down to Alcester tonight,' George Maffey advised. 'Because the sooner you finds out whether Styler is telling the truth about Carrie Perks and this bloke, Scambler, the better it'll be.'

Tom thought hard for some moments, then nodded. 'I'll need to call on Reverend Clayton and explain what's happening. If I have indeed got the wrong man in our cell, then laying the real killer by the heels must, for this night at least, take precedence over those poor babies' burial.'

It was late at night when Tom rode into the empty, quiet streets of Alcester. Only the occasional glimmer of candlelight showed where people might still be awake. Tom was thankful for the full moon which lighted his path over the rutted roadway and breathed a sigh of relief when he reached the large detached home of Edmund Scambler and saw light shining through its lower windows.

Being a clumsy and ungainly horseman, he breathed another heartfelt sigh of relief when he dismounted and tethered his mount to the railings which surrounded the building. He stood for some moments, rubbing his sore buttocks and legs and easing his aching joints before walking up the long shrub-bordered path to the front door.

A tall, gaunt-featured woman wearing an oversized mob cap and voluminous apron answered his knocking and shone a lamp beam on to his face. When he gave her his name and asked for Edmund Scambler, she grunted, 'You must wait there.' And closed the door.

Eventually the door reopened and this time it was Edmund Scambler, coatless, wobbly bellied and smelling strongly of brandy, who shone a lamp on to Tom's face and demanded pettishly, 'Why have you come here disturbing me at such a late hour, Constable Potts?'

'My sincere apologies for disturbing you, Master Scambler, but the matter is urgent and could not be postponed.' Tom managed to keep a pleasant tone. 'May I come in and explain it to you?'

Scambler clucked his tongue irritably and snapped, 'No, you may not! I do not accept unwelcome pests into my house.'

'I'm here on official business, Master Scambler. I would not otherwise have troubled you at this hour.' Tom was struggling to keep his tone pleasant. 'And it is a major, not minor matter that I'm come about.'

'Then you'd best tell me what this matter is, Potts. I do feel that perhaps I am better qualified than yourself to make a judgement

on it being a minor matter or major matter. After all, in this parish
I hold a position of considerable importance which ranks far higher
than any mere Parish Constable.'

Tom abandoned the struggle to be pleasant and snapped curtly,
'I'm searching for a young woman who has disappeared. I've
been informed that you have had a close personal acquaintance
with her. Her name is Carrie Perks.'

'And who has told you that I know this woman, I wonder?'
Scambler assumed a theatrical pose of being in deep thought for
a few seconds, before suddenly crying out triumphantly, 'Eureka!
I have it! I'll wager my entire fortune that the man who has given
you this information is that same vile beast who has so recently
murdered Carrie Perks. I do believe his name is Jared Styler!'

'So you do admit to knowing her then?' Tom challenged.

'I briefly encountered her many months past, when she applied
to me for the Parish Poor Relief. Since she no longer had Right
of Settlement in this parish, I sent her packing and heard no more
of her until I was told that you had arrested her murderer – Jared
Styler.'

'How well do you know Jared Styler?' Tom asked.

'I've never set eyes on that piece of scum. And if you come
pestering me again I'll lay complaint against you before My Lord
Aston himself!' Scambler slammed the door shut.

Tom walked slowly back down the path, evaluating his own
instinctive reactions to what Scambler had said. A line from
Shakespeare's *Hamlet* passed through his mind. *The lady doth
protest too much, methinks*. He grimaced wryly. Only in this
case, it's the man, methinks!

As Tom neared the gate he heard a sibilant hissing. 'Pssstt!
Pssstt! Master Potts! Pssstt!'

He halted and, from within the shadowed shrubs, sounded a
hoarse whisper.

'Don't look about! Walk on!'

Tom obeyed, and the hoarse whisper continued, 'He's lying
about that wench! I'll come to your Lock-Up on Wednesday, but
nobody else must know about it.'

There came a rustling of leaves, then silence.

Excitement pulsated through Tom's mind at this confirmation
of his instinct that Scambler had lied to him, and he could only

surmise that his hidden informant must be the woman who had answered the door.

As he untied its reins from the railings the horse tossed its head and snickered loudly. Tom chuckled happily and patted its neck. 'Hush now! I've no more wish to mount you than you have to have me do so. But we'll journey slowly and gently; and you may draw some comfort from the thought that my horsemanship causes me more physical pain that it causes you.'

THIRTY-TWO

Tuesday, 11 August, 1829

While he was performing his early morning, chill-watered ablutions at the pump, Tom's thoughts turned to the missing personal possessions of Methuselah Leeson and the realization of his own investigative lapse suddenly hit him.

'I should have got a warrant to confiscate Styler's personal belongings from whoever held them before making the arrest.' He couldn't help but smile at the irony of the present situation. 'Instead of confiscating the baggage to help prove his guilt, I'm now proposing to confiscate it to help prove his innocence. I wonder how Joseph Blackwell will react when he hears of my change of direction?'

An hour later, standing face-to-face with Joseph Blackwell in the study of the Red House, Tom stated that change of direction.

'What are you saying, Constable Potts?' Joseph Blackwell's expression radiated utter incredulity. 'Are you telling me that you are now trying to prove that Jared Styler is innocent of these murders?

'Are you drunk, Constable Potts? Or shall I take the charitable view, that the hot sunlight we are experiencing has addled your brain?'

Tom fought down a fleeting impulse to accept this last offer and steeled himself to reply, 'I am neither drunk nor addled by sunlight, Sir. I can only repeat that my doubts as to Styler being guilty of these murders are proportionately increasing as my investigation proceeds.'

Blackwell shook his head in apparent bewilderment. 'But it's you who proclaimed his guilt to the world by arresting him for these murders in the first place.'

'I fully accept that fact, Sir.' Tom suddenly found himself imbued with a certainty of purpose he had never before experienced so forcefully.

'And it's for that very reason that I am driven to make absolutely sure that this man is indeed guilty. I can only achieve that surety by a painstaking exploration of any possible likelihood of his innocence. To aid that exploration I now urgently need a warrant empowering me to confiscate Styler's personal belongings, which are presently being held for him by Andrew Parkman.

'I'm expecting to receive information tomorrow, which renders it vital that I thoroughly examine Styler's personal possessions this very day.'

Blackwell shook his head again and said wearily, 'There are times, Thomas Potts, when you try my patience to the utmost. You know very well that I'm not empowered to issue such a warrant and Lord Aston is still absent from the parish. However, I will give you a note to present to Andrew Parkman, which may persuade him to pass Styler's possessions over to your keeping.'

Even as Tom began to thank him, Blackwell's hand shot up to clamp across Tom's mouth.

He snapped angrily, 'Do not dare to offer me thanks, Thomas Potts! I shall never forgive you for forcing me to humiliate myself by asking for a personal favour from such an ignorant, greedy, dishonest, slave-driving clod-hopper as Andrew Parkman!'

Tom found Andrew Parkman in the barnyard superintending the building of a large corn-stack and could not help but feel a nervous tension as he walked towards him. To his surprise, however, the farmer greeted him with a friendly wave and told the men building the stack, 'Look who's here, you lot. This is the very same Constable Potts who helped me to capture that murdering bastard, the Devil's Monk. Now then, Constable Potts, how can I help you today?'

'I've brought you a note from Joseph Blackwell, Master Parkman.'

He handed the note to the other man, who quickly scanned it and exclaimed, 'Bugger me! Blackwell's being uncommon civil, aren't he just. Of course you can take the bastard's baggage, Constable. Go to the house and ask my wife-to-be to hand it over to you. Just tell her I said it was alright to give it to you.'

He turned away and shouted at the labourers, 'Get on wi' the fuckin' job, will you. It's got to be finished today, not next fuckin' week!'

Tom quickly walked away.

An old crone answered the door at the farmhouse and Tom asked, 'Excuse me, Ma'am, but are you the wife-to-be of Master Parkman?'

'Who told you that?' the crone demanded suspiciously.

'No one, Ma'am, only Master Parkman said I was to ask for his wife-to-be, and naturally I assumed it might be yourself.'

'Well it aren't that old bat you're talking to!' a youthful voice shouted indignantly and a pretty young girl, resplendent in a fashionable satin gown and foam-plumed bonnet, came hurrying down the passage. 'It's me! Mistress Jenny Tolley! I'm Master Andrew Parkman's betrothed Lady-Wife-to-be.'

Tom lifted his tall hat and bowed slightly. 'I hope I find you well, Mistress Tolley?'

'You do indeed, Master Potts.' She winked pertly and giggled. 'You did me a real favour, even though you scared the shit out o' me that night you come and took that bastard, Styler, away. The Banns am to be called this coming Sunday, and three weeks after that I'll be Mistress Andrew Parkman. I shall be living like a High-Born Lady for the rest o' me days! Now what's you come here for?'

'For Styler's personal baggage and belongings. Master Parkman said to tell you that it was all right for you to give them to me.'

'Florrie 'ull get his bag for you. Go on, Florrie, you daft old bat! Go and fetch Styler's bag for this Gentleman. Now I must bid you Good Day, Master Potts. You knows what they say about a Fine Lady's work never being done. These days I'm a very busy woman indeed.'

With that, she was gone, and Tom could only smile and feel that, for her at least, Styler's arrest had been a stroke of exceptionally good fortune.

THIRTY-THREE

B ack in the Lock-Up, Tom emptied the contents of the large canvas bag on to the floor of the kitchen alcove. The subsequent examination of Jared Styler's personal belongings revealed a pair of boots and assorted items of clothing. A cut-throat razor and small looking glass. Two hunting knives in leather sheaths. Several wire snares, three spoons and a pewter tankard. A flint, steel and tinder box set. A comb and a hair brush. A short-stemmed clay pipe and four twists of tobacco wrapped in a piece of rag. A middle-sized, cork-stoppered stone bottle which, when Tom pulled out the cork, he found to be half filled with gin.

Tom sat for a while musing over the twists of tobacco being wrapped in a piece of rag. It was this single discovery above all else which convinced him that Jared Styler's assertion of only ever having had Methuselah Leeson's silver snuffbox and the two pieces of silk in his possession was the truth. As a smoker himself, Tom knew that given the choice between storing any grade of tobacco in a leather pouch or a piece of rag, even a stolen pouch would win the day, since it would be virtually indistinguishable from so many thousands of similar pouches.

'So where are the objects that Nellie Leeson insisted had been stolen from her husband?'

Tom abruptly stood up and, leaving the contents of the bag strewn across the floor, shouted to George Maffey, who was sitting on the rear-yard privy.

'I need to go down to the Old Monks Graveyard and speak with Hector Smout, Corporal. I'll return as soon as possible.'

Smoking a pipe, Hector Smout was sitting on a mound of earth at the side of an open grave. When he saw Tom, he shouted: 'Where's the Reverend Clayton, then? He told me both of you was bringing them babbies down for burial today.'

'Oh my God!' Tom came to an abrupt halt as guilty shame struck him like a physical blow. 'Oh my God, Master Smout! I'd clean forgotten about them! Oh my God! I don't know what to say!'

'Then it's best you say nothing till you can remember why you've come here, other than to bury the babbies,' Smout advised sourly.

'I needed to make a search of Nellie Leeson's cottage. But instead, I think I'd best go up and see Reverend Clayton and make amends for having forgotten the babies.'

'Is this search summat to do with the murders?' Smouth asked.

'Yes, and it needs to be done as quickly as possible.' Tom nodded.

'Where are the babbies?'

'In the Lock-Up.'

'Well, you'd best do the search, and I'll go up to see Reverend Clayton. He can get the babbies from the Lock-Up. I got a good big basket to carry 'um in, and I've made a nice box to lay 'um to rest in. When we're ready you can join us and we'll do the burial.'

'That's a very good plan, Master Smout,' Tom agreed immediately.

Smout got to his feet and grinned. 'Come on then, let's go and open up Nellie's cottage.'

After Hector Smout prised out the final nail securing the door, he handed a small lavender-and-mint-filled pouch to Tom. 'You'd best put it on, Master Potts. It'll still be stinking inside.'

Tom did as advised, and when Smout pushed the door open a foul stench enveloped them.

'I'll get the shutters up as well to give you more light to see with.' Smout moved away from the doorway and Tom stepped into the shadowed, sparsely furnished room.

Like its neighbours in the row the thatch-roofed cottage was single-storied with a low-pitched thatched roof and consisted of two fair-sized rooms and a rear lean-to which served as kitchen and scullery with its own small water pump. A door in the rear wall of the lean-to opened on to a long, narrow garden plot which had a wood-built privy at its end.

Tom couldn't help but think that compared to most of the workers' hovels in alleys and courts throughout the Needle District this could be considered a very superior dwelling place.

When Hector Smout lifted the shutters sunlight flooded the rooms and Tom moved slowly through them. Noting that, despite the lingering foul miasma of rotting flesh, the walls, floors, sparse furnishings, the beddings and the contents of the lean-to were all exceptionally clean.

When his companion joined him, Tom remarked on this fact and Hector Smout nodded. 'Ahrrr! She's been a very fussy house-keeper, has Nellie. And fair play to Methuselah – until he went loony he was a good worker and provider.' Smout chuckled and winked. 'A bloody good poacher as well. They always had fresh meat for their table, or fish or eels whenever they fancied a change. I'll go up to the Reverend now, Master Potts.'

'Thank you very much for helping me yet again, Master Smout.'

'Youm always welcome to my help, Master Potts.'

They parted with a warm handshake, and Tom began his search.

He minutely checked every piece of furnishing, the garden plot, the privy and where possible, the thatch of the roof.

Search completed, he sat at the table in the front room of the cottage contemplating the varied objects strewn across it. Objects which he had found secreted in the lean-to, the roof thatch and the privy.

They were a Hunter watch. A pocket flint, steel and tinder set. Three new cambric handkerchiefs. A tobacco pouch and a silver-banded meerschaum pipe with an engraved bowl. The same personal possessions that Nellie Leeson claimed had been stolen from the pockets of her dead husband.

But Nellie had made no claim concerning one of Tom's finds: a flat, rag-wrapped packet containing five tightly folded lengths of soiled white silk cloth. Each measured two yards by one yard, and were crudely sewed together from smaller pieces, identically with the two silk cloths from the Ipsley cottage.

So why had Nellie not listed them with the other articles she claimed to have been stolen from her husband?

For some time, Tom remained seated at the table, the same questions continually passing through his mind, and for which he could find no ready answers.

Had Methuselah concealed all these articles without Nellie's knowledge? If so, why?

Was it Nellie who had done the concealing without her husband's knowledge? If so, why?

Had the concealments been made by both of them acting in concert?

His train of thought was disturbed by Hector Smout and John Clayton shouting at him from outside; he picked up his new finds and went outside to join them in giving a Christian burial to the tragic, nameless babies.

THIRTY-FOUR

Wednesday, 12 August, 1829

Since early morning Jared Styler had been pleading with Tom to tell him what was happening in the investigation. But Tom had ignored him, and ruefully admitted to George Maffey, 'I know I'm behaving like a spiteful child in not telling him what is going on, Corporal, but I abhor men who treat women so brutally. I freely admit that it's only for the satisfaction of my own vanity that I'm continuing these investigations, which regrettably might well end in saving the evil bastard from the gallows. Should that be the case, I will still only ever be wishing him a lifetime of misery.'

Nevertheless, these heartfelt feelings didn't stop Tom dreading that his eagerly awaited informant might fail to put in an appearance.

The bells signalling the end of the working day were ringing, and swarms of weary toilers were erupting from their workplaces when the bells of the Lock-Up finally jangled. Tom hurried to open its iron-studded door, while George Maffey bundled the leg-ironed and manacled Jared Styler out into the rear yard and barred that door before concealing himself in a cell.

The tall, gaunt-featured woman pushed Tom aside as she entered and, standing next to the door, demanded, 'Am you here by yourself?'

'I am,' he answered.

'Right then! Now just keep your mouth shut and listen careful to what I say. That wench, Carrie Perks, who Jared Styler's supposed to have killed, well he never! And her aren't dead! Her come to the house real late at night on the Tuesday before last.

Scambler thought I was sleeping, you see. But I've known for years about the tricks the dirty old pig gets up to that he thinks I don't know about! He gives the young sluts extra "Poor Relief" that they aren't entitled to, providing they opens their leg for him. He must have had more than a dozen of them over the years. The dirty old pig! And he thinks I don't know about it, because to him I'm just his thick-yedded skivvy of a wife!

'Anyway, I can tell you true that Carrie Perks is alive and kicking, and she's staying in a tramp's lodging house down by Evesham, which is kept by a sneaking thief called Slimey Blair. Scambler's paying Slimey Blair a fortune to keep her hidden away in secret until after Styler's been hung, because he's been wanting to get Styler hung for years. And in all truth it would be a good riddance to bad rubbish. But what makes me so angry is that while Scambler begrudges me every miserly ha'penny I spends for me own needs, the dirty old pig is paying for that slut to live on the fat o' the land and drink herself senseless each and every night. And I have to go down on me knees each and every night and pray to Our Blessed Lord and Saviour to give me the strength to bear this disgrace, and not commit the mortal sin of murdering Scambler for being the rotten dirty pig he is!

'Now I got to get back home, and these days I finds it a long hard walk, I can tell you. The only reason I could come today was because I knew the dirty old pig would be sneaking down to see the little slut, and he'll sure not be back till late tomorrow.'

'Well, I thank you very much for this information, Ma'am. I'll go and borrow transport and I'll carry you back to Alcester,' Tom offered.

'Ohh, no you won't!' she declared emphatically. 'I'm a respectable married woman, I am. Scambler might be a dirty old pig but I'm his lawful wedded wife and I'll never break me marriage vows. Not never! So with all your fine manners and way o' talking, and offering me rides in carriages, it's still no use you trying to tempt me into mortal sin!'

Tom could only blurt out in shock, 'I do assure you, Ma'am, that I have no . . .'

The door slammed behind her even as he spoke.

George Maffey emerged from his hiding place with a broad grin. 'Well, that went well, didn't it, Sir? Apart from her turning you down when you tried to sweet talk her into being your fancy-woman.'

Elated by what she had told him, Tom could only laugh and reply, 'That didn't surprise me, Corporal. Of late I've known nothing else but rejection from women. Anyway, I'm going to borrow a horse from Blackwell and go down to Evesham this very night. It shouldn't take long for me to find this lodging house she spoke of.'

'Can I say summat, Sir?' George Maffey appeared to be somewhat uneasy.

'Of course you may, Corporal.' Tom was disturbed by his friend's abrupt change of mood.

'Well, Sir, Slimy Blairs place is a "Thieves' Ken". I've stayed there a few times, and it's a fact that nigh on every jailbird and ne'er-do-well for fifty miles around uses it sometime or other'

Tom sensed what was to come, and interrupted, 'Very well, Corporal, I fully accept that this reconnaissance patrol should be left to you. I shan't try and direct such an experienced soldier as to how you carry it out. But what I shall strictly order is that you do not in any way put yourself into danger. Is that understood?'

Maffey snapped to action and saluted. 'At your orders, Sir!'

'At ease, Corporal.' Tom smiled and realized just how fond he had become of this man. 'Now take as much time as you need on this patrol, Corporal; and for the sake of our friendship, do not take any chances which might bring you into danger.'

They parted with a warm handshake, and Tom experienced a sudden pang of loneliness as Maffey walked out of the door. He went out into the rear yard.

'What's happening? Has you found Carrie Perks?' Jared Styler questioned anxiously.

'No!' Tom snapped curtly.

Styler sank to his knees, shaking his head slowly from side to side and whimpering in despair, and for the first time Tom was shocked by a sudden realization of Styler's physical and mental deterioration.

The arrogant, youthful-looking, powerfully built man in his prime had abruptly metamorphosed into this whimpering, haggard-featured, bent-backed old man, slumped on his knees upon the dusty cobbles.

Tom experienced a fleeting shaft of pity. Then images of women's bloodied faces and broken bodies and pitifully help-less dead babies forced themselves into the forefront of his mind, and he ordered harshly, 'Get on your feet, Styler. Once you're back in your cell I'll take the leg irons and manacles off you.'

THIRTY-FIVE

Monday, 24 August, 1829

It was mid-morning when George Maffey returned to the Lock-Up and the grin on his face bore evidence that his almost two weeks' long mission had met with success.

'Carrie Perks is in Slimy Blair's all right, Sir. Going under the name o' Carrie Brown and living on the fat o' the land wi' a bed and cubicle all to herself. I got friendly with her straight away, and we'd beg and drink together every day and night. When she got drunk enough she got loose-tongued and let things drop. Like how she'd never got pregnant in her life, although she'd been very free and easy with blokes, because her mam had showed her how not to.

'Scambler came to see her twice while I was there, but he never came to the ken himself. He sent a message to her by way of one of the casuals, asking her when it got dark to sneak out to meet him. She told me who he was, and asked me to follow her close, in case he turned on her, so I followed her both times. They just had a quick shag behind some bushes, then she came back to the ken. One night she asked me if I'd been in trouble with the law. I told her I'd been in trouble with it lots of times, but that you'd been all right to me when I was begging in Redditch. Then she told me how this one bloke she was with broke her nose, and that it was you who'd helped her and got the doctor to mend it. She said that this same bloke broke her nose again, and she was going to see him hung for it, even though she knew for certain he hadn't done the thing what he was going to be hung for.

'I asked her what his name was, but she wouldn't tell me. She passed out then and wouldn't speak of it again.'

'So she definitely knows what's happening to Styler,' Tom remarked.

'Ohh, yes! But I'd wager the whole of the bloody Midlands knows what's happening to him by now. That broadsheet about you arresting him is all over the place.' Maffey chuckled and teased, 'You're well on the way to becoming a famous hero, Sir, and I reckon the King 'ull be offering to make you the Constable o' the Tower o' London when Styler's hung.'

'I'm wondering what Lord Aston will be offering me when I meet with him tomorrow at the Petty Sessions.' Tom was no longer smiling. 'He came back on Friday from Malvern and sent word to Joseph Blackwell that he wants Styler brought before him tomorrow. He intends to commit Styler to Worcester Jail on five murder charges: the Haystack Woman, Methuselah Leeson, Carrie Perks and the babies.'

'Well, he'll have to be satisfied with two charges instead o' five.' Maffey chuckled. 'Styler can only be hung once, so whether it's for two or five murders it'll make no difference to his neck.'

Tom was now grimly serious. 'Come up to my bedroom, Corporal. I've something I want to show you.'

Up in the garret, Tom opened the storage chest and took from it the packet of silk pieces and the other articles he had found in Nellie Leeson's cottage.

'Finding these hidden away is proof that they weren't robbed from Methuselah, as his wife claimed, and that Styler was telling the truth when he denied having ever had them. We now know that his denial of killing Carrie Perks is also the truth, and that she's never borne children. So as Will Shayler said, those babies most likely belonged to tinkers, tramps, gypsies or even some desperate local woman. Also, I've found no proof whatsoever that he knew or killed the Haystack Woman, or killed Methuselah Leeson. As for the attempted murder of Judas Benton, I just do not believe it was anything more than Styler slathering a would-be blackmailer in mud.'

He paused for several seconds, then stated firmly, 'In fact, at this very moment, Corporal, I'm becoming increasingly fearful that I've arrested the wrong man!'

'So what will you do tomorrow, Sir?'

'I truly don't know yet, Corporal. But if you'll be good enough to take command here, I do know what I'm going to do this very minute. I'm going directly up to the Poorhouse to have a word with Nellie Leeson.'

This time it was Hilda Lewis who met and accompanied Tom upstairs to the cramped room, telling him with a beaming smile, 'Nellie's quite her old self again, Master Potts. She's ruling the other old women with a rod of iron, just like she did poor Methuselah. But so long as they does what her says she makes good and sure they get their pipes and bacca regular, and none of the old men dares to try and bully them when she's about.'

In the narrow room he found Nellie Leeson, now dressed in the 'TP'-badged grey dress and bonnet, sitting with her ancient crone companions on the wooden bench, all three of them noisily sucking in and blowing out clouds of smoke from their clay pipes.

'Now then, Nellie, here's a Gentleman come to visit. Do you remember him?' Hilda Lewis asked gently.

Nellie Leeson screwed her eyes until they were mere slits embedded in red-rimmed flesh and stared up at Tom for several seconds. Then demanded angrily, 'Where's me husband? What's you done wi' him?'

'He's received a Christian Burial in the Old Monks Graveyard, Mistress Leeson. The Reverend Clayton read the service, and Hector Smout and myself were mourners.'

'Who was it who had me brung up here?' She scowled.

'It was myself, Ma'am. You were taken ill and needed constant care. However, your home and belongings are all well secured, and Master Smout keeps a close watch on them.'

Her withered features contorted in fury and she screeched, 'You had no rights to bury Leeson! There was still plenty o' folks paying to have a look at him! And the bugger owed me money for the valuables he'd stole from me!'

Tom instantly seized upon this opening she had given him. 'Well, that is why I'm come here to see you today, Ma'am.'

There was a small table at the end of the room and Tom

dragged it in front of the three seated crones. Then, from his canvas bag he started pulling out the articles he had found in her cottage, and one by one laid them on the table in front of Nellie Leeson, identifying them aloud as he did so.

'The silver-banded meerschaum pipe with an engraved bowl. A tobacco pouch. The Hunter watch. A pocket flint, steel and tinder set. Three new cambric handkerchiefs. Do you not recognize them, Ma'am? They are some of the articles that you told me had been stolen from your husband.'

She made no reply, only sat rocking her body backwards and forwards, noisily sucking in and blowing out clouds of strong-smelling smoke.

He waited briefly before taking out the flat packet of silk pieces and opening the packet lifted one piece and shook it out before her.

'These pieces of silk are exactly similar to other pieces which I found in the possession of the man who is accused of murdering and robbing your husband, Ma'am. But these particular pieces I found concealed in your cottage, together with all these other articles I've just shown you. I'm wondering why you didn't include the pieces of silk with the other articles you told me of? I'm also wondering who it was that concealed all these things in various hiding places in your cottage?'

Nellie Leeson's head bent low, her body started rocking, lower and lower, faster and faster until she suddenly toppled off the bench and thumped on to on the floor, her head, legs and arms jerking, her body convulsing erratically, her breaths whooping gasps.

'Oh my God!' Hilda Lewis shouted. 'Quick! Help me get her on to the cot, Master Potts.'

Tom sprang to her side and they lifted Nellie Leeson and laid her on the cot, where she continued convulsing and whooping.

'I do apologise most sincerely for this, Mistress Lewis. I fear I should have not badgered her so. I'm very, very sorry for doing so!' Tom was feeling truly guilty and blaming himself.

Hilda Lewis shook her head and told him, 'Don't go moithering yourself, Master Potts. She's been having these fits for as long as I've known her. Don't forget I've had years of dealing with Nellie and Methuselah. Every time he's been put in here Nellie's come up regularly to see him, and as sure as little apples she's

had one o' these turns at some time or other during the visit.
Perhaps I'm a wicked cow for saying so, but there's been times
when I've wondered if she can throw a fit whenever it serves her
best. Anyway, you'd best leave her to me now and go about your
business, because you'll get no sense from her when she comes
back to her senses. I'll bid you Good Day, Master Potts.'

Tom bowed. 'Thank you for being so forebearing, Ma'am.
Good Day to you.'

As he walked back to Redditch, memories of various incidents
were flooding into his mind.

Nellie Leeson waving the rusty hatchet and threatening, 'Hold
your bloody tongue, Thomas Potts, and bugger off from here
afore I cuts your bloody yed off!'

Nellie Leeson, brandishing a rusty hatchet above her mob-
capped head, screeching furiously at her husband, 'Get back here,
you barmy bugger! I told you to stop in the house, didn't I! Get
back here afore I has your bloody guts for garters!'

Methuselah Leeson howling in pain as his wife grabbed his
long beard with her free hand and hobbled back along the lane,
dragging him with her.

Nellie Leeson screeching in fury, 'He'd gone off by hisself
again! I told the bugger time and time again that he'd got to wait
for me, and not go gallivanting off by hisself! But he would keep
on sneaking off like a slithering snake. We was fighting day and
night about it, so we was.'

A grossly obese woman snapping curtly, 'It's a wonder Nellie
Leeson aren't put this chopper into old Methuselah's head long
afore now! Her's tried to do it enough times afore when her
bloody temper's up. Like a mad thing at them times, so her is.'

Nellie Leeson whirling the rusty hatchet around her head,
howling, 'I'll kill you! I'll kill you! I'll kill you!' at this same
obese woman, who was sobbing in terror and struggling to raise
her gross body from the ground while Tom himself was grappling
with Nellie Leeson, to restrain and disarm her.

Now a voice whispered from the depths of Tom's mind: If
Nellie Leeson had killed Old Methuselah, that would leave only
the Haystack Woman to charge Jared Styler with, and you have
no evidence against him for it. So what are you going to say to
Lord Aston tomorrow?

Tom smiled wryly, and thought: I'm buggered if I know. But personally, I'm sure that it was Nellie who, in a fit of rage, buried the hatchet in Old Methuselah's head after finding out about his stealing their money to go whoring. But I'm not relishing the thought of a poor old madwoman ending her life on the gallows because of my investigation. As he continued on his way a plan began to formulate in his mind, and when he reached Redditch he went directly to the house of Joseph Blackwell.

After a long and extremely detailed conversation with Blackwell, Tom was on horseback, leading another saddled horse behind him, heading towards Studley Village.

THIRTY-SIX

Tuesday, 25 August, 1829

By eight o'clock in the morning the Select Parlour, Tap Room, Snug Room and the entrance and corridors of the Fox and Goose were packed. Outside a noisy crowd were clustered along the entire length of the front wall of the inn. The roadway was lined with carriages and carts loaded with people. Another large rowdy crowd was gathered outside the Lock-Up. Roaming hawkers and pedlars cried their wares, sweetmeats and drinks vendors offered refreshments, Broadsheet Sellers brandished their sheets of bloodthirsty reportages. The atmosphere was that of a festive occasion, with everyone present eagerly awaiting the entrance of the 'Star Attraction'; in this case, the 'Star Attraction' being Jared Styler, the notorious Devil's Monk.

Inside the Lock-Up a small group of men were standing in the central passage between the cells, when from outside there came a sudden hubbub of shouting, followed by the jangling of the bells.

'Attend to the door, Corporal Maffey,' Joseph Blackwell ordered. 'You'd best go with him, Constable Shayler, and you also, Deputy Constable Bint, in case any of the roughs try to follow My Lord Aston inside.'

The Right Honourable and Reverend Walter Hutchinson, the
Lord Aston, had taken great pains with his toilette and dress this
morning, and entered the Lock-Up emanating mingled scents of
colognes and pomades, freshly laundered linen and clothes, and
highly polished leather. But when he spoke his breath carried
strong scents of wines, spirits, tobacco and snuff.

'Blackwell, my good fellow, why did you not inform me
yesterday that it was imperative I call here before taking my seat
to open the Sessions?' he demanded pettishly. 'Why have I only
been informed this very morning? This laxness displayed by
yourself has most dreadfully discommoded me!'

Joseph Blackwell bowed apologetically. 'Alas, My Lord, I am
truly regretful if you have been discommoded in any degree.
However, since midday yesterday until the early hours of this
morning, myself, together with Constables Shayler, Potts, Bint
and Corporal Maffey have been fully engaged upon official duties.
These particular duties were carried out with the sole intent of
protecting yourself, My Lord, from being hooted and jeered and
insulted by this mob outside.'

'Hooted? Jeered? Insulted?' Each word was an explosion from
Aston's purple ballooned jowls. 'Have you not heard or read of
the praises being showered upon my name for instigating and
directing the investigation which has brought this vile mass
murderer to face justice?'

'Exactly how many murders constitute a mass, My Lord?'
Blackwell hissed sibilantly.

'In this case, five! As you well know, Blackwell! Furthermore,
as you well . . .'

Aston suddenly halted in mid-sentence, and he blinked several
times in rapid succession as realization dawned. His bombastic
bellowing dropped to a virtually whispered plea. 'What is it, Sir?
What is it that you have discovered which creates this need for
protecting me from abuse?'

Joseph Blackwell turned towards the kitchen alcove and called
gently, 'Miss Carrie Perks, will you please come here to me.
Don't be afraid, my dear. No one will harm or shout at you, or
offer you insult in any way.'

Carrie Perks slowly emerged into view and approached the
group, head bowed, hands kneading nervously together.

'Goddammee! Carrie Perks! The murdered woman, whose babies were murdered also! Goddammee! Is this really her?' Aston was shaking his head as if he could not believe what his eyes were seeing.

'It is indeed, My Lord.' Blackwell smiled thinly. 'Constable Potts and Constable Shayler brought her here from Evesham last night, where she has been staying in a lodging house of the type commonly called a "Thieves' Ken". She has given me a full account of her relationship with Jared Styler. She has confirmed that Jared Styler's account of her prostituting herself with Methuselah Leeson in return for money and certain other articles is accurate. She has also sworn on the Bible that she has never borne children, and that Jared Styler, to her certain knowledge, did not murder the babies that were found in Ipsley. So, My Lord, would you not agree that the number of the Devil's Monk suspected murders has now dropped to two?'

Knowing Blackwell as he did, Aston became very wary, and now his tone sounded almost humble. 'Blackwell, my dear fellow, I do sense that you have more disturbing news to impart. Let me hear it.'

'One moment if it please you, My Lord.' Blackwell turned and told George Maffey, 'Corporal, will you escort Miss Perks out of earshot and ensure she remains so.'

Maffey snapped to attention and saluted. 'At your orders, Sir.'

He took Carrie Perks arm and said gently, 'You come on upstairs wi' me now, my dearie, and you can sit and be comfortable while I make you a nice breakfast.'

Blackwell then said, 'Constable Shayler, Deputy Constable Bint, will you accompany them and come when I call.'

When the pair had also gone, the moment for which Tom had been waiting with grim anticipation arrived.

Blackwell almost imperceptibly nodded to him.

Tom stepped forward, bowed slightly to Aston and told him firmly, 'I have to report, My Lord, that the accusation of attempted murder made by Judas Benton against Jared Styler is false, and Benton has proven himself to be lying. There is as yet no positive evidence to link Styler with the murder of Methuselah Leeson, and there is as yet no positive evidence to link Styler with the murder of the individual termed the Haystack

Woman. I freely admit that I now have strong doubts that he is guilty of either of those two murders, and that I was too hasty in concluding that he was the so-called Devil's Monk. Therefore, My Lord, I offer you my immediate resignation, or my dismissal without protest, from the post of Constable of Tardebigge Parish.'

Aston was so taken aback that he could only stare incredulously at Tom.

Blackwell intervened smoothly. 'My Lord, I do not believe that anything would be gained from dismissing Constable Potts, or accepting his resignation at this time. If you will permit, I will give you my reasons.'

Radiating a confident surety, he fluently presented those reasons at considerable length while giving Aston scant opportunity to present any counterargument.

Slowly, inevitably it seemed to Tom, Blackwell persuaded Lord Aston that he would gain fresh kudos if he followed his, Blackwell's, advice. Listening and watching intently, Tom's already high respect for Blackwell's expertise in handling Lord Aston rose to fresh heights.

When Blackwell was satisfied he had prevailed, he then gave Aston the opportunity to comment upon and alter slightly some of the advice he had received. By the time all was settled, Aston was left believing that it was he himself who had formulated the course of action they were to follow.

Blackwell bowed submissively and in admiring tones declared, 'Very well, My Lord, it shall all be done exactly as you have advised. May I make so bold as to offer you my sincerest admiration, and also my grateful thanks, for the masterful way you have dealt with this crisis. I fear that without your wise counsel we would be facing the most riotous disorder.'

Aston waved his be-ringed hand in casual acceptance of his rightful dues. 'I need no thanks, Blackwell. I am merely doing my duty to my sovereign and my country.'

'As you always do, My Lord.' Blackwell bowed again before turning to Tom. 'Constable Potts, go immediately and fetch the Crier here.'

As Tom left he heard Blackwell advising, 'My Lord, I think it wisest for you to leave in these next moments, whilst the rabble will undoubtedly be focussing all their attention on Constable Potts.'

As Tom walked across the Green he was assailed from all side with questions.

'Where's the Monk?'

'When's he coming out?'

'Is it true he's slaughtered more than a dozen?'

'Is it true he roasted and ate their hearts?'

Jimmy Grier was standing by the door of the inn fully accoutred in all his garish professional splendour. Tom beckoned for him to follow and walked back across the Green, still being assailed by a barrage of questions.

Lord Aston's four-horsed carriage had gone when Tom and Grier entered the Lock-Up, and his fellow constables were returned downstairs.

Joseph Blackwell emitted a reedy chuckle. 'I do hope we're not faced with a riot when this news is Cried. Now listen carefully, Master Grier.'

He quickly recited the words, then waited expectantly.

Jimmy Grier cleared his throat and repeated in a low voice. 'OYEZ! OYEZ! OYEZ! By Order of the Magistrates, let it be known that the man, Jared Styler, being held in custody in the Redditch Lock-Up, is presently lying unconscious after suffering a seizure at the hour of three hours and seventeen minutes of this morning, the twenty-fifth day of August, in the Year of Our Lord, 1829. The Petty Sessions called for this day, the twenty-fifth day of August in the Year of Our Lord, 1829, is hereby cancelled. The Magistrates warn that should any disorder occur following this announcement, the perpetrators of such disorder shall be punished with the utmost severity the law allows. GOD SAVE THE KING!'

'As always, you have committed that to memory without any error whatsoever, Master Grier. I do declare that you are the finest Crier in the Midlands, and likely in the whole kingdom,' Blackwell praised as he produced a gold sovereign and handed it to the old man. 'Now Cry that message until this is fully earned. Then call at my house and you shall be given a full bottle of whatever drink you wish for.'

Jimmy Grier was let out on to the Green. Almost immediately

his bell rang out and his stentorian shout rebounded from the wall of the Lock-Up.

'OYEZ! OYEZ! OYEZ! By Order of the Magistrates . . .'

Blackwell emitted another reedy chuckle. 'I'll wager that with a strong enough wind to carry it that shout can be heard a hundred miles away or more. Now, Deputy Constable Bint, call Corporal Maffey and have him bring the girl back downstairs. I want you, Constable Shayler, to deliver her safely back to her lodging house. Give her this when you arrive there.'

He handed a sovereign to Shayler, and turned and beckoned Tom to follow him to the front door. As he exited he emitted yet another reedy chuckle and whispered, 'Now, Thomas Potts, make good use of the extra time you have to lay the real Devil's Monk by the heels, which I have no doubt you will succeed in doing.' He winked broadly and in a louder voice instructed, 'Constable Potts, I want you and Deputy Constable Bint to patrol the town until the crowds disperse. Corporal Maffey can watch over our "Sleeping Beauty".'

Locked away in the cell nearest the rear door, breathing hoarsely through his wide-open mouth, Jared Styler lay unconscious under the effects of the laudanum he had been dosed up with earlier that morning.

THIRTY-SEVEN

Wolverhampton, Black Country, Staffordshire.
Tuesday, 25 August, 1829

T he grey dampness of early afternoon did nothing to lift Amy Potts's spirits as she walked slowly along the canal-branch towpath which led into the wide-spaced yard of the huge Union Mill.

When she reached the edge of the yard she halted and sighed despondently as she scanned the view before her. The south-east directly overlooked a gasworks, the main canal and a large foundry, in that order, surrounded by an ever-spreading smoke-shrouded panorama of the multi-terraced housing, heavy industries, coal and iron mines which stretched more than a dozen miles to meld in parts with the outskirts of the city of Birmingham.

This was the Black Country. One of the ever-increasing, wealth-producing industrial powerhouses which had propelled Great Britain to its present preponderance among the nations of the world. A fact which, although she was a proud patriot, did not at this moment serve to raise Amy's low spirits as her gaze switched to the western edges of the yard where the huddled tents of the Vincent Sorenty Grand Aerostation Company were pitched.

Again she sighed despondently, lost in thought: I thought being an Aeronaut Maiden would be different from this. I've only been up in the balloon that one time in Brum, and the bloody balloon hasn't been up either since then. And I never thought we'd be camping out in the Black Country. I thought that by now we'd be travelling over the seas to France and all those other countries I want to go to. Why did Vincent bugger off and leave that nasty sod to boss over me and work me half to death?

The thought of that 'nasty sod' entered her mind and his shout sounded in her ears, and Mario Fassia came running from the huddled tents.

When he reached her he challenged her angrily. 'Why aren't you practising?'

'I was just taking a walk before I started,' she explained.

'We don't pay to you to go swanning about like a High-Born Lady,' he snarled.

'You haven't paid me for anything at all yet, have you!' she retorted.

His dark eyes blazed with fury and he spat back, 'What about the fine bed and board we give you?'

'Bed and board!' she scoffed scornfully. 'A straw mattress and two blankets on the ground in a leaky tent, and mutton stew twice a day with the cheapest beer that money can buy to drink. That's not what I call fine bed and board!'

'Well, you're still living better than any other skivvy I've ever known.'

'I'm no skivvy!' She erupted now in fury. 'I'm married to a man who was born a Gentleman and who's a much respected and praised Parish Constable. He's just arrested that murderer called the Devil's Monk. Read the latest broadsheets if you don't believe me. My husband, Thomas Potts, is worth a dozen like you, and the whole world knows that now!'

She stepped around him and walked towards the tents.

For brief seconds he stood agitatedly gnawing his lips, then ran after her, shouting, 'Where are you going now? Where are you going?' His voice rose to a feminine-like shriek. 'Where? Where are you going? Where?'

'I'm going to do my afternoon practice! Where else do you think I'd be going at this hour? Where else is there for me to play in this scruffy hole? You bloody great Molly.'

Mario Fassia jerked to an abrupt halt, lifting his hands to his mouth in shocked consternation. 'Molly! She called me Molly! What the fuck has she found out?'

In a temporarily vacant section of the extensive mill buildings there was a multistoried enclosed courtyard where Vincent Sorenty had had his crew rig high scaffolding from which ropes and trapezes could be hung to swing freely. It was here every morning and afternoon that Amy, under Mario Fassia's tuition, had learned to do a variety of acrobatic movements on both trapeze and ropes.

It was later that afternoon when Vincent Sorenty returned to the encampment and came to watch Amy at practice. Dressed in a dark blue, close-fitting, ankle-length dress, she was swooping and soaring through the air on the trapeze. Repeatedly pulling herself upright so she was standing on the bar. Hanging by her hands at full length from the bar. Laying balanced on her stomach across the bar and performing stomach-anchored spins around it. Doing all this as the trapeze continually swooped and soared through a hundred and eighty degrees radius backwards and forwards at top speed.

When she finally let the trapeze slow to lessen the radius of movement and gradually come to rest, Sorenty clapped and cheered loudly as the crew men lowered the trapeze to the ground.

As Amy landed Sorenty hurried to meet her and, clasping both her hands, praised genuinely, 'That was absolutely superb, Amy. You've progressed so wonderfully well in such an amazingly short time. There's no doubt that you were born to be an Aeronaut Maiden, and so you shall be. You will perform your first balloon ascent with the trapeze this coming Saturday, and I truly believe you'll create something of a sensation!'

He smiled warmly at her. 'You've earned a reward for all your hard work, my dear. So tonight, let's you and I seek whatever in the way of diversion Wolverhampton may have to offer. I'm told that the Swan Inn at High Green serves passable food and wine, and the town theatre at rear of the Swan is lit by so many gaslights we shall believe ourselves to have been transported to London.'

Amy's low spirits had been lifted by her exercise on the trapeze which, now that she was mastering the techniques, charged her with an exhilarating mingling of intense excitement and the crowning exultation of accomplishment.

She giggled delightedly. 'Oh, yes, please, Vincent! I shall really enjoy a change from mutton stews and watery porter.'

Five hours later in the Swan Inn, after devouring servings of turtle soup, baked carp, pigeon pie, roast beef, potatoes, cauli flower, fried apple fritters and jelly, ginger beer and claret, Amy was contentedly replete.

'Well, Ma'am, I trust that was to your satisfaction?' Vincent Sorenty smiled.

'Oh my God, yes!' she assured him emphatically. 'And I've made a real pig of myself, haven't I? I'm not a bit ashamed of it either.'

'Nor should you be.' His white teeth gleamed fleetingly in a smile. 'When I was a small ragamuffin in London without kinfolk or friends I knew nothing but hunger and want. I had to beg and steal and scavenge dirty scraps to try to fill my belly. Now I'm a famous Aeronaut I can eat and drink whatever I fancy, and whenever I fancy . . .' His teeth gleamed white again, but now in a vicious snarl of menace, '. . . And the Devil will have whoever tries to drive me back into poverty. Because whoever it is who tries to do that, I'll save the Devil the work of taking them himself. I'll present them to him as a gift from me.'

For the first time since she had met Vincent Sorenty, Amy experienced the shock of a nervous wariness of him. Then in the next instant he was laughing and instantly transmogrified into the genial, kindly, charming man she had become familiar with. 'Pay no attention to my drunken nonsense, Amy. I have this pathetic fault of occasionally feeling sorry for myself without any justification. When, truth to tell, I was a spoilt brat who was treated like a little prince by all his kinfolk.'

He beckoned to the waiter, and when the man came to him,

asked, 'Is there anything in the way of a performance at the theatre tonight?'

'No, Master Sorenty, there won't be nothing doing there till Saturday. But yesterday morning a Gyppo woman named Madame Heptiza Lee, who's a fortune teller, parked her caravan on that bit o' open ground just along from the theatre. You might be interested in going to see her?'

'Why? I've seen more than enough Gypsy fortune tellers in caravans already in my life.'

'Well, begging your pardon, Master Sorenty, but I couldn't help but hear you mention the Devil. Have you read the broadsheets telling about those Devil's Monk murders on the other side o' Brummagem there? Well, this Gyppo wench, as well as being a fortune teller, is also saying that she was set on and nearly murdered by the Devil's Monk, and that for a good fee she'll tell the story of it. So you can have your fortunes told and meet somebody who knows the Devil's Monk, at one and the same time.'

Amy was thrilled. 'The Devil's Monk! That's who my husband arrested! Ohh, do let's go to see this woman, Vincent. I'd love to hear her story.'

'Then you shall, my dear Amy. Just give me time to drink a Brandy Toddy, and then I shall take you there and wait patiently while you talk with her. But on one condition, and that is that I must pay her fees.'

'Can you please tell her, Master Sorenty, that it's Willy Kelly, the waiter at the Swan, who's sent you to her? You see, she's promised that if I sends her enough customers she'll read me fortune wi' the cards, and I'm real desperate to know if me rotten luck is ever going to change.'

Sorenty laughed and nodded. 'Of course I'll tell her that you sent us, Willy. And your luck's already beginning to change because when you bring me my Brandy Toddy I'll settle the bill for our feast and give you a florin for yourself on top of it.'

Willy hurried away, and Amy could only smile warmly at her companion and think to herself what a nice man he truly was.

'Madame Heptiza Lee. Fortune Teller and Star Gazer to the Crowned Heads and Nobility of Europe and Asia.'

The crudely shaped lettering dominated the other garishly

coloured designs smothering the large caravan. To one side of the caravan stood a small square marquee, also covered with the same lettering and garish paintwork. A shaggy-coated horse tethered to the caravan's rear wheel was the only sign of life.

As the couple walked on to the plot of land, Vincent Sorenty called, 'Are you here, Madame Lee? Willy Kelly, the waiter at the Swan Inn, has sent us.'

The top half of the caravan door swung open and a mature woman leaned out. She was bedecked in a profusion of golden earrings, necklaces, bangles and brooches, a mass of turban-topped black hair framing her plump, dark-skinned features.

'Welcome to you, my Good Gentleman and Lady. I am Madame Heptiza Lee, Fortune Teller and Star Gazer to the Crowned Heads and Nobility of Europe and Asia. What is it you wish of me? Is it to foresee and tell your futures with the cards, or the crystals, or by consulting with the Wise Spirits who dwell among the stars of the heavens?'

As she and Sorenty had arranged while walking here, it was now Amy who took over the negotiations.

'No, Madame Lee, we haven't come to have our fortunes read. It's me alone who wants to talk with you, not this Gentleman, who is Master Victor Sorenty, the very famous Aeronaut. You see, it was my husband, Constable Thomas Potts, who arrested the Devil's Monk. So I'm very, very interested to hear all that you can tell me about that awful villain and how you managed to escape from him.'

Heptiza Lee's black eyes narrowed as if she were calculating odds, and after a pause she smiled and told Amy, 'O' course I'm willing to tell you the tale, my Pretty. But the fee is a heavy one, and who's going to pay it?'

'I am, Madame Lee, and if my friend Amy enjoys your tale, I'll most probably pay you something extra on your fee.'

'You don't need to pay me anything at all, Master Sorenty, if you'll do me one small favour.' She spoke rapidly for a brief while and, when she had fallen silent, Sorenty nodded. 'Be my guest, Madame Lee.'

'Come then, my Pretty.' Heptiza Lee beckoned Amy. 'Step into my van and be comfortable, while I tells you a tale that'll make your blood curdle.'

THIRTY-EIGHT

Redditch Town.
Monday, 31 August, 1829

J oseph Blackwell's manservant came at eight o'clock in the morning to summon Tom to the Red House.

'My Master says to tell you that he needs to speak with you straight away.'

'Please tell your Master that I'll be with him directly once I've dealt with an urgent problem here.'

As he watched the man walk away, Tom felt self-disgust at his own cowardly reluctance to face Joseph Blackwell and report on his continued investigative failings, and chastised himself: It's no use you trying to put it off any longer, you damned coward! You'll just have to tell Blackwell the truth: that you've made no bloody progress and don't know where else to go with it.

As Tom left the Lock-Up he saw Maisie Lock coming across the Green with the daily rations for himself, George Maffey and their prisoner.

In his current depressed mood, Tom had not the slightest desire to meet her, so quickened his pace and kept looking straight ahead.

'Tom Potts! Don't you try making out you aren't seen me coming! I knows you saw me, so just hold where you am!' Her strident shouts bounced off walls on all surrounds of the Green.

He halted and faced her, enquiring wearily, 'What do you want from me, Maisie Lock?'

She halted at a distance and tossed her head scornfully. 'I don't want nothing from you, Tom Potts. And the only reason I'm shouting you is that Amy wants to tell you summat and she asked me, her best friend, to pass the message on to you when I brought the grub to the Lock-Up.'

She went on towards the Lock-Up and Tom, heart pounding with shock, forgot all about Joseph Blackwell and ran after her, shouting, 'Where is she? What is it she wants you to tell me? Where is she?'

Maisie Lock's only answer was to jerk her mob-capped head backwards in the direction of the Fox and Goose.

Tom changed course and ran towards the inn. As he neared it an upstairs casement window opened and he heard Amy calling, 'Wait there for me, Tom. I'll come out to you.'

Body stiff with tension, he stood telling himself over and over again: Don't raise your hopes! Don't raise your hopes! Don't raise your hopes!

She came out from the front door, wearing a simple unadorned green gown. Her long blonde hair was hanging loose, framing her rosy cheeks and wide blue eyes. And for Tom the years rolled back and it was as if he was meeting her for the first time.

Oh, Amy, you look as you did when I first met you and thought you the most beautiful girl I'd ever seen.

But those words remained unspoken, for it was all he could do to stop himself from bursting into tears and begging her to love him again as she once did.

'Hello, Tom. Are you well?' she asked smilingly.

'Yes, I thank you,' he replied hoarsely. 'And you? Are you well?'

'Never better!' She radiated an air of bubbling excitement. 'I did my first trapeze performance from beneath the balloon last Saturday. It was the most wonderful feeling I've ever known, Tom. And when the crowd shouted and cheered me I felt like I was the Queen of England. And Sam Thomas has sent word to Vincent that it's this coming Saturday he wants to open his gasworks, so I'll be giving a performance there. You will come and watch me, won't you, Tom?'

Momentarily his genuine pleasure that she had achieved her goal, almost, but not quite, overlaid his bleak sense of absolute loss.

'Ohhh, that's wonderful, Amy. I'm really happy that it went so well for you and that you're having such a great success. Of course I'll be watching you on Saturday.' He coughed to try and ease the painful tightness in his throat, and asked tentatively, 'Is it true what Maisie said? That there is something you want to tell me?'

He waited in dread for her to answer. 'Yes, Tom, very soon I'm going abroad with Vincent. So after Saturday you might never see me again.'

But when she did speak, he couldn't fully absorb what he was hearing at first.

'I've met with a woman in Wolverhampton, Tom. She's a fortune teller. A Gypsy who calls herself Madame Heptiza Lee. Well, she told me that the Devil's Monk had tried to murder her, but that she'd fought him off.'

He held up his hands and said slowly, 'Don't be angry with me, Amy. But can you please tell me all this again – I'm fearing that I haven't understood correctly what it is you're saying. Did you say that her name is Heptiza Lee?'

'Bloody hell, Tom!' she complained pettishly. 'Are you going deaf in your old age?'

'No! Of course not! But what you said is of the utmost importance to me and I need to hear it again. And with the fullest and most minute details of exactly what she told you. This is truly a matter of life and death, Amy. So it's of the utmost importance that I have everything you tell me absolutely clear in my mind.'

She instantly felt guilty for reacting so pettishly. 'I'm sorry for snapping at you, Tom. And I didn't mean what I said about you getting deaf in your old age, because I don't see you as being old. Now listen carefully, and stop me straight away if you want me to say something twice.'

Within minutes Tom was repeating her information to Joseph Blackwell, and directly after that conversation he was on horseback, heading for Wolverhampton.

At this hour in the afternoon, with virtually the entire able-bodied population of Wolverhampton at their work or household tasks, the theatre's immediate surrounds and environs were deserted.

Tom tethered the horse to the front wheel of the caravan and called, 'Are you inside, Madame Lee?'

The top half of the caravan door swung outwards and Heptiza Lee stared speculatively at this exceptionally tall and lanky caller.

Tom lifted his tall hat and bowed. 'Good Afternoon, Ma'am. Am I addressing Madame Heptiza Lee?'

Her eyes glinted shrewdly. 'Indeed you are, and am I right in thinking that you're Constable Thomas Potts, husband to Amy Potts?'

'You are, Ma'am.'

She pushed the bottom half of the door open and came down the caravan steps to stand facing him. 'Your Missus told me that you'd very likely come calling once she'd told you about me. I hopes she also told you that I charge a very high fee for telling my story?'

'How much might that fee amount to, Ma'am?'

'How much is it worth to you to hear it? Maybe five sovereigns?'

'Can I respectfully remind you, Ma'am, that a man's life might well depend on what you tell me today. How can you or I set a valuation of price on a man's life?'

'Pfffff! I don't give a bugger about Jared Styler's life! He's naught but an animal!' she spat out contemptuously and held out her hand palm upwards. 'Cross this with five sovereigns worth o' gold or silver and I'll tell you my story. Give it to me now or bugger off, because I'm not going to waste any more time haggling the price wi' you.'

Tom smiled and said at a tangent, 'My wife told me that last Saturday Master Sorenty allowed you to set up your tent on the same ground as his balloon, and that you did good business because of that pitch. I believe that you'll be doing the same next Saturday – setting up your tent on the balloon field in Redditch Town.'

She shrugged her meaty shoulders dismissively. 'So? What's that to you?'

'Well, since Jared Styler is the talk of the entire Needle District, you'll make a veritable fortune displaying yourself there as one of his victims. The local people will be clamouring to hear your story and will pay a very large price for it.'

'So? What's that to you? I'll do whatever I choose, whenever I choose, wherever I choose, and there's naught you can say or do about it. Now, are you going to pay me or what? Because I've had more than a bellyful of you now!'

Her attitude was so unpleasantly arrogant that Tom's patience abruptly evaporated and he told her, 'You should know that if you practice your fortune telling in the Tardebigge Parish, I could, if I chose, lawfully arrest you for making, "False and Pretended Prophecies". The penalty for a first offence is a Ten-Pound fine and one year's imprisonment. For a second offence, Forfeiture of All Goods and Chattels and imprisonment for life.'

Heptiza Lee put her hands on her hips and roared with laughter before shaking her head and telling him, 'You knows as well as I do, Tom Potts, that that law was passed in the days of Old Queen Lizzie and that what I does in my tent is seen in this day and age as just a bit o' fun and nonsense – nothing more.' Her hand came forward. 'If you wants to hear my story, you'll cross my palm wi' five sovereigns this instant or you can bugger off! So what's it to be?'

Tom stepped to the horse and freed his yard-long, crown-topped staff from the saddle straps. He stepped back to confront Heptiza Lee and told her quietly, 'Heptiza Lee, when I'm carrying this staff I'm acting in the King's Name, and now I am arresting you, in the King's Name, for the offences of Battery and Wounding and Robbery, committed by you upon the person of Jared Styler. One of the wounds you inflicted upon Jared Styler being the biting off of the lobe of his right ear.

'I warn you that I'll use force if you make any attempt to resist arrest or to escape. You now have choice of being manacled and pulled at rope's length behind me, or riding pillion on the horse with me. What's it to be?'

She seemed totally dazed with shock and was shaking her head, muttering, 'You can't do this! You can't arrest me for biting that bad bastard! You can't do it!'

'Oh, but I can. And I have. So you'd best tell me right away. Do you walk or do you ride back to Redditch?'

He gripped her arm and pulled her to the side of the horse, where he opened a saddlebag and lifted out a set of manacles.

'Noo!' she wailed. 'No, please, no! Just let me go and I'll tell you! I'll tell you everything what happened! Everything! I swear on me mam's grave! I'll tell you everything!'

After a long pause, Tom told her quietly, 'Very well. I'll give you a chance. We'll sit inside your van and you must tell me everything and answer all my questions truthfully. Should

I be satisfied that you've done that, I shall release you and you'll be free to continue your fortune telling.'

An hour later, after questioning in great detail and listening to Heptiza Lee's answers and explanations concerning her relationship with Jared Styler, Tom fully accepted the truth of what he had heard.

'Very well, Madame Lee, you'll hear no more from me concerning Jared Styler. But until it is proven in a Court of Law that he is indeed the Devil's Monk, I would advise you to stop calling him by that title.' He smiled wryly. 'As I shall stop doing so myself, now I've met with you and heard your story.'

'Will it be all right for me to come to Redditch with the balloonists?' she asked.

'Oh, yes.' Again, he couldn't help but smile wryly. 'And the way my life is going at this time, I may well be seeking to have my own future prospects foretold.'

In the lamp-lit study of the Red House, Joseph Blackwell listened in silence while Tom described the meeting with Heptiza Lee, ending with the admission, 'So, Sir, yet another of my suppositions have been proven to be completely without substance. It's my own stupidity to blame, for assuming without an atom of proof that Heptiza Lee must be the Haystack Woman.' Tom sighed heavily and shook his head. 'Truth to tell, at this moment I've not got any idea at all as to how I can now further the investigations into the Methuselah Leeson and Haystack Woman murders. I fear that I've arrested an innocent man, and feel that I should now release him.'

Blackwell smiled bleakly. 'You may well fear and feel, Thomas Potts. But the fact remains that you have not yet proven Styler to be innocent of either of these two murders, and until you have done that he must remain in custody.

'Imagine the outcry should we release him and within a space of time another murder is committed in the Needle District. Who would be blamed for it, d'you think?'

Tom could only accept. 'Jared Styler for the murder, and ourselves for letting him go free to commit it.'

'Exactly!' Blackwell slapped his hand down sharply upon the desk. 'Now go and attend to your normal duties, Constable Potts,

and for a brief period push this matter of the Devil's Monk to
the back of your mind. I'm confident that in God's good time
you will find another avenue of this investigation open up for
you to journey down.'

He chuckled dryly. 'And above all else, give no thought to any
nonsense such as Habeas Corpus. Bear this in mind that Jared
Styler is enjoying the absolute surety of warm, dry shelter and
free bed and board. There are countless thousands of the homeless
and hungry in this country who would greatly envy him for having
such material blessings. I bid you Good Night, Constable Potts.'

In the Lock-Up, George Maffey greeted Tom with a smart salute.

'All present and correct, Sir. The prisoner has been quiet and
orderly. Ritchie Bint called in to say he'd report for duty early
Saturday morning. Master William Maries from the Red Lane
come in to lay a complaint against his neighbour, the Widow
Reilly, for chucking the contents of her chamber pot on to his
head when he was passing underneath her bedroom window. The
Widow Reilly come in to make a complaint against Master
William Maries for abusing her with foul language and threatening to kill her. Doctor Laylor sent a message to remind you
it's the Apollo Club meeting at the Fox and Goose tonight; and
that your attendance would be much appreciated. Your Missus
called in on her way back to the Black Country to say tarrah to
you, and that she was looking forwards to seeing you again next
Saturday after her's done her performance. And I've got a nice
bit o' beefsteak and some potatoes for our supper, which I can
start cooking right away if you want me to, Sir.'

'I do indeed, Corporal, because I'm bloody starving,' Tom
accepted gratefully. 'And while you're doing that I'll have a word
with Styler.'

The cell stank of unwashed flesh and the reeking bucket in its
corner when Tom entered, and ordered sharply, 'Pay attention to
me, Styler.'

The prisoner stood up from the bed slab unshaven and, with
hair left unoiled and uncombed for more than two weeks, Jared
Styler's face and throat were thickly stubbled with grey whiskers.
His shaggy hair now displayed grey streaks and roots.

Tom felt no pity as he regarded the other man's physical

deterioration; the battered, bloodied features of Carrie Perks were still too vivid in his mind.

'I've found Heptiza Lee and have spoken with her this very day, Styler. She confirmed that after suffering a week of brutal ill-treatment at your hands she bit off part of your ear and ran away.'

Styler vented a shout of exultant relief. 'That's it then! I told you I'd never murdered nobody, didn't I? You've got to let me go now, haven't you?' He scowled menacingly and snarled, 'I'll be looking for payment in gold for the wrong you've done me, Potts!'

Slowly and deliberately, Tom shook his head. 'No, Styler. I'm not letting you go. So far I've only proven that you didn't murder Carrie Perks or Heptiza Lee, and given you the full benefit of doubt about the babies. You're still the main suspect for the murders of Methuselah Leeson and the Haystack Woman and, unless I prove otherwise, you'll stay in here.'

He turned and went out, locking the cell and bolting the hatch cover in place while Jared Styler cursed and raved and howled like a madman.

THIRTY-NINE

Redditch Town.
Saturday, 5 September, 1829

When the clock chimed the morning hour of eight, it signalled the end of a discussion which had lasted for nearly two hours in the Select Parlour of the Fox and Goose.

Joseph Blackwell raised his hand and announced, 'Very well, Gentlemen, I'm satisfied that our business here is done. I move that we now partake of breakfast. Is the motion agreed?'

Samuel Thomas, Vincent Sorenty, Tom Potts and William Shayler chorused agreement and Blackwell rang his hand bell to summon Tommy Fowkes.

'Bring in five of your excellent breakfasts, Master Fowkes,

with whatever these Gentlemen care to drink, and a bottle of
your best claret for myself.'

'And put everything down on my tab, Tommy,' Samuel Thomas
ordered. He instantly quelled any possible dissent by insisting
loudly, 'No! I'll not stand for anybody paying a penny. This will
be the best day o' my bloody life today, and you chaps am the
ones who'll be making it all run smooth for me, so just get on
and fill your bellies with whatever you fancies. This day 'ull
be long remembered as the greatest day in the history of the
whole bloody Needle District, and it'll be stamped forever with
the name o' Samuel Thomas, Needle Master!'

At the bottom of the steep Fish Hill, flat fields spread northwards
from the complex of buildings which constituted the Needle Mills
of Samuel Thomas. Close to the complex on its north-eastern
side stood the new gasworks. An impressive, high-storied Retort
House with an exceptionally tall, smoke-belching chimney stack
and three adjoining Gas Holders: huge inverted steel bells
contained within frameworks which allowed them to rise and fall
as gas was pumped in or drawn out.

On the north side of the mills was a spacious enclosure in
which a large grandstand had been erected, directly overlooking
the balloon launch site.

High lath-and-canvas screens were positioned to shield the
launch site from the gaze of those unprivileged individuals who
had paid their sixpences for entry to the main field.

Now, at the launch site the preparations were being made for
the first of the two separate ascents the balloon would be making.

Mario Fassia was telling Amy, 'The first one will only be up
to 150 feet. Depending on what wind we get, the winch and the
four tether lines will be tied to the netting at different places
around the widest curve of the balloon. So no matter what direction the breeze might shift to, the balloon stays in the same
position and the lines won't impede your swing path. Once the
trapeze is lowered you go down to it by rope ladder, which is
then pulled up. You make your swings and do your tricks. When
you're done, Vincent will lower the rope ladder to you and you'll
climb back up into the gondola. Vince will deflate through the
top valve and down you'll come.'

'It'll cost a deal of money to inflate again, won't it?' Amy remarked.

'Not a penny.' The young man grinned. 'Sam Thomas is supplying all the gas for free, and the use o' this preparation ground and whatever extra casual labour we needs to take on. So me and Vince will not have to pay anything out of our fee for the show for any of that. Plus there'll be men patrolling all the hedges and guarding the gates surrounding this field here where you'll be performing, and everybody who comes in is going to be charged sixpence. That includes all the stall-holders and traders, right down to even the bloody beggars. And me and Vince are going to get a half of all those takings as well. If me and Vince could get a show on these terms every week, we'd soon have as much gold as the bloody Lord Mayor o' London.'

At ten o'clock the group from the Fox and Goose came to the mills and walked down the broad sunlit sweep of the central concourse, both sides of which were lined with drink and refreshment stalls already supplying the needs of the multi-variegated traders, pedlars, hawkers, street entertainers, travelling musicians and licensed beggars who were awaiting the crowds.

Ritchie Bint, dressed in Pointers Rig, and George Maffey in red tunic and black shako, both wielding constables' crowned staffs, were standing guard and taking the entrance fees from the early-comers at the concourse gate. Near the gate, thirty of Samuel Thomas's mill hands, armed with lead-weighted cudgels and wearing white sashes across their chests, were standing in a long line.

'Well now, Tom Potts, Will Shayler, what do you think of my lads? My Lord Aston has sworn them all in as Special Constables for this day.' Samuel Thomas grinned. 'There's none o' them who'll turn tail and run from a scrap, I can assure you. I've handpicked the roughest buggers from the whole o' my works.'

Tom and his friend briefly eyed the lines of stocky, tough-looking men, noting the brawl scars many of them displayed.

'They'll do for me, Master Thomas.' William Shayler nodded.

Tom saluted Samuel Thomas. 'My friend Constable Shayler and myself are of the same mind, Master Thomas. We think they are most satisfactory for our purpose.'

'We shall leave you to it then,' Joseph Blackwell intervened. 'The Yeomanry band and gun team will be arriving shortly. They, of course, will not be charged entrance, nor will any of the carriage folk who might chance to come in this way.'

He, Vincent Sorenty and Samuel Thomas walked back towards the grandstand.

'All right, lads, gather round.' William Shayler called the sash-wearers to him while Tom went to the entrance gate.

'Ritchie, you'll be patrolling the ground like myself and Will Shayler. Corporal Maffey, you'll command the gate guard. I'll give you six men. Did you have any trouble with Styler?'

'No, Sir, not a bit. He's becoming a real greedy pig for his porter and laudanum shandy. He'll still be bloody snoring when we gets back. You'll be wanting to take the money we've collected so far and put it somewhere safe, Sir? It amounts to—'

'Be silent! I don't wish to know that!' Tom snapped curtly. Then laughed, shook his head and stated very firmly, 'And furthermore, I most definitely do not wish to take the money with me, Corporal Maffey, because I don't know of a safer billet for whatever amount is paid here today than to leave it in your keeping.'

Maffey glowed with gratified pride. His chest swelled visibly. He snapped to rigid attention and saluted, 'At your orders, Sir.'

FORTY

I t was late afternoon and the concourse was a seething, uproarious mass of men, women, children of all ages, shapes and sizes; and by this hour the majority were in conditions of greatly varying degrees of coarse-mannered sobriety.

In the now open to view but still fenced enclosure, the resplendently scarlet-and-golden uniformed band of the Worcestershire Yeomanry Cavalry were playing to entertain the occupants of the grandstand. These Gentlefolk also comprised men, women and children of all ages, shapes and sizes, the majority of them also displaying varying degrees of sobriety, but in a more refined manner.

In a small tent near to the now grounded, half-inflated balloon,

Amy was still elated by the success of her trapeze performance earlier that afternoon, which had been rewarded by long-sustained tumultuous applause.

Vincent Sorenty, elegantly clad in the very latest High London Fashion, came into the tent and scolded: 'Come now, Amy, no more daydreaming! You should already be changed. There's a slight breeze risen and a bit of shifting in the highest cloud strata. We need to launch as quickly as we can and get the show done in case the wind freshens too much.'

Carrying a brass speaking-trumpet, Mario Fassia came to tell them, 'The gondola's ready and the lads and sheep are loaded; we're waiting to inflate. So come the moment you've changed, Amy.'

Both men hurried away, leaving Amy to change into a garishly ornate costume styled on the nursery rhyme shepherdess Bo Peep.

Her reappearance was greeted with loud applause, which she acknowledged by waving her shepherd's crook. The Yeomanry gun team fired a charge of gunpowder to alert the crowded concourse that another balloon launch was imminent.

In the middle of the concourse, Tom Potts, standing talking to Josiah Danks, heard the loud bang, stiffened and exclaimed, 'Ohh, no! She's going up again!'

Danks chuckled. 'Bloody hell, Tom. Youm as big a scaredy-cat as my Missus is. Her wouldn't come out of the house today or even look up through a bloody window, just for fear she might happen to catch sight of our Amy flying over in the balloon. Amy knows exactly what she's doing, and her's loving doing it. You should be proud to have a Missus as brave and able as her is. And bear in mind that it's a sight more dangerous going to sea than it is flying about in a balloon on a nice calm day like this is. I knows that, because I've climbed a lot o' rigging on a lot o' ships when gales have been blowing the rain into your face like double charges o' small shot and the ship's been jumping about like a mad flea.'

A sudden commotion erupted at a drink stall and Tom heard his name being shouted. 'I have to go, Josiah.'

They shook hands and parted. Tom ran to the stall to find two of Samuel Thomas's men holding a man face down on the ground.

'He's a pickpocket, Constable Potts,' one of the men informed him.

'It was my watch he pinched, Constable,' a respectably dressed, elderly man explained. 'And these chaps spotted him doing it, and they've give it back to me.'

'And he had these others on him.' One of the captors showed Tom two watches.

'Very well done, Lads!' Tom praised. 'Please take him down to the gate and hand him over to Corporal Maffey. He knows what to do with the bugger.'

At the launch site, the previous gondola had been exchanged for a larger one and was now carrying four sheep and two of the ground crew together with Vincent Sorenty and Amy.

The gunpowder charge was exploded, the winch brake released and the balloon rose, accompanied by a roar of cheering from the spectators and the Yeomanry band playing the National Anthem.

In the gondola Vincent Sorenty was telling Amy, 'If you don't feel fully confident then all you need to do is the one touch.'

Amy's eyes were gleaming, her cheeks flushed, her heart thudding. She was totally in the grip of the adrenaline coursing through her body. 'I'm confident, Vince!' she declared forcefully. 'I'm very confident!'

Standing before the grandstand, Mario Fassia was using the brass speaking-trumpet to inform his audience of Gentlefolk: 'My Lords, Ladies and Gentlemen. What you are about to witness has never before been performed anywhere in the world. I pray you to keep your gaze fixed upon the gondola so that you do not miss a single second of this world-first performance.'

On this second ascent the balloon rose much higher than the first, and onlookers were speculating aloud: 'Must be up a hundred yards or more?' 'No, got to be nearer two hundred!' 'How far is it up, d'you reckon, Charlie?' 'Looks like a good half a mile to me!'

Tom Potts could only stand with his fists clenched, silently entreating over and over again, 'Dear God, I beg you, keep her safe! Dear God, I beg you, keep her safe!'

Suddenly a white object plummeted from the side of the gondola and bounced to a halt to swing wildly on the end of a rope. A concerted outcry of shock erupted from the watchers. In rapid succession three more white objects toppled from different sides of the gondola to bounce and swing on ropes, and each time the outcries and roars of the crowd intensified in noise and wild excitement.

After a few brief seconds the sharper-eyed onlookers realized: 'Theym sheep!'

'Theym all bloody sheep!'

Mario Fassia was screaming through his trumpet, 'Oh my God! Bo Peep's sheep are running away! Bo Peep, where are you? Your sheep are running away! Bo Peep's sheep are running away! Bo Peep! Bo Peep! Bo Peep!'

The Gentlefolk in the grandstand took up the shout. 'Bo Peep! Bo Peep! Bo Peep!'

And like a wildfire the shout flashed through the concourse and thousands of voices were bawling, shrieking, screaming, '*Bo Peep! Bo Peep! Bo Peep!*'

In the gondola, Amy was having a harness fitted around her waist and shoulders, which was then secured to the end of a rope being held by the two crewmen.

'Now try to keep all your moves as smooth as you can. Remember, it's got to look graceful,' Vincent Sorenty was telling her repeatedly.

'Graceful, graceful, graceful.' Amy muttered the word to herself as Vincent Sorenty opened the large, wide rectangular trapdoor in the middle of the gondola floor then took his place on the rope with the crewmen.

Amy sat down on the edge of the aperture, her legs dangling in the air. She gripped her shepherds crook tightly to her chest and said, 'At the count of three, Vincent!'

'All right.' He nodded. 'Take your grip, lads. Good luck, Amy. One! Two! *Three!*'

She propelled herself into the void; fell only a yard and was jerked to a stop then slowly and evenly lowered down, swinging gently from side to side, waving her multi-tasselled crook at the roaring mass of upturned faces below.

'Here she comes, My Lords, Ladies and Gentlemen! Here comes Bo Peep to drive the flock back where they belong. Here comes Bo Peep!'

Again the Gentlefolk took up the cry. 'Bo Peep! Bo Peep! Bo Peep!'

Again the concourse followed suit. '*Bo Peep! Bo Peep! Bo Peep!*'

Amy's descent halted when she was at the level of the noisily terrified, wildly wriggling sheep. She drew a series of deep breaths and began her performance.

Tom was physically and mentally transfixed as he watched Amy swooping and circling, going from sheep to sheep, using the crook to pull and push them in different directions. Drawing them after her. Clasping them close to her. Spinning them with her. Swooping and circling beneath them as, one by one, they were drawn upwards to be taken back into the gondola.

Mario Fassia screamed, 'There now, another runaway sheep is sent back to the flock. Bo Peep is a truly wonderful shepherdess, is she not?'

The answer roared back from a thousand throats. 'Yes, she is!'

The final sheep began its rise upwards, frantically wriggling and struggling to be free. Amy began swooping round in increasingly wide circles, waving the tasselled crook and glorying in the tumultuous applause from the crowd.

Then suddenly the final sheep was toppling downwards and a shouting, screaming uproar erupted as those beneath its fall path scrambled and fought to get clear. It crashed on to the ground, bounced once only and lay motionless.

Mario Fassia reacted instantly, running into the crowd shouting through his speaking-trumpet, 'That sheep is Bo Peep's present to the Poorhouse, to give the paupers a fine, fresh meat supper!'

A storm of appreciative cheering erupted and people resentfully made way for Tom to push through towards the dead sheep.

Vincent Sorenty released gas through the top valve and the balloon began to slowly descend. The Yeomanry band struck up the tune 'Rule Britannia'. Interest in the dead sheep almost instantly evaporated and the crowd began to crush as near as they could to the launch site.

Tom was standing staring down at the bloodied, bulge-eyed sheep when another man pushed through the crowd to join him.

'Well, this is a stroke o' luck for my lodgers, aren't it, Master Potts?' Edwin Lewis grinned happily. 'And the other stroke o' luck is that I've got the horse and cart wi' me. I'm too long in the tooth now to tote a heavy pack o' rations like this 'un all the way to Webheath.'

'Indeed it is a stroke of luck, Master Lewis,' Tom replied, not taking his gaze away from the sheep. Then, kneeling down, he pressed his hands on different parts of the animal, kneading the flesh with his fingers.

When he stood upright, he was so deep in thought that he appeared to be unaware of anything around him.

The Poorhouse Master regarded Tom curiously for some moments, then queried, 'Am you all right, Master Potts? Only you don't seem altogether like yourself today.'

There was no reaction from Tom, and Lewis waited several more seconds before touching Tom's arm and asking in a louder voice, 'Am you hearing me, Master Potts?'

Tom blinked hard, shook his head, turned to face his questioner and asked, 'Will you be butchering this beast today, Master Lewis?'

'Oh, yes. My lodgers aren't tasted a bit o' fresh mutton for a month or more, so this 'ull be a nice treat for their suppers.'

Tom coughed to ease the tightness which was gripping his throat, and requested hesitantly, 'Will you please allow myself and Doctor Laylor to butcher it for you, Master Lewis? We'll do it in his dispensary this very hour, and I can guarantee it will be done very neatly, with not a morsel of edible flesh being lost to you. I do assure you that I have a very good reason for making this request, which at a later date I will fully explain to you.'

Lewis emitted a shout of laughter and answered, 'You don't have to explain, Master Potts – it'll save me a bloody, messy job. So you and Doctor Laylor am very welcome to do the butchering. But there's one condition on me letting you do it! You both must come back wi' me to the Poorhouse to have some of it for supper wi' me and the Missus, and our lodgers.'

'I'm sure we'll both be very happy to do so, Master Lewis, and many thanks for your kind invitation,' Tom instantly agreed. He called to a nearby Special Constable, 'Please go to the grandstand and tell Doctor Laylor that I need him to come here to me straight away.'

FORTY-ONE

'What's this, Constable Potts?' Joseph Blackwell exclaimed incredulously. 'Are you drunk? Is that your excuse for having me summoned out from church in the middle of My Lord Aston's sermon? Certainly My Lord Aston will be extremely displeased with you for this blatantly insolent discourtesy.'

Tom shook his head. 'Indeed, I'm not drunk, Sir. I'm come here to tell you that yesterday I discovered the true cause of the Haystack Woman's death.'

'But we already know that she was battered to death!' Blackwell now stared at Tom in utter disbelief. 'I do declare, Master Potts, if it's not the drink that's addled your mind then you're afflicted by a brainstorm!'

'In that case, Sir, Doctor Laylor is also suffering from that affliction, because he is in complete agreement with what I'm trying to tell you.' Tom's manner and tone of voice abruptly hardened. 'I don't give a damn for Lord Aston's displeasure! But I do expect you to have the courtesy to hear me out. Will you do so, Sir? Without further insult or interruption?'

After a long pause, Joseph Blackwell bowed and said quietly, 'Firstly, allow me to apologise for my own churlish rudeness, for which I do most sincerely beg your pardon, Thomas Potts. Secondly, I will listen without interruption to all you have to tell me. So please, will you be good enough to do so without further delay.'

Tom bowed to acknowledge the apology, then began, 'It was the sheep that fell from the balloon yesterday that enabled me to discover the true cause of the woman's death.' He went on to describe in detail how he and Hugh Laylor had carried out a post-mortem on the animal and discovered that many of its skeletal,

muscular and internal organs injuries coincided so closely indeed
to those of the Haystack Woman, that it was beyond all doubt.
'The woman's injuries can only have resulted by her falling from
a considerably greater height than even that sheep did.'

'Will you please walk with me, Thomas Potts, while I give
consideration to what you've told me,' Blackwell requested, and
the pair went side by side out from the churchyard and along the
neighbouring lane exchanging no words, both wrapped in their
own thoughts.

The lane eventually took them downwards to the canal, and
as they slowly strolled along the towpath, Joseph Blackwell
remarked reflectively, 'And now you believe that the Haystack
Woman must have fallen from a balloon, do you not?'

'I do, Sir,' Tom confirmed. 'We've already established that she
had only been dead for a matter of hours when she was discovered by Corporal Maffey. The type and extent and gravity of her
injuries can only have resulted from a very great height of fall.
To my knowledge there is no man-made edifice or high place of
such a great height that lies close enough to Redditch Town to
have enabled her to be transported and discovered here with her
body still in the process of Rigor Mortis.'

'So tell me, Thomas Potts, how do you propose to identify
this particular balloon that you believe she fell from? How do
you persuade me to pressure the Vestry into allotting sufficient
money to finance any continuance of investigations?'

The question triggered immediate waves of successive relief
and elation pulsing through Tom's mind. He knew from experience that the simple asking of it signalled that Joseph Blackwell
had already decided to pressure the Vestrymen into financing that
continuation. 'Well, Sir, because of my late Father's, and my
own, lifelong interest in the science of Aerostation, I do believe
I know someone who can advise me on how I might identify
that particular balloon.'

'That will be this fellow, Sorenty, of course,' Blackwell accepted.

Tom hesitated momentarily, then shook his head. 'No, Sir, I
think not.'

Blackwell frowned interrogatively.

Tom again hesitated before stating bluntly, 'Because I'm
jealous and resentful of the close relationship he has formed

with my wife, at present that would influence my judgement of whatever he told me. I'm hoping to obtain sufficient information from the Gentleman I am proposing to talk with so as not to be unduly influenced by my personal feelings should I find cause to ask Master Sorenty any questions concerning the Haystack Woman. So, I'm asking for your permission, and the necessary help with funds and transport, to enable me to travel to London.'

'Humph! That will deprive me of the services of my best mare and cost the Parish Chest a small fortune,' Blackwell grumbled and sighed resignedly. 'Ah, well, I can at least draw comfort from the fact that My Lord Aston and myself shall take full credit for the successful conclusion of this new direction of investigation.'

'Of course, Sir,' Tom agreed. Then ventured, 'When might it be possible for me to go to London to make a search to find this Gentleman I spoke of?'

'Come and see me tomorrow at noon, Thomas Potts. Money and my mare will be waiting for you.'

When Tom returned to the Lock-Up, it was Amy who was waiting for him. He rang the bells for entry. The front door opened and she was facing him, angrily demanding, 'Where've you been? I've been in here for hours waiting for you! Why didn't you come and talk to me after I finished me performance, like you promised you would?'

Tom knew well that he had made no such promise, but such was the hold that this young woman still had on him, he instantly lied. 'Oh Amy, I wanted to with my heart, but . . .' He gestured to the row of barred cell doors. 'I've got a pickpocket, two pedlars who were selling stolen goods and three brawlers in these. I was so busy with them that by the time I came to look for you, you were already abed. I feared you'd be very angry with me if I'd had you woken up to speak with me.'

'Oh, no, Tom.' She shook her head and her blue eyes moistened. 'I'd not have been angry.'

Vincent Sorenty brought his gig to a halt outside, and shouted, 'Amy, we have to go right now. If we're late for the meeting with His Nibs there'll be hell to pay.'

'I have to go, Tom. We've got to meet a noble lord in

Brummagem. I'll send word to the Fox where we'll be performing next, and you must come and see me there. Promise you will!'

'I promise.' Sadness overwhelmed Tom, but he managed to force a smile. She pulled his head down and kissed him on the lips. Then, dabbing her eyes, she ran to the waiting gig.

With tears stinging his own eyes, Tom watched the gig until it had gone from sight.

FORTY-TWO

Highgate, London.
Wednesday, 16 September, 1829

Tom reined in by spiked railings enclosing a villa fronted by a large, well-kept garden where a rubicund-featured, stocky man dressed in the blue apron, breeches and gaiters and straw hat of a gardener stood smoking a cheroot.

He stared hard at Tom, and then called, 'Excuse me, Sir! I beg you to oblige me by being so kind as to dismount.'

'Very well, Sir,' Tom agreed. Grimacing from the pain of sore buttocks and inner thighs, aching muscles and joints, he clumsily levered himself off the horse.

Famed Aeronaut Charles Green chuckled and slapped his thigh. 'I thought so when I glimpsed your face, and now I can see your length I know it's so. What a very pleasant surprise to encounter the son of an old and very dear friend again after all these years. I sincerely hope this encounter was not merely by chance, Tom Potts?'

'Indeed no, Master Green!' Tom was suffused with pleasure at this recognition. 'I set out more than a week since to come and find you. I'm in sore need of your help.'

'And you shall have it and welcome, Tom Potts, because I owe my very life to my dear friend, your father, for the caring and curing of me all those years ago – at great sacrifice to himself, I might add.' He pointed to the portmanteau bag tied behind Tom's saddle. 'I trust that contains your spare clothing and necessaries.'

'It does,' Tom confirmed.

'Excellent!' Green smiled, and roared at the top of his voice, 'Lucy! Betsy! Martha! We have an honoured guest! Prepare his bedroom and some refreshments immediately, and don't forget to lay an extra place for dinner.'

FORTY-THREE

Redditch Town.
Thursday, 24 September, 1829

I t was late at night when Tom reined in and dismounted in the dark shadows of the Red House stable yard. He stroked the travel-jaded mare's neck and apologised sincerely aloud: 'I'm truly sorry for having ridden you so clumsily these last weeks, but I beg you to draw some comfort from the fact that God is punishing me for doing so by lacerating my arse and joints with flames of fire.'

'And that's exactly what My Lord Aston is lusting to do to you as well. Before throttling you with his own hands.' Joseph Blackwell emerged from the shadows. 'I was leaving the privy, Thomas Potts, and heard you entering the yard. Have you called at the Lock-Up?'

'No, I've come directly here,' Tom answered.

Blackwell turned his head and shouted, 'Jenkins! Come and tend to the mare.'

When the stableman appeared, Blackwell beckoned Tom. 'Come into the house. Jenkins will deliver your baggage to the Lock-Up.'

In the study, Blackwell ushered Tom to a chair and placed a large, full glass of brandy on the small table to the side of it. He handed Tom a filled pipe of tobacco and a box of Lucifer Friction Lights and said, 'I truly want you to enjoy this refreshment before I give you the final gift of the evening.'

Tom blinked in bewilderment at this sequence of behaviour.

'Do as I say, Tom Potts! Smoke, drink and enjoy until we've

finished the bottle,' Blackwell insisted. 'And no talking until I say so.'

Tom willingly obeyed, greatly savouring the fragrant Egyptian tobacco, finest French brandy and the balm of mental and physical inertia.

They sat in companionable silence, heads wreathed in the smoke from their pipes, sipping their frequently replenished drink.

When the bottle was finally empty, Blackwell queried with a flicker of a smile, 'Tell me now, Thomas Potts – was your journey worthwhile?'

'Very much so, Sir.' Tom smiled back. 'Charles Green is a veritable fount of knowledge concerning balloonists and their flights – not only in this country but abroad also. He has given much information which I'm convinced will greatly aid me.'

Blackwell's manner became grave. 'I'm glad to hear that, because I fear when you read this you may feel somewhat demoralized.'

He rose and went to the desk, took a broadsheet from a drawer and held it in front of Tom's eyes.

The front page bore a headline in large letters: 'TOM FOOL! THE CONSTABLE OF TARDEBIGGE PARISH!'

'I'll save you the discomfort of reading the rest of this bilge.' Blackwell almost snarled the words. 'What has happened is that on the second day following your departure, Nellie Leeson announced that she was dying. But like Charles the Second, she took a long time in doing so, and during that period she repeatedly confessed to the murder of her husband. Doing this in the presence of My Lord Aston, Reverend Clayton, Doctor Laylor – all our illustrious Vestrymen and any other odds and sods who managed to squeeze into the room.

'She said that she had murdered him because, in her own words, "The dirty old bastard was robbing all me money and giving it to them filthy whores he was fucking in the Abbey Meadows!"'

Blackwell smiled acidly. 'A justifiable enough reason for killing him, I suppose . . . Then this broadsheet appeared in the town a few days since, and apparently copies are now circulating throughout the entire Needle District and beyond. The day after its appearance, My Lord Aston insisted on releasing Jared Styler from custody and has ordered him to be given money from the parish chest as recompense for wrongful arrest and detention on

the five counts of murder. However, My Lord has retained Corporal
Maffey in the post of Turnkey.' Another acidic smile twitched his
lips. 'Perhaps to keep your good self securely in custody.'

'May I, please?' Tom held his hand out and Blackwell passed
over the single sheet.

Tom duly noted that it had been printed by Solomons Bros.,
Birmingham. Then quickly read the jeering diatribes directed
against himself as being a proven village idiot who only ever
arrested innocent men. He smiled ruefully. 'Being called these
names don't hurt me. But I do hope that I'm not greeted with
volleys of sticks and stones when I next appear in public view.'

'And I can only hope that you will pardon me for having so
stupidly doubted you, Thomas Potts, when you asserted Styler's
innocence of any murders.' Blackwell held out his hand. 'Will
you shake hands with me as token of that forgiveness?'

Tom rose to his feet, grasped the outstretched hand firmly and
shook it long before asking, 'Can I take it, Sir, even though I
can't guarantee any success? You'll continue to assist me with
funds and transport, for the furtherance of my investigation into
the death of the Haystack Woman?'

For the first time ever, Tom saw tears glistening in Blackwell's
eyes as he answered gruffly, 'You most certainly can rely on that
continuance, Thomas Potts. As long as I have a breath in my body!'

'Many thanks to you, Sir.' Tom's own voice began choking
up and he quickly wished the other man, 'Good Night, Sir,' and
departed before his own tears welled.

FORTY-FOUR

Redditch Town.
Friday, 25 September, 1829

I t was six o'clock in the morning, a full hour before sunrise
when Hector Smout rolled out of his bed, roused by the repeated
volleys of loud knocking. Scratching hard at the grubby skin
covered by his grubby nightshirt and long johns, he shuffled to

open the cottage door, shouting angrily, 'Stop that bloody hammering 'ull you! Aren't it bad enough you've ruined me rest? Am you trying to smash me door down as well?'

'Indeed not, Master Smout, but I've urgent need to speak with you,' a voice answered.

'Bloody hell! Is it you, Master Potts?' Smout quickened his pace and unbarred the door, declaring, 'Well, this is a surprise, Master Potts! Folks said you'd gone to London. And when that new broadsheet come around a few days since, everybody said that was the reason you'd run off to London and that you'd never be showing your face in these parts again for the shame of it.'

Smiling wryly, Tom answered, 'Believe me, Master Smout, I am not feeling any shame whatsoever that Jared Styler has been released. However, I do pity whichever unfortunate woman becomes his next concubine. But now, I wish to ask you a question.'

'You ask away, Master Potts.'

'Clothes-lines, Master Smout. The ropes people hang their wet washing on. Did Nellie Leeson have any longish ones?'

'What sort of a bloody question is that?' Smout seemed almost bemused by the query. 'O' course her did! Everybody's got bloody clothes-lines o' some sort or other.'

'Might you know where her clothes-lines are now?'

'Ahrrr, I does. Theym coiled up in me shed wi' a lot of other bits and pieces of ropes and suchlike. When the Poor-Law bloke come clearing out her furnishings to sell to the dealers, he said I could have the lines and oddments for helping him do the work.'

'D'you think I might take a quick look at them, Master Smout?'

The gravedigger's gnarled features displayed utter bewilderment as he mumbled, 'O' course you can, Master Potts. But why would anybody in their right mind come all the way down here, just to look at some pieces of old rope?'

Tom chuckled and told him, 'Ah, well, Master Smith. You know the old saying, "It takes all sorts to make a world". I might find some ropes and oddments in your shed that I would like to buy from you.'

'Well, you knows the old saying, Master Potts, it takes all sorts o' ropes to make a clothes-line, don't it!' Hector Smout cackled with laughter. 'And if you finds any pieces in my shed that you likes, then youm more than welcome to take 'um wi' you for nothing.'

'Many thanks, Master Smout, and I'll only be borrowing them temporarily.'

'No thanks needed, nor wanted, Master Potts. Youm one o' the good blokes in this wicked world, and can keep 'um for good if you wants to.'

The final 'Warning Bells' were ringing and men, women and children were hurrying to their workplaces. Tom's return to the Lock-Up was made to the accompaniment of jeering insults, mocking gibes, raucous laughter and the universal chanting of 'Tom Fool! Tom Fool! Tom Fool!'

But to his own self-wonderment, he felt completely unscathed by the verbal tirade. So much so that he made his next call at the Fox and Goose, knowing full well what his reception there would be.

'My God, Maisie! Just look at what the bloody cat's dragged in!' Lily Fowkes shrieked in shock.

'What's you doing coming here, Tom Potts?' Maisie Lock challenged angrily. 'Am you come back here to bring more shame on poor Amy's head? Folks am sneering at her and saying she must be the stupidest cow in England to have ever wed a bloody great Tom Fool like you!'

'I would just like to know if Amy is well and her present whereabouts,' Tom explained quietly.

'Fuck off, Tom Fool!' Maisie hissed, and both girls turned their backs to him.

Tom could only turn also, and walk out of the inn. But as he exited, the window casement above the door opened slightly and Gertie Fowkes's voice sounded softly, 'Amy went with the balloonists to Warwick nigh on a week since.'

An hour later, outside the Lock-Up, Tom did the final check of his saddlebags contents and mounted the mare.

'With all respect, Sir, but you really ought to let me come wi' you. I could scout around and find out what strength they're in,' George Maffey urged.

'Many thanks, Corporal, but your post is here. Holding the fort until I return.' Tom touched the brim of his tall hat in salute.

George Maffey snapped to attention. 'I wish you Good Luck and God speed, Sir!'

He remained at rigid salute until Tom had disappeared from his view.

FORTY-FIVE

Warwick.
Friday, 25 September, 1829

Adjoining the canal basin in the Saltisford suburb of Warwick was the most elegant gasworks in the whole of Europe. Its front resembled a white-stuccoed ducal mansion, double-storied, with rows of windows and a central portal and flanked either side with tall octagonal towers, enshrouding the massive gasholders.

The 'Vincent Sorenty Grand Aerostation Company' were encamped on a large tree-lined field on the opposite side of the canal from the gasworks.

Every morning, when Amy came from her tent, she would gaze at this white building gleaming in the sunlight and take pleasure from its elegance. For her it was a foretaste for the wonders she would see when Vincent Sorenty took her across the seas.

Every day since her arrival here, she had wandered throughout the city, marvelling at the towering grandeur of Warwick Castle. The grim walls of the massive County Gaol, the great County Hall and Judges' Lodgings. The close-packed half-timbered houses, shops, taverns, inns, chapels and churches from earlier centuries. The wide Market Square and the ceaseless noise and bustle of commerce.

This morning Sorenty was waiting for her when she left her tent. She had not seen him or Mario Fassia since the day of her arrival.

'Where have you been, Vincent? I've been wondering where you'd got to?'

He smiled and held up a roll of paper. 'Among other matters, I've been having these posters put up in Birmingham and

Coventry, and at this very moment they're being put up all over Warwick and Leamington.'

With a dramatic flourish he unrolled the poster and held it up before her.

Amy gasped at the garishly coloured picture of a woman wearing a black mask a black hood and billowing robe, which had scarlet wings rising from the shoulders. Topping the poster in large scarlet lettering was a caption: 'THE FALLEN ANGEL.'

Beneath the picture smaller lettering proclaimed, 'She will fall from Heaven at the Saltisford Canal Basin Meadow, Saturday, 26 September. Admittance to the meadow is Two Shillings. By gracious permission of the Right Honourable the Earl of Warwick, Lord Lieutenant of Warwickshire.'

'Is that me?' Amy queried excitedly. 'Am I the Fallen Angel?'

'Of course you are. Now look over there.' He pointed to the meadow gate where a large wagon and a group of men on foot were entering. 'They've come to build the grandstand and fence off the field, and they'll be keeping the crowd in order and guarding the gates on both sides of the basin. We're going to make a fortune from this show, and you'll get your fair share of it!'

Amy giggled mischievously. 'Well, that won't be much will it? Not after you've paid for the billposting and the gas and all these men, and the fencing and grandstand.'

Sorenty threw back his head and roared with laughter, then told her: 'My new patron is paying me four times over the biggest fee I've ever had, and on top of that he's paying for everything else. This show is a present for his Missus.'

'Pheww!' Amy's eyes widened. 'He must be a really loving husband, and a very rich one.'

'Oh, he is, and he's promised to make me a very rich man in the years to come.' Sorenty beamed with satisfaction. 'He's Henry Richard Greville, the Earl of Warwick.'

'What will I be doing as the Fallen Angel?' Amy asked.

He lifted his forefinger to his lips. 'It has to be my secret until tomorrow. But when you do it, you'll become the most famous Aeronaut Maiden in the world.'

Amy was thrilled to hear the words. 'The most famous Maiden in the world! That'll be wonderful!'

* * *

Tom reached Warwick midway through the afternoon and asked another horseman, 'Sir, do you know of a troupe of balloonists being here in the city?'

The man pointed at a garish poster on a neighbouring wall. 'If those are the ones you're looking for, they're camped at the Saltisford canal basin. Just take that road over there and you'll come to a canal bridge. Cross over and follow the towpath eastwards. It will bring you to their camp.'

'Many thanks, Sir.' Tom went near to the poster and stared at it for some time before riding on with very mixed feelings.

'You, nor nobody else, can't come on to the field till tomorrow, and then it's two bob for entry,' the cudgel-wielding man at the meadow gate told Tom.

'But I'm a personal friend of Master Sorenty, and it's he who has sent for me to come today,' Tom argued.

'And I'm a personal friend o' the Earl o' Warwick, and it's him who gives the orders in these parts, not bloody Sorenty. So just clear off and come back tomorrow wi' two shillings entry money.'

Tom realized the futility of arguing, turned his mount and rode back into the city, where he found lodging at an inn.

FORTY-SIX

Warwick.
Saturday, 26 September, 1829

It was two o'clock in the afternoon, and since mid-morning the numbers of men, women and children in the great meadow had been increasing until they were a noisy, seething mass of many thousands.

Close to the tree line the balloonists' camp, launch pad and the grandstand for the Earl's family and guests were concealed behind a high wall of laths and canvas, its entrance guarded by men armed with muskets and bayonets. As were the men taking the entrance money at the meadow gate and those patrolling the field fence.

Tom had come early, and on foot, with his saddlebags slung over his shoulder. He'd tried to gain entrance to the canvas-walled enclosure but had been brusquely turned away. Now he could only watch and wait.

Sitting inside her tent, Amy had been fully costumed for over an hour, except for the scarlet wings which could be fitted in seconds to her shoulders. But Vincent Sorenty had given her strict orders to remain concealed in the tent until he himself came for her. Sorenty had not yet said what form her performance was to take, and her mood now was a melee of longing for the crowds roar of approbation, resentment at still not knowing what she was to do, and nervous tension.

She heard him shouting orders as he came towards the tent and jumped to her feet, excitement flooding through her.

He came in, declaring elatedly, 'It couldn't be better, Amy! The clouds are blanketed, and they're low, Amy! They're low! It's what I was praying for!'

He grabbed her hand. 'Come on. The Earl's party are in sight and I want you to be hidden in the gondola before they arrive.'

As they hurried towards the still flat balloon, she asked, 'What am I going to do today, Vincent?'

'Hold your bloody tongue, will you, Girl!' He spat the command.

Amy was shocked into a resentful silence by this sudden display of temper, and her resentment still festered when she was lay concealed from view in the large gondola.

Tom heard the loud report which signalled the start of the balloon inflation, and nervous tension gripped him. He begged silently, over and over again: Please God, I beg you to protect Amy and keep her safe from death or injury

There came another loud report and the great silvery orb of the balloon soared up from the enclosing canvas walls. The crowd erupted, deafening roars of cheering filled the air and, in the gondola, Vincent Sorenty doffed his top hat and bowed repeatedly in acknowledgement of this tremendous storm of continuous applause.

The balloon rose higher and higher and thousands of voices howled in shock and protest as the silvery orb was abruptly swallowed into the blanketing clouds.

Tom's knowledge of ballooning had been much refreshed by Charles Green, and on the first sight of this balloon he had noted that there were two tether ropes attached to the orb's net cover, but could not see a winchline. Now Tom reasoned, 'Sorenty must have already known he'd be going into the clouds, but why would he want that?'

As if in answer bright streams of sparks suddenly fell from the clouds and exploded. The crowd were momentarily dumb-struck into silence. Up in the gondola, two crewmen were igniting the touch papers of maritime flares and throwing them earthwards. More spark streams tumbled down, more explosions sounded and the crowd's roars erupted afresh.

Vincent Sorenty rapidly attached the scarlet wings to Amy's shoulders, fixed a harness around her waist and under her armpits and led her to an opened gateway in the gondola's side.

All the time, she was continuously asking him, 'Tell me what I'm to do, Vincent? What is it you want me to perform?'

He reached up to the circular hoop of the balloon's mouth, pulled down a rope, clipped it on to the back of the harness and shouted, 'This will make you the most famous Aeronaut Maiden in the whole world, Amy!'

He hurled her through the open gateway. She was screamed in terror-stricken shock as she dropped, jerked violently upwards, dropped, slowed and swung into an angled gliding descent through the clouds.

On the ground all eyes were fixed on the tumbling streams of sparks and explosions.

At the grandstand, Mario Fassia glimpsed what his eyes had been straining for and screeched with hysterical relief through his speaking trumpet. 'Look there, My Lords and Ladies! Look there! The Archangels have won the battle! The Fallen Angel has been cast out of Heaven! Look up over our right-hand side! The Fallen Angel has been cast out of Heaven!'

At that same instant Tom also saw the Fallen Angel. 'It's a parachute! Amy's flying a parachute!'

Though assailed by a surge of panic, he desperately tried to assess the rate of descent of the gliding parachute and judged that she would land further to the east. He pushed through the crowd, out of the entrance gate and ran eastward as fast as he could.

The crowd's attention suddenly switched to another sensational sight: the balloon slowly spiralling down from the clouds, trailing a vast plume of flame and smoke then suddenly plummeting earthwards and smashing down on to the launch pad.

Totally fixated on the parachute, Tom was unaware of the balloon's fall. Gasping for breath, legs and arms pumping furiously, he went on, struggling to speed across the rutted ground, tripping and reeling, recovering balance and forcing his body on. Then a protracted stumble brought him crashing to the ground, and when he struggled back to his feet the parachute had disappeared beyond some rising ground.

'She must have landed! But what damage might she have done to herself?'

Panic again dominated his senses and he ran up the long slope of rising ground, breasted its crest and saw a row of tall trees. Entangled in the branches of two adjoining trees was the white sheet of the parachute and, dangling beneath it, the hooded, black-robed, scarlet-winged Fallen Angel.

'Dear God, let her not be hurt! Let her not be hurt!' Tom gasped frantically as he stumbled down the slope.

The dangling figure's hands were now scrabbling at the mask and Tom cried out in relief: 'Thank you, God! Thank you.' And then called, 'Amy, I'm here! It's Tom! I'm here, Amy!'

As he reached her, Amy managed to tear the mask away, and stare in dazed shock at Tom's face, now several inches below her own.

Disbelievingly, she uttered, 'Tom? Is it you? Are you here, Tom?'

Fighting to control his rampaging emotions and speak calmly, he told her, 'Oh yes, I'm here, my dear. And I'm going to get you down from there. But first I need to know, are you hurting at all? Do you feel as if you've any broken bones or have other wounds? Move very slowly and carefully as you check yourself. I'll be back soon.'

While she did as he had asked, Tom ran back to where he had fallen and retrieved the saddlebags he had dropped there.

When he returned to Amy, she announced in wonderment, 'It's like a bloody miracle, Tom! I think I've only a few little scrapes and bruises by the feel of things!'

'Thank God!' he exclaimed, found a knife in a saddlebag and stepped up to her dangling body. 'You take this knife, my dear. I'm going to lift you as high as I can. That'll free the harness of your bodyweight and you should be able to cut through enough points of it to free yourself. Do you think you'll be able to manage to do that?'

To his amazement, she giggled mischievously and retorted pertly, 'It's certain that I'll manage to do that without half the struggle you'll have trying to hold my weight up, Master Sampson Potts.'

It took a brief instant for the sly humour to dawn on Tom, and then he burst into helpless laughter. Laughing with him, Amy reached out and clutched his head to her breast. His arms enfolded her waist and they stayed for long, long moments locked together, their mingled laughter rising up through the tangled leafy branches above.

Later, when Amy cut through the last binding section of the harness and Tom lowered her gently to the earth, she wondered aloud, 'It's strange nobody's come looking to see what's happened to me, aren't it?'

'Indeed it is, but they'll no doubt be coming soon,' Tom agreed thoughtfully, and asked her to describe her jump from the gondola.

A troubled frown crossed her face and she shook her head as if to clear it. 'Do you know, Tom, the strange thing is it's only this instant that the jump's come into me thoughts. Bloody Vincent Sorenty threw me out o' the gondola! The cheeky bugger thought I was feared to do it. But I wasn't feared to do it! He just acted all day like he thought I'd be, and wouldn't tell me what we were going to do for the performance. I'll be giving him a real earful when I get hold of him, no matter how famous and rich this performance has made me!'

'What?' Tom couldn't credit he had heard correctly. 'He threw you out of the gondola?'

'He bloody well did,' she declared emphatically, and went on to relate in detail the sequence of events. Tom listened with ever-intensifying anger, but at the same time another emotion was also burgeoning ever more strongly.

Amy had finished her account when the first distant shouts sounded from the other side of the rising ground.

Tom came to an instant decision. 'Amy, what I'm going to ask you to do might sound very strange but believe me, I have good reason for it. Go and meet them, and tell them that you freed yourself from the harness. Don't say I was here, and get them to take you straight back to the camp. Tell them the parachute is so tangled up in the high branches they'll need to come back with ladders to free it without ripping it to bits.

'I beg you to do this, my dear, without further questions. I'll come to you tomorrow morning and explain everything. Please! Trust me, and do as I ask.'

She reached up, pulled his head down, kissed his lips and was gone, running up to the top of the slope and shouting, 'I'm here, lads. I'm coming!'

It took Tom more than an hour of clumsy climbing and edging his way up and along branches, slashing cloth and cutting ropes, tugging, pulling with all his strength to free the voluminous parachute. He bound it into as tight a bundle as he could and carried it away in the opposite direction to the canal basin.

It was long past midnight when, utterly weary, he returned to his room above the rear courtyard at the inn, still carrying the bundled parachute and his saddlebags. He stowed them in his room, locked the door and went in search of food and drink.

Among the few people still drinking in the bar room, the main topic of conversation was the flaming balloon crashing to earth and the deaths of Vincent Sorenty and the two crewmen. Amy's parachute descent was only mentioned in passing. When Tom's shock at hearing about the crash had passed, he couldn't help but feel aggrieved on Amy's behalf for the way her exploit had been relegated to something of little or no importance.

Back in his room, he stowed the seal-bearing parchment of 'Magisterial Authorization of Right of Arrest in Warwickshire and Worcestershire' in his innermost pocket. Primed and loaded his brace of pistols. Then lay fully dressed on the bed to snatch a couple of hours' sleep before the inn's night-watchman came to wake him as arranged.

FORTY-SEVEN

Saltisford Canal Basin.
Sunday, 27 September, 1829

There were no musket-armed guards on the meadow or enclosure gateways when Tom rode through them at dawn. The charred remains of the balloon and gondola lay across the launch pad and the tented encampment looked deserted.

But as he rode into it Amy came running from her tent calling, 'Tom! I'm so glad to see you, Tom!'

He dismounted and folded her in his arms. 'I didn't hear about the crash until quite late in the evening, my dear, and I couldn't come to see you because I urgently had to find some people. Now, are the crew still abed?'

She shook her head and told him excitedly, 'Oh, no! They all left last night, after having a great big row with Mario Fassia. They were blaming him and Vincent Sorenty for their mates' deaths. But he was blaming their mates for being too careless with the lighted flares.'

'Has Fassia left also?' Tom questioned tensely.

She shook her head. 'He got as drunk as a lord when they'd gone and he's snoring his head off in his tent right now.'

'Which tent is it?'

'That one there.' She pointed.

He gently released her and took holstered pistols and chain-manacles from the saddlebags.

'Will you tether my horse, please, while I arrest Fassia.'

'Arrest Mario?' she exclaimed. 'What for?'

'For the murder of his sister, Graziella Fassia,' he said quietly, and walked away, leaving her gaping after him in shocked disbelief.

Mario Fassia was fully clothed, laying spread-eagled on the low cot, snoring loudly. A half-full bottle of wine was on the floor beside him.

Tom picked up the bottle and emptied it over Fassia's face. Fassia woke up coughing, snorting, cursing. He sat upright, rubbing his eyes, as Tom told him loudly, 'Mario Fassia, I'm arresting you in the King's Name. If you make any aggressive moves I'll shoot you dead!'

Blinking constantly, eyes watering, Fassia squinted up at Tom and croaked hoarsely, 'Arrest me? Shoot me? What for?'

'For the murder of your sister, Graziella Fassia.'

'Aaaaagggghhhh!' Mario Fassia's long-drawn-out, piercing scream carried across the meadow, startling the horseman riding into the enclosure.

Fassia rolled off the cot and fell face downwards on the ground, venting loud, choking sobs.

Amy came running to the tent, shouting, 'Tom, are you all right? Are you all right?'

'Shhh!' Tom signalled her to be silent and stay outside, then knelt at the side of the sobbing man and began stroking his head, telling him soothingly, 'I know that you didn't want to hurt her, Mario. I know that she drove you to do it. It's not really your fault, my poor Mario. You and Vincent truly loved each other. Why did she have to be so evil? So cruel? Why couldn't she accept that you and Vincent were meant by fate to be together?'

The horseman dismounted and came quietly to stand by Amy.

'Poor, poor Mario,' Tom crooned in rhythm with his stroking hand. 'Fate had brought you and Vincent together and your cruel, selfish sister was going to destroy you both, to destroy you for being in love. You were forced to destroy her first, my poor Mario. You had no other choice if you were to save your own beloved, Vincent. No other choice, my poor Mario.'

'No choice! I'd got no choice!' Mario sobbed.

Tom urged gently, 'Tell God now! Tell God that you had no choice, my poor Mario. God will understand. He'll reunite you with Vincent. Tell God now, how she forced you both to kill her. How she forced you both, my poor Mario!'

'We'd no choice!' Fassia whimpered brokenly. 'I swear to you, God, she forced us to do it to her. She persuaded Vincent to take her up for the flight to London. Then, when we were flying she told us she knew we were fucking each other, and she was going to take us all to the Devil. She pulled out a box o' Friction Lights and some oily rags, and screamed she was going to set fire to the gas and burn us in the Fire of Hell. I took hold of her and she knocked me down, and Vincent, my lovely, sweet Vincent, came to help me, and we had a hell of a fight with her before we managed to get her out of the gondola. And still she managed somehow to grab hold of the parachute we'd got tied to the mouth-hoop, and it tore away. It was the Devil who gave her that strength, God! Because she was so cruel and evil. So fuckin' cruel and evil!'

He collapsed, sobbing helplessly.

Tom rose and opened the tent flap. 'Did you hear all that, Amy?'

'We both did, and remember every word of it.' The horseman grinned broadly. 'Well now, Constable Potts, youm putting me in the shade again aren't you?'

Tom laughed. 'Good God, no! I'm sharing the glory with you, Constable Shayler. Tell me, what time did the messenger reach you?'

'The bugger woke me up just after I'd gone to bed and got to sleep, so you owe me a very large favour for coming here.'

'And you will receive it, my friend, because we're sharing this arrest and prisoner escort back to Redditch. I'll give you the full story on our way back.'

Piqued by this switch of Tom's attention, Amy snapped pettishly, 'You can arrange separate transport for me, Tom Potts. Because I'm going back to live with my friends in the Fox and Goose.'

FORTY-EIGHT

Redditch Town.
Monday, 28 September, 1829

At midday in the Lock-Up, Lord Aston and Joseph Blackwell were seated on a bench in the kitchen alcove with Tom, Will Shayler, George Maffey and Ritchie Bint stood facing them. Mario Fassia, dosed with laudanum to quiet his constant loud lamentations, was locked in a cell.

'Now, Thomas Potts, let My Lord Aston hear the full story of how you achieved this remarkable success.' Joseph Blackwell beamed like a proud father at Tom. 'Which I never for one single moment ever doubted that you would so achieve.'

Tom bowed. 'Very well, Sir. The major credit for this success must be given to Charles Green, Constables Shayler and Bint, and Corporal Maffey, because without their unfailing help I wouldn't have succeeded in arresting the murderer of the Haystack Woman, Graziella Fassia. Charles Green has intimate knowledge of Vincent Sorenty and the Fassia family. He told me the family are afflicted by an extremely rare, hereditary physical deformity, the third and fourth fingers on both hands being peculiarly deformed by malformation of the proximal, middle and distal phalanx joints. Mario Fassia and his sister, Graziella the Haystack Woman, shared that deformity.

'Because Aerostation is a singularly rare profession with very few practitioners, Charles Green is kept constantly informed of any balloon flights made in this country and Europe, such as the flight made by Vincent Sorenty and Mario Fassia from the Saint Michaels Street Gasworks in Shrewsbury, with the object of reaching London. This flight was due to take off on Saturday, 11 July. But because of adverse winds could not be made until the late afternoon of Sunday, 12 July when the wind was favourable, which carried the balloon over the Needle District.

'Now Graziella had been Vincent Sorenty's mistress for some years, and was carrying his child. It was through her that he and Mario Fassia came to meet. But among certain London circles Sorenty had long been rumoured to be a queer Molly. As was Mario Fassia. Sometime after their meeting, and unknown to Graziella, they became lovers. She eventually found out that fact, which resulted in her tragic end.

'With reference to Methuselah Leeson's claim to have met with the Devil's Monk, and being enveloped in the Monk's robe, I think those robes were the parachute which was taken by the wind and blown into the Abbey Meadows. Methuselah or his wife found it later and cut it up into separate pieces. After Nellie's death, Hector Smout came into possession of the ropes and the harness which he gave to me. Those and the pieces of silk are in the end cell if you wish to see them.'

'I'm a busy man and not at leisure to spend time gawping at bits of rope and cloth like some country mawkin,' Aston snapped irritably and rose to his feet. 'I must be off, Blackwell. I've very important matters to attend to. I'll remand this fellow, Fassia, to Worcester Jail at tomorrow's Petty Sessions. I bid you a Good Day, Sir.'

'Good day to you, My Lord.' Blackwell rose and bowed as Aston hurried out of the Lock-Up and shouted at his coachman, 'Take me to Birmingham and make haste to get there. I've not a moment to waste!'

Blackwell turned to Tom. 'My Lord Aston is rushing to a business concern he owns in Birmingham, Thomas Potts. It's a printing shop which trades under the name of Solomons Bros. Have you ever seen that name, I wonder?'

Blackwell chuckled and slyly winked.

When his friends had left, Tom checked on the prisoner, who was still snoring, and then went up to his garret bedroom. He sat down on the narrow cot and a wave of loneliness welled over him.

'I shouldn't have given George Maffey the rest of the day off.' He sighed. 'He's always pleasant company for me.'

The bells suddenly jangled. Tom went wearily down the flights of stairs and wearily opened the door. Dressed in bonnet and gown, her large travel trunk at her feet, Amy smiled nervously at him.

'I want to come back home, Husband. I want more than anything else in this world to be your true-hearted, faithful wife again.' She paused. 'And your lover, my dear, sweet Tom.'

He stood for some moments absorbing her words. Then told her quietly: 'You have just made me the happiest man throughout all of this earth, my beautiful Amy.' And folded her gently in his arms.